HANDS ON

HANDS ON

AMIE STUART

APHRODISIA

KENSINGTON BOOKS
http://www.kensingtonbooks.com

APHRODISIA BOOKS are published by

Kensington Publishing Corp.
850 Third Avenue
New York, NY 10022

All Kensington Titles, Imprints, and Distributed Lines are available at special quantity discounts for bulk purchases for sales promotions, premiums, fund-raising, and educational or institutional use.

Special book excerpts or customized printings can also be created to fit specific needs. For details, write or phone the office of the Kensington special sales manager: Kensington Publishing Corp., 850 Third Avenue, New York, NY 10022, attn: Special Sales Department, Phone: 1-800-221-2647.

ISBN-13: 978-0-7582-1892-6
ISBN-10: 0-7582-1892-3

First Kensington Trade Paperback Printing: June 2007

10 9 8 7 6 5 4 3 2 1

Printed in the United States of America

For the boys

Acknowledgments

First off, thank you to my boys for putting up with a grumpy, distracted mommy.

A hearty thanks to Jaqueline Bdudard for the great title, Michelle Miles and Denise McDonald for being my pinch hitters, Raine Weaver for refusing to let me give up, and last but certainly not least, AKA for showing the way.

CONTENTS

Lexie 1

Lanie 77

Carlotta 161

Lexi

1

Hot bath; cold beer. Hot bath; cold beer.

This mantra sustained me on the long drive home, on the long walk up my driveway, and even as I'd shoved the key in the back door and unlocked it.

I was so tired that I almost regretted the fact it was Friday night. Friday was Girls' Night. And there was no getting out of it.

Weekends were this blue-collar girl's guilty pleasure. Weekends were spent on the white-collar side of town, in white-collar bars, dancing and teasing and flirting with men who didn't think burping should be an Olympic sport. No blue collars allowed. Not after Melanie, Carlotta, and I spent our week dealing with them daily.

Dealing being the operative word.

I dropped my hard hat on the washer and struggled out of my filthy work boots. They were covered in mud, as was I, from the knees down. Thanks to the heavy spring rains that had saturated the site and put us behind schedule. And a rogue forklift that had gone crashing through a wall with a load of bricks. Luckily no one had been hurt, but this afternoon's descent into hell had killed any excitement or anticipation I had about going out tonight.

And you wanted to go into construction why, Lexi Kimball?

Stripping out of my jeans and work shirt, I padded into the kitchen and retrieved an icy cold beer from the fridge. That first long drink hit my empty stomach at lightning speed and didn't stop until it reached my feet. After being trapped in steel-toed boots all day they practically steamed on the tile floor. With a sigh, I rubbed the chilly bottle against my hot neck.

Momentarily satisfied, I headed for the bathroom and a nice long soak. One of the first things I'd done after I'd bought the house two years ago was gut the extra closet in the master bedroom and put in a Jacuzzi tub for days just like today.

While the tub filled I stripped off my tank top and tossed it into the hamper. The rest of my clothes quickly followed. I ran a hand across the flat plane of my stomach and smiled. Tanned and fairly firm, I certainly didn't get many complaints. My breasts were average, but still perky. Working construction had always kept the arms and legs in shape. Yoga took care of the rest.

Hmm, not bad for 34.

Despite the fact that I'm a natural redhead, I'm lucky enough to be of the variety that tans easily. Rare, but not unheard of. I leaned in closer to the vanity mirror and ran a hand through my short, shaggy hair. Soon I'd have to do something about those silver threads starting to peek through.

The tub was almost full and I added a generous amount of jasmine bath foam, inhaling the relaxing fragrance. Relieved to see the end of another awful day, I sipped at my beer and set the bottle on the edge of the tub, then slid in with a deep sigh.

I liked the satisfaction of seeing something I'd helped build as a finished product, and the money was really good. But construction workers are a breed unto themselves. Being a female

Assistant Job Supervisor on an all-male crew had been stressful enough. Adding Safety Supervisor to my title had made things ten times worse, and I didn't believe for a minute that the rest of the job would be any less difficult than the last eighty-eight jobs had been. Nothing like overseeing a group of men who resented the hell out of you to take the wind out of your sails. I'd worked tough gigs before but none this bad.

My sex meant everything to them; my femininity meant *nothing*.

Shaking off my reverie, I took another long pull of my beer. The combination of warm water and Miller Lite were definitely doing the trick, unworking knots of stress and loosening tense muscles. With another sigh, I closed my eyes and relaxed, my mind drifting to Wade Wilkins, as it had far too often lately.

He didn't strike me as the typical construction crew guy—married, settled, kids, running to fat around his middle and bitter at the chances he'd pissed away or let pass him by. Instead, Wade seemed like the type who enjoyed gambling, and he was the only man on the crew who didn't seem fazed by my sex or my charms (or lack thereof, depending on whom you ask). Too bad his part of the job would be done soon.

Compact, tanned, and muscular, Wade topped my own five feet six inches by only a few more, but the man knew how to fill out a pair of Levi's, and he had these thick, tanned forearms that rippled and flexed from all the manual exertion. You could tell he spent a lot of time outdoors shirtless: no "farmer's tan" for him. I heard he played sand volleyball on the weekends. With his easygoing personality and bright green eyes, he had charmer written all over him. I'd miss watching him work once his drywall crew finished up, but then again, he was a distraction I couldn't afford. After hours was a whole 'nother matter.

I closed my eyes to block out the sight of the tiled walls surrounding me and let my hands have free rein, imagining they were his. They drifted through the silky water until they reached my breasts, cupping them as I imagined Wade's hard length behind me, surrounding me, instead of the fiberglass tub. The throbbing between my thighs quickly intensified as my excitement grew. Lifting one leg, I draped it over the side of the tub, moaning as the water caressed my sensitive pussy lips. My hands continued to squeeze my breasts until my nipples were hard, achy little points. I groaned at the thought of my vibrator tucked away in my nightstand drawer. My muscles were so jellified from the heat and beer, I didn't feel like climbing out of the tub for it. With no other relief in sight, I closed my eyes again and stroked the insides of my thighs, kneading and stroking my way higher and drawing every ounce of anticipation out of it. This was a race all about endurance, not speed.

A picture of Wade driving inside me filled my head, so vivid I could almost believe he was really there with me. Need overcame all other thoughts and I stroked my clit, which swelled under my fingertips. I bit my lower lip as the ache intensified and my labored breathing filled my ears as I neared my goal. Feverishly, my emboldened fingers continued until my body took on a will of its own. Toes curled and hips involuntarily thrust upward out of the water as the waves of my orgasm traveled through me, released by the stroke of my fingers and thoughts of Wade.

Afterward I lay there, listening to my harsh breathing and the soft plunk of water dripping from the faucet.

With a smile of satisfaction, I reached for my beer and sipped the lukewarm brew, contemplating dinner—only to dismiss such a mundane thought, dismayed at the reminder of my solitary existence.

The unexpected sound of the doorbell echoing through the house reminded me that the clock was ticking. Knowing my luck it was Lanie or Carlotta, come to rob my closets.

I climbed out of the tub, wrapped my wet, flushed body in

my old robe, and dashed down the hall to the front door. Sliding the chain off, I yanked the door open to discover it wasn't either of the girls.

It was Wade with my lunchbox.

"Wade." *How nice to see you, since I just masturbated in my bathtub while thinking about you.*

As his full lips curved into a grin, I tightened my robe around my waist, conscious of my legs still trembling from the aftermath of my orgasm. Despite his aviator sunglasses, I had the strange feeling he knew I'd been . . . well . . . *thinking* about him. Then again, maybe it was the wet robe and the hard nipples.

"Evening, Alex. You forgot this."

So it wasn't really a lunchbox but a small cooler. I'd left it sitting on the steps of the construction trailer when I'd gone tearing across the site after the forklift crash.

I had no choice but to take the damn thing from his outstretched hand and couldn't work out anything beyond a mumbled thank-you. How could it be legal to work all day in the blistering Houston sun and still look as good as he did?

"Didn't mean to interrupt anything."

I pulled my robe tighter still and forced myself to breathe. "It was time for me to get out anyway."

"Hot date?"

"Girl's Night," I replied with a smile.

He slowly nodded, his grin deepening as he took a few steps backward. "Then I won't keep you. Have fun."

If he had any idea! "I will."

"And stay out of trouble!" With that parting shot, he spun on his heels and disappeared down the walk and around the corner to the driveway, where I heard his truck start up a minute later. Ducking back inside, I shut the door before he saw me standing there, wishing I'd invited him in.

* * *

Two hours later I stepped through Jimmy Z's shiny black double doors, smiling to the burly bouncer who greeted me by name. Located just down the road from the Houston Galleria, Jimmy Z's catered to an eclectic, but mostly upscale, clientele which was reflected in the chrome, black, and red decor. I took the long way downstairs to where the girls were waiting, barely giving the booths full of snuggling couples a glance. However, I paid close attention to the packs of men on the prowl. They weren't the only ones hunting tonight. My earlier tub adventures and Wade's visit had left me hungry for more. And if I couldn't have *him*, then I'd just have to make do.

At our table (positioned strategically beside a set of stairs that led to the dance floor), the girls were already digging into appetizers and admiring the evening's early, yet so far slim, offerings. They both stopped eating long enough to hug me while we admired each other's outfits. Carlotta looked great, as usual, dressed in a multicolored, watered silk skirt and red halter top that showed off her natural tan and curly blond hair to perfection.

"Lanie, is that new?" Smiling, I motioned to the leopard print dress with turquoise trim that hugged her lush curves and swirled around her knees. Only Lanie would or could pull off leopard print. And with her chocolate brown hair, framing deep blue-green eyes, she pulled it off well. No one would ever guess that up until a few hours ago she'd probably been elbow deep in grease and engines.

"Just a little something I dug out of my closet." Her deep coral-colored lips curved into a Cheshire-cat grin as she crossed her legs.

"She went shopping," Carlotta and I chimed in unison.

I waved at Brian, our regular waiter, as he went breezing by, and hollered out my order for a Woo Woo—peach Schnapps, vodka, and cranberry juice—then settled on the vacant stool.

"Looks like she's not the only one who went shopping," Carlotta observed with a grin.

"I bought this two weeks ago, thank you very much!" I'd spotted the funky yellow, orange, and royal blue paisley outfit on a Sunday afternoon shopping expedition and hadn't been able to leave it behind. It went perfectly with my orange Christian Lacroix sandals.

I snitched a chicken egg roll off the platter in the middle of the small table, dipped it in some of Jimmy's homemade salsa duck sauce, and bit in with a sigh of appreciation as the spicy, tangy flavor filled my mouth. Jimmy Z's made the best egg rolls in all of Houston.

"So how was your day?" Carlotta asked while she scoped out the bar.

"I'll be so glad when this job is over!" I accepted my Woo Woo with a smile for Brian and handed him my credit card to run a tab. He was hot, but then most of the waitstaff at Jimmy's were. A crisp white T-shirt hugged his well-defined pecs and sharply creased black pants accented the rest of his assets.

"You ladies ready for something more substantial?" He pointed to our platter of appetizers, then wiggled an eyebrow at Carlotta, who giggled.

Indeed! My visit from Wade had definitely left me in the mood for something "more substantial."

I didn't miss Lanie's eye-rolling either. She'd had one of her notorious flings with Brian about six months back, but he'd refused to quit serving us. He probably did it just to irk her. But as long as we'd been coming here, he'd been our waiter; he was a great guy, even if he was too young for me. Whereas Lanie didn't discriminate on the basis of age—too much.

"I'm fine." With a soft sigh, I turned and scoped out the almost empty dance floor and tables surrounding it. It wasn't that I minded being single but sometimes it had its downside—though I'd decided long ago the good far outweighed the bad.

I didn't have to share my bed for more than a night if I didn't want to (and usually I didn't).

I could come and go as I pleased.

I didn't have to answer to anyone about money.

I didn't have to cook if I didn't feel like it.

I could ogle men to my heart's desire without someone getting jealous.

And if I got tired of a man, I just dumped him (no nasty divorces and splitting of assets to deal with).

I polished off the last of my egg roll and turned to Carlotta. "Did you finish up that wiring job today?"

She pursed her lips and nodded, an "it was a shitty day" look on her face.

"That bad, huh?"

"Have I told you how much I hate my new boss?" she asked with a curl of her lip.

"Noooo," I drawled, grinning.

"Asshole wants me to wire his nephew's office Monday for phones and Internet. God forbid I fuck *that* up." Carlotta's new boss was all we'd heard about for the last two months. He was, in her words, a control freak, who constantly felt the need to double-check her work and censure her for the slightest infractions, imagined or real. Never mind that she was the best field technician the company had, and had been there longer than he. Other than the fact she'd applied for his job (and been passed over for him, an outsider), none of us had been able to figure out what his beef was with her, so we'd decided he was just a Chauvinistic Pig.

"I swear to God, he wants me to quit!"

"Well, maybe you should," Lanie threw in. "You're too damn good to put up with that shit."

"Hell no! Why should I quit because he's got issues? He can just get the fuck over it." With a scowl, Carlotta slipped off her bar stool.

I gave her an understanding smile, then watched as she turned and headed downstairs toward the dance floor. Carlotta could wire damn near anything, from a small office phone system to a computer network for a multistory office building.

"I don't blame her a bit, you know," I sighed, scooping up a quesadilla filled with cheese, cilantro, and bits of pork. "She shouldn't have to quit because some asshole is determined to make her life miserable."

"Yeah, but you know how hardheaded she is. I wouldn't be surprised if she did stuff just to piss him off." Lanie thoughtfully sipped her dirty martini, focused on something—or someone—over my shoulder, while I polished off what amounted to my dinner.

"What?"

She grinned and nodded to a spot behind me, pure female lust making her blue eyes sparkle. "Check *him* out."

With a grin of my own, I checked. Lanie might like 'em young, but she had really good taste in men. Not six feet away stood a tall slender young *thang* with dark hair and even darker eyes. He quirked an eyebrow at us and we waved and laughed.

"Back soon!" Lanie cheerfully announced as she circled around me and headed straight for him.

By the time I'd nursed my way through half of my second drink and let the girls drag my tired body onto the dance floor, the bar was packed. And the three of us were dancing to the Freestylers with any man brave enough to get close. After fifteen minutes Lanie had ditched Freddie, the sexy brunette with the baby face, and rejoined me, announcing he was only twenty-one. Even for a hottie like him she wouldn't break her ten-year rule. Besides, all he seemed to talk about was chicks—yes, he used the word *chicks*—cars, rims on cars and doing X (Ecstacy).

The Freestylers segued into No Doubt, something sexy for

showing off, and I did, despite the fact that Lanie and Carlotta had now deserted me, claiming they were ready for a break.

Shyness had never been a problem for me and I was a good dancer. While Gwen Stefani sang, I danced, letting the sensuous rhythm of the sexy song roll through me. Before I knew it, I found myself pulled up on one of the podiums positioned at the end of the dance floor, grooving with a hot blonde in a psychedelic pink minidress.

We danced with each other as much for the crowd as ourselves. With a grin, she grabbed my hips and we ground against each other. We both laughed at the hoots and appreciative whistles from the group of men below us. I returned her smile and spun around, wiggling my hips and inviting her closer. My bones turned fluid as the vodka, heat, and admiring cheers of the crowd worked their magic.

I shimmied down the length of her body, tilting my head back as I came in contact with her heavy breasts, then paused in a crouch at her feet, gathered up my skirt, and pulled it up to the tops of my thighs as I slowly wiggled my way back up. We danced belly to back, me with my skirt pulled up as high as I dared and her with her incredibly soft hands stroking my bare thighs. Hands that raised goosebumps on my skin and ventured dangerously close to my panties more than once, causing the silky material to rub my crotch, exciting me even more.

Then I saw *him*. The bottom fell out of my stomach and ice-cold shock, horror, dread even, washed through me, replacing the heat brought on by our little show.

What the hell was Wade doing in a place like this?

Lucky for me the song ended and the DJ spun a faster groove. But before I could stop her, my erstwhile dance partner spun me around and kissed me full on the lips, giving my ass a squeeze in the process. I had no choice but to hang on to her to keep from falling off the ministage.

"Thanks for the dance," she mouthed. "Maybe later we can do it again." She spun on her heels and accepted a hand down from our group of admirers.

I turned for a quick peek over my shoulder. Wade still stood at the top of the stairs, a level above the dance floor. On shaky legs, I followed her down and headed his way.

With clammy hands I climbed the stairs, forcing a bright smile on my face, but nerves, adrenaline, and the heat of too many bodies was too much. As I neared the top, Wade grabbed my wrist, a frown of concern on his face.

"Air," I gasped, my head swimming.

He led me through the thick crowd and up to the main level, cruising through the two muscled-up goons who guarded the entrance to the VIP Lounge.

Interesting, but my head was swimming too much to even contemplate how he'd managed what Lanie, with her arsenal of wiles, hadn't been able to. I gratefully sank down on a gaudy, crushed red velvet couch that Wade led me to in some VIP hidey-hole. Then I watched as he closed the opaque screen that made up the door, muting the music in the process.

God, my whole crew was gonna know I'd kissed a woman in a bar. My stomach rolled over and the two Woo Woos I'd drunk threatened to come back up.

I'd heard all the rumors about how I was a ball-busting dyke. I was five foot six, for crying out loud. I could bust someone's balls if I had to, but dyke? Nuh-uh. I figured that was the price I had to pay for working in a man's world, and I was more than willing to pay it. At least blue-collar men were honest in their bias, rather than shielding it behind some glass ceiling. But that didn't mean I wanted them finding out I'd been dirty dancing with a woman in the hottest bar in Houston—and enjoyed it.

I forced my eyes open, fully aware of his firm grip on my

wrist, the crisp starch of his shirt against my bare arm and the woodsy scent of his cologne tickling my nose. "What are you doing here?"

His deep green eyes widened slightly then narrowed. "I'm here with friends. Do you need to let your girlfriend know where you went?"

"She's not my girlfriend. Gawd, Wade—" I just stared at him, my stomach lurching as he gave me a slow once-over.

"Hey, it's okay if she is. To each his . . . her own." He gave me a conspiratorial wink that made me want to slap him. "I won't say anything."

"It was just a . . . show," I said with a wave of my hand. "For the guys. Just for fun."

"Coulda fooled me, honey."

"Fool you or not, what I do in my off-time is no one's business." Refusing to give in to the nausea that threatened, I struggled out of the too-soft cushions.

"Especially your crew's," Wade softly observed.

"Yeah, especially them." I gently tugged my arm free. "I'm going back downstairs before my friends wonder where I went. Please . . . *please* keep this just between us."

Outside of our little private hidey-hole I debated going back inside and seducing him into silence. I could do it. I knew I could do it. Hell, I wanted to do it.

No way had I forgotten Wade was the stuff of fantasies—specifically mine—but as a member of my crew, he was also forbidden fruit. Luscious, tempting, *forbidden* fruit. I gave a quick smile to the two men dressed head to toe in Tommy Hilfiger, standing at the rail, then pivoted around and stepped back inside the room.

Ready or not, I was about to get my man.

2

Wade eyed me, a wary expression on his face, as I slid the door closed.

"Did you decide not to let me live?" he asked, his lips quirking into a wry smile.

"Did you mean it when you said you wouldn't tell anyone?" With a slow roll of my hips, I closed the short distance between us and gave him a leisurely once-over. Sharply creased khakis hugged his thighs and outlined the erection between them. More than once this week—hell, today—I'd walked the strip shopping center we were building just to watch him hang sheetrock. The tool belt that rode low in his hips, the jeans that hugged his ass, the sweaty, sleeveless T-shirt, those thick arms raised above his head.

"I'm not the blackmailing kind, if that's what you're afraid of."

I lifted my skirt, spread my legs, and straddled his lap, biting the inside of my lip to keep from laughing at the look of surprise that appeared on his face.

"You don't have to do this."

The eyes focused on my breasts said otherwise, as did the hard-on pressed against my already damp panties. I rubbed against him, then exhaled sharply, my thighs tightening at the friction against my sensitive clit.

"I'm not worried about blackmail," I said, pushing my blouse up over my head to reveal a sheer white demi-bra that barely covered the tops of my nipples.

A loud burst of laughter from outside briefly penetrated the thick cloud of need that surrounded us. "You do realize that, at any given moment, someone could walk in here."

In lieu of a reply, I unhooked the bra and let it slide down my shoulders. Dropping it on the couch beside him, I leaned in, wrapped my arms around his neck, and buried my face in the collar of his shirt. And Wade didn't resist. Warm, strong hands skimmed across my back and gave my shoulders a firm squeeze as I nuzzled his neck. "Jesus, Alex!"

"It's Lexi," I whispered, nipping at his earlobe.

"Lexi"—he gasped—"suits you."

I eased upright to a sitting position and cupped my breasts, squeezing the puckered tips hard enough to feel deep in my belly. "I like to watch you work." Licking my lips, I forced myself to focus on my hands. Like my earlier race, this one wasn't about speed. I rolled my nipples between my fingers and forced myself to keep talking. "Earlier, when you came by my house . . ."

"Yeah." His fingers slid up my thighs and under my skirt. As much as I was enjoying the show he was getting, I wanted him to touch me. I wanted his fingers inside me, for starters.

"I was all . . . wet."

Both of his hands slipped under the elastic of my panties.

"I'd just finished masturbating." My hips started a sinuous roll as Wade's fingers spread my swollen pussy lips. I glanced up at him from under my lashes and gave my nipples a painfully slow tug as anticipation curled outward from my belly and seeped from my skin like the musky sweet smell of sex that filled the room. From outside the door, the music and laughter of another world faded away at the first light caress of Wade's finger on my clit.

"I was thinking about you," I said.

"What were you thinking about?"

"This." I pulled up my skirt and watched as he slipped two fingers inside me, stretching me. Flexing and stroking, fucking me as I closed my eyes and forced myself to breath. The need to climax gathered force, doubling on itself and picking up speed even as Wade kept a slow, steady pace, his fingers sliding in and out of my pussy. Until it was beyond even my control, and my heavy breathing turned to low moaning. My nails cut into the palms of my hands, and furious with need, I grasped a nipple between my fingers and gave it a hard squeeze as I came with a long sharp shout. I watched my hips buck against his fingers as the sound of loud raucous laughter and "Get it, honey!" reached my ears. Apparently we had an audience nearby, and the thought that someone had heard me and knew what we'd done only made it that much sweeter.

I eased myself away from him and off his lap, reaching for my blouse and pulling it over my head. "Be a good boy and maybe you'll get the rest later."

On shaky legs, I headed back downstairs, pushing my way through a group of college students toward our table, my purse, and another drink. I forced a smile on my face for the benefit of Lanie's latest pickup (despite the fact he screamed "gigolo"), then watched as they cooed and giggled while I drained the last of my watered-down drink and motioned to Brian to bring me another.

Carlotta's hand on my arm caught my attention. "You okay?"

With a sigh, I leaned over and yelled in her ear. "One of my guys is here." At her puzzled frown, I continued. "From my crew!"

"Oh . . . my . . . God, you are shitting me!" she mouthed, wide eyed.

I slowly shook my head, then started to giggle. By the time I filled her in on what I'd done, we were both in stitches.

"He is hot." She put on her best limpid-eyed look and eased back in her seat, lips pursed. Mata Hari had nothing on Carlotta when it came to getting her man.

Before I could turn to investigate, an arm slid around my shoulder and Carlotta's come-hither look morphed into shock as she realized the hottie she'd been ogling was the same hottie who'd just gotten me off upstairs.

Wade.

"Hi!" The deep rumble of his voice as he introduced himself to her tickled my stomach . . . and other, more sensitive, parts of my anatomy. He pressed his lips to my ear and said, "Thanks for the boner, for leaving me high and dry like that. You owe me."

As casually as you please, I reached for my little purse, and more lipstick, before uncrossing my legs and slipping off the bar stool. I pressed myself against the length of him and smiled. "We can always finish what we started someplace else."

I wanted to drag Wade to bed as soon as we hit my front door, but he apparently had other ideas. Thoroughly puzzled, I followed him through to the living room, then stood behind the couch and watched while he fiddled with my stereo across the far wall.

He'd practically dragged me out of the bar and now he had cold feet? With just a few pushes of a button the sound of Seal filled the room through the surround-sound speakers, wired for me by Carlotta.

"That's a lot better than that bouncy-ass shit they played at the bar." Wade turned to me with a smile.

"I like that bouncy-ass shit." I strolled the length of the

couch, running my finger along the caramel suede cushions. By the time I reached the end, only a few feet separated us. Excitement over what was to come made me slightly jittery. I quickly covered the short distance between us.

"Won't your friends worry about you?" I asked as he pulled me into his arms. I gave myself over to the feel of his heavy hands on my hips and his broad chest plastered against my breasts.

"Nah," he said with a grin, pulling me tighter to him.

With heels on I was in the perfect position to snuggle up close, and gave in to the urge. Cheek to cheek, my lips less than an inch from a tantalizing earlobe, I closed my eyes and relaxed against him. His warm breath tickled my ear and danced down my neck as his hands slid down my back and cupped my bottom, leaving heat trails in their wake as he pulled me even tighter against him. Tight enough to feel the erection I'd left him with. As I inhaled the tang of sweat and crisp, citrusy cologne, I felt a rumble deep in his chest as his head dipped lower to nuzzle my neck. His hands traveled the length of my back, leaving a heat trail in their wake, and months of anticipation and lust caught up with me.

I opened my eyes, that earlobe still temptingly near. Near enough to . . . I flicked my tongue out and gave it a tiny quick lick. When Wade didn't respond—negatively, anyway—I leaned up and pulled it between my lips for a slow, hard suck, then traced the delicate ridges of his ear with my tongue.

"Do you have any idea what you're doing?" His grip on my ass was now almost painful.

Laughing in the back of my throat, I nipped the tender flesh, then sucked again to take the sting out.

"Where's your bedroom?" he whispered.

"Who needs a bed?" I countered, chuckling softly to myself.

"I'm an old-fashioned kinda guy." He pushed me away and smiled.

With a nod, I led him down the dimly lit hall to my bedroom. I grinned at his soft snort of laughter. The girls and I had affectionately named it "my harem room," and for good reason. Multicolored sheers shot through with gold thread hung at the windows and a coordinating duvet cover made up of silk squares covered the king-size bed. Bright purple, orange, and yellow throw rugs on the floor completed the look.

Feminine just didn't cover it.

"Not exactly what I expected from the boss lady."

"Mmmm, what did you expect?" I peeled my shirt over my head and tossed it on the floor. "Condoms are in the nightstand."

With a grin, Wade pushed me back onto the slippery silk and fell on top of me. He wiggled his hips, nudging my legs apart and settling between them. "I didn't expect anything this colorful, but then, I never expected to see you French-kissing another woman either."

"*She* French-kissed *me.*" I thrust my hips against his. "Is that a banana in your pocket?"

"No, I'm just happy to see you, darlin'." He slowly thrust back, pressing against my tender, nerve-filled mound.

We stayed like that for a while, his fingers combing my hair, his lips hovering over mine, teasing, testing, exploring until I found myself insistently grinding my hips against his, seeking release. His stamina surprised me—pleasantly so. I'd expected him to be all over me the moment we hit the door.

"Hmm mmph. Not yet." He worked his way down my chest, biting and sucking at my taut nipples until I'd arched up toward him as high as I could, frustrated and achy as little sharp spikes of pleasure radiated through me. Then he slowly worked his way lower to the valley under my ribs, and lower still. I squirmed and giggled as his warm, wet tongue circled my belly button.

He laughed and sat up. Just sat there, staring at me with those warm green eyes until self-consciousness forced me to speak.

"What?"

"Just admiring the view." He continued to make long sweeps up and down the outsides of my legs. I heaved a sigh of relief and anticipation as he finally reached for the waistband of my lacy panties and pulled them down, flinging them over his shoulder with a grin.

Sitting up, I returned the favor, making it as far as shirt off, pants unzipped before I started teasing him. I couldn't help myself: he was right there, in all his glory, hot and hard and thick in my hand. With my legs still forced wide open by his position between my thighs, I cupped the smooth, round cheeks of his buttocks and wrapped my lips around his cock. He was smooth and deliciously alive against my tongue.

He slowly pumped into my mouth, one hand fisted in my hair. His other hand found my nipple and gave a gentle tug that sent little electrical impulses straight to my pussy. Grunting as my need and frustration grew, I swirled my tongue around the head and gave an extra-firm suck.

"Did you know that girl you were dancing with?" he whispered as his fingertips lightly caressed my back.

"Hmmph mmm," I muttered with my mouth full.

"I liked watching you dance with her. It turned me on," he said, tangling a hand in my hair.

With a smile of thanks I kept up a slow, steady movement, using my hand to jack him off at the same time.

"Ever been with a woman?" he asked, pushing me back on the bed and reaching for a condom.

"Maybe." I gave him an easy smile as I straddled his hips. "But I prefer men."

"That's good to know," he hissed as I eased him inside me.

"How do you want it? Slow? Fast? Hard?" I wiggled my hips experimentally and bit my lip as my oversensitive clit ground against his pubic bone.

"Fast is good," he acknowledged with a painful grin.

I fucked him hard and fast, not at all surprised when he didn't last very long. After all the teasing, I didn't either, and collapsed on his chest a few hot and sweaty minutes later.

"Damn," he huffed, "that girl at the bar has no idea what she's missing."

3

Sunday I forced myself to run Wade off. He left with a good-natured laugh and I barely made it to Baroque in time for brunch with the girls. Sunday was our weekend recap day. Who got lucky. Who didn't. Was it any good? And it came with a five-star rating system: lowest star buys. We were as bad (and as thorough) as any man, and completely unapologetic about it.

If we didn't go shopping or Lanie didn't have paperwork to catch up on, we'd spend the afternoon in her pool or at the pool at Carlotta's condo—depending on whether we felt like being ogled or not.

Sunday was all about relaxing and making it to work on Monday with no one the wiser about our weekend activities.

"So," Lanie said, once we'd all been seated and served our mimosas, "how was Wade, you hussie? Carlotta told me what you did."

I eased back in my chair and gave her a satisfied grin. "Five shiny gold stars, Miss Cradle Robber." Maybe I should feel bad talking about him, rating him—but he did get five stars! And besides, he was probably telling his roommate all about his wild weekend anyway.

Men talk. Women talk. Deal with it.

"He didn't even leave until this morning."

"He stayed all weekend?" Carlotta whispered with a sly smile. "What have I told you about hog-tying men?"

"I think the important question is, what is she gonna do tomorrow?" Lanie asked between snorts of laughter.

"Go to work just like normal and pray he doesn't tell his crew that the Safety Supervisor screwed his brains out!" I finished with a laugh of my own. I was worried, but not terribly so. Wade and I hadn't discussed any post-sexual relationship. I figured he knew the rules—a lay is a lay is a lay (not a relationship or a commitment)—and if he knew not to tell the guys about me kissing a woman, he surely knew that applied to our weekend of sexual acrobatics.

We stopped gossiping long enough to order and waited till our server was out of earshot before continuing. Around us, diners were dressed in their Sunday best, doing their post-church socializing, and the low chatter of people filled with God surrounded us.

Then there were us three heathens discussing sex, with just as much reverence, I might add.

"Lanie deserted me Friday night," Carlotta said, then paused to take a sip of her drink. "So I ended up going home alone."

"It's not like you didn't have any offers," Lanie said with a frown.

"After Friday work, I wasn't in the mood, but trust me, I made up for it Saturday night."

We were forced to wait for details until the waitress served us each a small plate of fruit.

"Rate it," Lanie ordered under her breath.

"Four stars, almost a five but"—Carlotta shook her head—"*not quite*."

"Details," I demanded, leaning forward in my chair.

"Details yourself," she countered. "What made Wade a five—God, he's so hot; never mind."

"He's got all the moves." I forked a piece of cantaloupe, practically moaning as it melted in my mouth. "Yum. Wade was the entire package—and you?"

"I think his name was Greg—"

"You *think* his name was Greg," I said, only to be interrupted by Carlotta, who gave me a dirty look.

"I was talking! He was a little sloppy, a little passive for my taste, but well equipped."

"Who isn't passive for your tastes," Lanie teased. She picked up a piece of strawberry and slid it between her lips and bit down slow enough to make me look around. I shook my head and cut a piece of kiwi in half, then chewed as I slowly scanned the room until I found what had caught her eye.

A Suit—a tall blond with a chiseled jaw and dimples, dressed to the nines in a navy suit with a coordinating red power tie. He sat with an older woman not three tables away.

"Quit flirting and give us the dirty skinny on your Friday conquest. Was it the gigolo, the babe in the woods, or what?"

"Three stars," Lanie said with a sneer of disgust, "small and lacking *serious* moves."

"Oops," Carlotta giggled.

"Not only did he lack moves, he passed out! Thank God we were at his place, so I just got up and left him there."

"Left him where?" I asked with a laugh.

"On the floor." Lanie rolled her eyes then sat back as the waitress slid a Belgian waffle in front of her.

"God, that smells good. I should have gotten one," I said, regretting my own omelet, and never mind that I knew it'd be to die for. The grass was always greener on the other plate.

Carlotta, on the other hand, was too busy tittering to even thank the waitress. While we ate, poor Lanie filled us in on her horrible pickup, making us laugh loud enough to disturb the church crowd and garner us more than a few frowns.

By the time the food was gone, the mimosas were drained from our glasses, and the waitress returned with our check, the dining room was nearly empty—except for the guy Lanie had spent the entire meal flirting with.

"Brunch is on you, since you had the three-star lay." I grinned and pushed the little tray with our check toward Lanie.

"No need to remind me," she said, throwing her Gold Card on top of the bill and smiling as the waitress took it. "I should have gone home with Carlotta."

I shook my head at the sight of her pulling an extra piece of paper from her purse. "You're not." I glanced at the tall Adonis who kept eyeing our table. His mother—or sugar mama—had disappeared, but probably not for long.

"I am, damnit. I have to redeem myself somehow. 'Cause I'm not buying breakfast next week too!"

Once she'd signed the receipt we stood and wound our way through the tables with Lanie bringing up the rear.

Neither Carlotta nor I stopped. Instead we stood at the dining room entrance, watching her work her magic.

"Well?" I asked once she joined us.

"He'll be at Jimmy Z's on Friday night."

"Slut," I muttered with a laugh.

None of us felt like being ogled or going shopping so by unanimous decision, we headed for Lanie's after brunch. Dressed in a skimpy and shockingly yellow bikini, I stood on the patio while Carlotta, in an equally skimpy red ensemble, slathered sunscreen on my back.

While I returned the favor, a topless Lanie went bouncing

by—literally—with a tray of margaritas in hand, her smile as impudent as her unfettered C-cups.

"Someday when her tits are down to her belly button, she'll regret that."

"In the meantime I get to enjoy the view," Carlotta giggled.

"Y'all are so bad!" I snapped the lid on the sunscreen and set it on the table before following Lanie to the pool.

"You okay, doll?" she asked, handing me a sparkly plastic glass rimmed with salt as I sat down beside her.

"Just thinking about Monday, is all."

"Oh don't do that! You're gonna ruin the whole afternoon."

"Thinking about Wade?" Carlotta left her top on the patio table, leaned down and took a full glass, then stepped daintily into the pool. Her golden brown skin gleamed from the suntan lotion, and her nut brown nipples puckered from the chilled water.

Lanie sighed and sipped her drink. "Fooling with the help is a bad idea, girl, and I'd hate to say I told you so but."

"You should know," Carlotta said.

"Y'all remember Jay?" Lanie chuckled and shook her head. "Jay was *hot*. Best damn mechanic I ever had and the best lay too, but he was an *ass*. Hated working under me outside of the bedroom. My point is men just don't like taking orders from women. It's tough but that's why we have rules."

4

I pulled into the construction site's freshly cemented parking lot, barely getting my truck in park before Wade had my driver's-side door open.

"What are you doing?" I hissed as I killed the engine. *God, don't go lovesick fool on me now!*

"We have a problem." The deadly serious expression on his face made me instantly queasy with fear.

"Someone saw us Saturday night?" We'd gone to a little Chinese restaurant just north of The Heights for dinner, then back to my apartment for more mattress acrobatics.

"No!" With a scowl, he yanked off his ball cap, ran a hand through seriously mussed hair, and then replaced the cap on his head. "We have nearly twenty-five thousand feet of fucking *ruined* sheetrock!"

The only thing that kept me from screaming in horror was the site of Wade's crew standing a few feet behind him. They shuffled from foot to foot looking as awful as I suddenly felt. I turned my head enough to take a good hard look at our strip shopping center sitting smack-ass in the middle of a lake of sour mud. It nearly brought up my English muffin and coffee. The entire footprint—the building layout—was fifty thousand feet. How the hell had half of it gotten ruined?

"This isn't happening."

"It is. And it gets worse, honey. Dolan is on his way out."

"Jerry or Junior?" I asked, grabbing my hard hat.

"Both."

"I'm dead." I killed my engine and slid out, pocketing my keys and ignoring Wade's empathetic "honey."

Jerry Dolan *was* Dolan Industries, the most prominent commercial builder in Houston. And his son, Junior, was the Senior Project Manager. If they were on their way, our jobs were in serious jeopardy.

My very first assignment as an Assistant Job Supervisor and nothing had gone right from day one. We were already behind schedule due to a dozen or so minor mishaps, including lost materials, which aren't my domain but Hal Langston's, the Job Supervisor. As Assistant Job Supervisor *and* Safety Supervisor I had more than enough to keep me busy. Barring any serious budget problems, I saw the possibility of us working around the clock to meet our deadline becoming a distinct probability.

I looked up at Wade and sighed. "Nice knowing you."

Despite his understanding chuckle, I knew *he knew* exactly what I was feeling. A company's reputation could be made or broken on a job and so could a crew's—and a supervisor's.

As we gingerly traversed the mud- and muck-covered sidewalk, I was as aware of Wade's hand on the small of my back as I was Hal Langston's eyes on me from just inside the building. He was a tall, stocky man, weather-beaten from years of construction work. Another crew stood at the edge of what would someday soon be a landscaped lawn, waiting for the word to start repairs on the eight-by-four hole located to the left of the door.

Sweat pockets were already forming under my T-shirt, and I

couldn't even shake Wade's hand off—not with forty or so men watching. As Mondays went, this one ranked somewhere in the seventh circle of Hell.

Hal hated me more than anyone else who worked for Dolan Industries. And for no other reason than because I was a woman. He was old school: women should be seen and not heard, I mean barefoot and pregnant. And he always smelled like he'd just swam out of the bottom of a can of beer.

"Alex." Hal wasn't one for formalities like "How was your weekend?" or "Good morning."

And I was always happy to oblige.

"Hal." As I stepped inside the building, I did my best to stay upwind of him but I had a feeling today it wouldn't do me much good. "How bad is it?"

"Some idiot left the water on, and after Friday's fuckup, Dolan's gonna have someone's ass!" His voice echoed off the concrete foundation as he spoke to be heard over the pumps currently sucking out the excess water. Someone, of course, meaning anyone but him.

As if someone had left a tap running. I shook my head and bit my lip to keep from calling *him* the idiot.

"Did anyone call the plumbers? Do we have *any* idea what caused this?" I demanded, focusing on the inch of water under my feet. I turned in a slow circle, surveying square foot upon square foot of newly sheetrocked walls that had sucked up water for two days, and my heart sank to my toes. A quick glance said everything from about waist-height down would have to be ripped out and replaced—sheetrock, insulation, and wiring—with another inspection, to boot.

"One of my guys found one of those oversized plumber's wrenches near the water main."

Hal butted in before Wade could continue. "I told you that could have been left by Little when he shut the water off."

"We don't know that for sure though." A scowling Wade shoved his hands in his pockets.

"Have we called the police?" I asked, even though I already knew the answer. Hell, *no*, Hal hadn't called the police.

"I don't see any reason to call the police. It was an accident!"

"I need a cup of coffee," I said, digging my cell phone out of my purse and dialing 911. Hal and I had our own little scowl battle while I reported the possible vandalism.

"It's your job," he muttered after I hung up.

"Yeah, it is. Now what about the bricklayers?" They were supposed to have finished up this week. I slowly started my initial walk-through, wanting a chance to assess the damage before the boss showed up.

"Sent 'em home." Hal shuffled along behind me. It wasn't just my reputation on the line but Hal's too, whether he liked it or not.

My steel-toed work boots made little sucking, sloshy noises as I silently walked the length of the building. The sight of the damage had a sobering effect on all of us.

By the time we stepped outside into the bright morning sunshine, all three of us heaved a sigh of relief. We watched as a shiny black Lincoln Navigator with dark tinted windows pulled into a space beside my Chevy. If it had been just Wade and me, I might have cracked a joke or something to ease the tension, but Hal didn't have much of a sense of humor. So we all just stood silently waiting as Jerry and Junior Dolan slid out of the shiny SUV. Jerry wore his customary cowboy boots, jeans, and pearl snap shirt, with a ferocious frown on his rugged face. Junior, a younger, taller version of his father, just looked concerned.

Jerry slipped off his sunglasses and silently greeted us, as if we were all attending a funeral. And I suppose in a way it was. *Someone's* funeral.

Normally Jerry was a likeable man, full of good humor and

quick with a joke. He'd earned his money the old-fashioned way and insisted his sons did likewise. He respected people who got the job done, but today he didn't look like he respected much and none of us had answers for him.

Junior gave me a nod and an understanding smile. "Morning, Alex. What happened?" he asked, as Jerry stepped around us and inside the building. The water on the floor came just shy of hitting the snakeskin on his boots, as if it knew better than to slosh.

"Friday—" Hal began.

"We already know about Friday," Junior said. The other reason Hal hated me? He wasn't my boss—Junior was—and Junior Dolan, who had also hired me, *liked me*. I quickly filled him in, earning another understanding smile at Hal's sputtering when I got to the part about calling the police.

"Let's not go assigning blame yet. Wade." Jerry sighed. "How long you think it's gonna take your crew to redo that sheetrock?"

"At least a week; ten days at the outside," Wade quietly said. "And that's just a guess."

"How far behind is this gonna put us?" Jerry pulled a cigar from his pocket and clamped it between thinly compressed lips.

I dreaded saying what I had to say but Jerry was man enough to take it, and besides, he knew what was coming even if none of us liked hearing it. "We'll have to have another electrical inspection, and all the insulation will have to be replaced. Ten days with overtime, and that includes fixing the hole."

"If they can get all the old sheetrock out by Thursday, I can have two insulation crews here to work all day," Junior said.

I didn't even have a chance to ask where he'd find the insulation so fast.

"Do it." Jerry turned my way with a shake of his head. "Get the electricians out here ASAP, and get this job in as close to on time as you can. With no more fuckups!"

* * *

The rest of the morning was like something out of my worst nightmare as I watched Wade's crew remove the saturated sheetrock they'd spent weeks installing, patching, and sanding. And when I wasn't supervising, I was dealing with the police, who finally showed up, or on the phone screaming at the electricians. After enough threats and cajoling they agreed to get their asses out on Tuesday and check our wiring, though they made no promises about how long fixing anything would take.

I collapsed in the chair in my tiny office, nearly deaf after a morning of listening to heavy equipment suck out water and the sound of my little window air-conditioning unit drowning out everything else. I was hot and tired and sure as hell not in the mood for anyone's shit when Wade showed up at my office door.

"How come you're not eating with your crew?" I asked between bites of my meatloaf sandwich. With his jeans and T-shirt covered in white smudges from the damp sheetrock, he looked as stressed and worn out as I felt.

"Thought I'd come see how you were doing." He dropped his cooler on the desk and collapsed in a chair across from me.

"Finally got the fucking electricians straightened around."

"And the police?"

"They said there's probably not much they can do but file the report and get us some extra patrol cars."

Wade pulled his lunch out and set it on the edge of my desk with almost military precision. "Did you tell them about that pack of skateboarders?"

"They're not a pack," I said with a laugh. "You really think it was them?" I nibbled on a Dorito, waiting for his reply. I have nothing against skateboarders. Hell they're up and down my street all the time and their tricks are . . . well, they take more skill than I'll *ever* have. But I don't want them darting in and out of a busy construction site and risking getting run over or hurt—and suing us.

"I think anything's possible, darlin'. They got mighty pissed at you last week." Grinning, he eased back in his chair, a small plastic cup and spoon in his hand. "Between you running 'em off and Hal nearly getting into a fistfight with one on Friday, anything's possible."

As if Friday's mess hadn't been enough, the three skateboarders, who'd been a total nuisance from the day the concrete had dried, had appeared out of nowhere to laugh at The Hole. Hal hadn't taken it well, but then there wasn't much Hal did take well, and a heated argument had ensued.

"It's a wonder we all still have jobs."

Nodding, Wade slipped a spoonful of something between his lips.

"What are you eating?" I frowned over the pile of paperwork at his lunch.

"Chocolate pudding."

"You eat your dessert first?"

"I got a sweet tooth," he replied with a grin that said he had *more* than a sweet tooth.

I chuckled and shook my head as Hal appeared in the doorway, the perennial frown on his face killing my desire to flirt with Wade. "How's it going out there?"

"We're making good progress." Wade didn't bother to turn around, just sighed and slipped another spoonful of pudding between his lips. I didn't miss the hard assessing look Hal gave the both of us. Or the way Wade slowly licked the spoon clean, a huge shit-eating grin on his face.

"Electricians will be out tomorrow," I said.

"Good." With one last nod, Hal turned and headed down the tiny hallway, his footsteps reverberating through the tiny trailer.

"Do me a favor," I said once the door slammed, announcing Hal's departure.

"What's that?"

"Don't call me darlin' when we're at work . . . or honey either."

I hadn't meant to say it quite so harshly but Hal just did that to me. With a curt nod, Wade had gathered up his lunch and quickly retreated from my office, leaving me all alone and pissed off at myself for not having more tact. I made it a point to stop him when they knocked off work for the day, then found myself hemming and hawing under his scowl until all of them finished streaming past.

"I have a reputation—"

"As a ballbuster. Yeah, I know."

Before I could respond, Hal went trolling by, giving us both another long hard look like he'd done earlier. "See you both tomorrow."

We said our goodnights, then watched him climb into his dusty Ford. The sound of the diesel engine starting up drowned out anything else we might have said.

I barely caught Wade's " 'Night boss" when he turned to go. With half the crew still waiting to get out of the parking lot there was no way I could stop him, as much as I wanted to. Turning, I headed inside the trailer to get my stuff. Tonight was yoga. I didn't really want to go, but I needed the stress relief and something to take my mind off Wade.

5

If anything, Tuesday was worse. The stench of sour mud hit me the minute I got to work and stayed with me the entire time I walked the site with the electricians, who, of course, confirmed my worst fears. We had wiring problems.

I stepped outside the building in time to see Wade, who'd ignored me all morning, coming my way with two biscuits and two cups of coffee, a smile on his handsome face. Sure, it was probably for the best that he'd ignored me, but that didn't mean I had to like it.

"You look like you could use this," he said, handing me a cup and a biscuit.

With a sigh of relief and a smile I accepted his peace offering.

"Where's mine?" Hal boomed from behind me with a raucous laugh. "Or do you just treat *the ladies* to breakfast?"

From nearby someone chuckled, and I swallowed a lump of dread as I picked up a few sly glances shot my way. As businesslike as possible, I filled Wade in on the electricians' verdicts while I ate. "They'll need at least two days to fix the wiring."

"It's a wonder Dolan hasn't shown up back out here to supervise." Hal stepped past Wade, giving him a slap on the shoulder.

Wade winced slightly, then turned his attention back to me. "Any other bad news you'd like to share, darlin'?"

More laughs, and louder to boot; this time from Wade's crew and the electricians who streamed past us on their way to the catering truck. It wasn't even noon yet and the humidity was so thick I could feel it pressing me into the sidewalk. My feet were so heavy, I couldn't move as fear and anger stiffened my spine. Somehow or other I had to make him understand that being at work meant business as usual. Though that didn't make me want him any less.

I sipped my coffee and gave him a cold, hard stare from under my hard hat. "Your guys are gonna have to work this weekend." I couldn't hold back a smirk at the sound of groans that accompanied my statement.

"I ain't working this weekend," Wade said with a nod.

" 'Fraid it looks like you are."

"I got a hot date."

I wanted to ask who with, since he hadn't asked *me* out, but I didn't.

"Your hot date will have to wait. You're working this weekend to get that sheetrock back up. And you're probably working late this Friday night."

"Which means you'll be here too, right?" He shot the crew a grin.

"Nope, but I will be on call." I made to step past him and escape to the relative peace of my office, where I could hide out and forget he'd called me darlin' *again*.

"What if we can't reach you?"

Because, of course, I'd be at Jimmy Z's while he was here hanging sheetrock by spotlight. "I'll have my pager on."

"So we can just page you if something goes wrong?"

I didn't miss the threat in his voice. If he paged me, and I had to come straight from the bar all dressed up in high heels and a skimpy dress, I was busted. I wadded up the biscuit wrapper and threw it into a nearby trash bin. "Let's take this in my office, shall we?"

On shaky legs I led him across the parking lot to the trailer and flung the door open. One of Hal's flunkies sat at a corner desk, talking on the phone in a low voice. At my scowl, he set his feet on the floor and turned his back to us, obviously not in the mood to be disturbed.

I led Wade back to my office, slammed the door, and threw my hard hat in the corner, thankful Hal was still outside. Kicking the extra chair out of my way, I leaned against the desk beside Wade.

"Do you think I asked you not to call me sugar or darling or honey just to be a bitch?" I asked, scowling down at him.

He set his biscuit and coffee next to mine and eased to his feet so I had to look up at him. "I think you're making a big deal out of nothin'."

"*Nothing?* How long have you worked for Dolan?" I hissed, wishing I could holler at the top of my lungs instead, but I damn sure didn't want anyone finding out the real reason I'd yanked him into my office.

"This is my first job for Dolan, but I've worked construction all my life."

"Ever work with a woman?"

"Yeah," he said, with a slow nod. He stepped in front of me so his legs straddled mine and reached up to give my shoulders a firm squeeze. Talking was nearly impossible with him distracting me.

"Wade, I've worked for three years to earn a little respect. Just a little and you're putting all of that in jeopardy. You see how Hal—what are you doing?"

He was unsnapping my dusty work shirt, then untucking my tank top. Fear and desire slid up my spine, competing with one another as his warm, firm hands grasped my rib cage. "No, Wade! Not here. We can't," I whispered as he leaned closer. *What I can do and what I should do are two very different things. What I should do is chase his ass out of my office.*

"The door's not even locked," he murmured, his lips curving into a smile.

Even though I knew I shouldn't, that I could kiss my job good-bye if we got caught, I let him kiss me. His mouth was as warm and firm as I remembered as his tongue slid smoothly against mine and his fingers dug deep into the sore, tired muscles of my back.

"You know if we get caught—" I stammered once he let me up for air. I felt hypnotized by his deep green gaze; my legs were heavy and my cunt damp and eager, in spite of—or because of—the possibility of getting caught.

"We're not gonna get caught. We didn't get caught Friday night," he added, unzipping the fly of my jeans.

I reached for his fly, pausing long enough to cup the erection outlined in worn denim. "That was a bar, though."

"Yell at me," he said, pulling a condom out of his pocket.

I snorted in shocked laughter at the little cellophane package. "Yell at you?"

"Yeah, and turn around, while you're at it."

I spun around in my heavy work boots, then bit my lip to keep from laughing. I could barely remember why I'd dragged him in here in the first place. He moved up behind me and leisurely pushed my jeans over my hips, as if he had all the time in the world. I closed my eyes and leaned against him as soft, worn denim caressed my bottom and caused my nipples to strain against my bra. His hand at the small of my back coaxed me to bend over my desk. I did, allowing frigid air to drift across my backside and send another shiver up my spine. I moaned and grabbed the edge of my desk for support as he slid a finger inside me.

"Yell!" he hissed, leaning over to cover my body with his. Anyone who walked in would have no doubt about what we were doing.

I sighed at the feel of his cock pressed against me, then forced myself to follow his instructions. "Y'all are working this weekend whether you like it or not!"

With one hard thrust, Wade was buried deep inside me, and I wasn't laughing anymore. I struggled to adjust to the feel of him inside me, stretching me, finally pushing myself up on my toes and arching my hips to better accommodate the both of us.

"No we're not! That sheetrock can get hung—"

From somewhere nearby a door slammed. I tensed slightly until my sex-fogged brain didn't pick up footsteps.

"This weekend, goddammit!"

The window A/C unit hummed loudly enough to drown out the moans we forced ourselves to stifle as Wade pumped in and out of me like a piston, filling me, only to pull back and tease me, then thrust inside again until skin slapped against skin.

"Harder," I ordered from between gritted teeth.

"Yell some more," Wade replied on a thrust I felt at the back of my throat.

"It's your turn."

"If you ain't workin', I'm not either." He pressed his face against my shirt so I could feel him laughing against my back.

"I'm not the drywall foreman!" came out somewhere between a yell and a screech at another extra-hard thrust. I could barely force the words out as I got closer and closer to climaxing. "And don't call me darlin' again or I'll have your ass!"

"I got your ass!"

Now we were both laughing. I shifted enough to get to my clit with my fingers and stroked myself while Wade raced to keep up. "Come on, baby," I hissed, ready to finish it before we did get caught. Groaning, I pressed my face into a stack of paperwork. "Hurry, Wade . . . oh God."

"Like that," he panted in my ear.

A door slammed again and footsteps bounced down the hallway, stopped, then started again and a door closed. *Hell!* "Hal."

"Hurry up, darlin'," Wade hissed.

"Call me darlin' again," I yelled for our audience, "and I'll have your fucking job!" I reached around and dug my fingers into his bare ass as my pussy clenched and my legs nearly gave out beneath me.

Wade didn't waste any time. A few sharp thrusts and a groan he muffled by biting my shoulder, and he sagged against me. The harsh, raspy sound of our heavy breathing filled my ears but I didn't miss the sound of the floor creaking somewhere nearby. I sat up as much as I could and tapped Wade's shoulder, then pointed toward the wall that separated Hal's office from mine. He gave me a nod of understanding.

We hurriedly dressed, then I sank down in the chair next to Wade on shaky legs.

"Does it smell like sex in here?" I asked, giggling.

"Probably," he replied with a soft chuckle. "But ya gotta admit, it was worth it."

"You're damn good, but you're not worth my job, Wade."

6

Wade and I reached an agreement about work. I don't think he was happy with it but he didn't have much of a choice. I agreed to go out with him Thursday night and he'd leave me be to have my fun at Jimmy Z's on Friday. I also had to work a couple of hours on Saturday and agree to spend Sunday night with him. Not all night, just hang out.

I ran home with just enough time to shower and change into a sunny yellow peasant blouse and my favorite broken-in pair of Silver jeans before trudging down to the Golden Cafe to meet Carlotta for dinner. She'd called late in the afternoon in a complete tizzy, and despite my fatigue, I didn't have the heart to turn her down. Once I got there, I immediately felt better about my decision to get out. Ginger, garlic, and stir-fried beef tickled my nose and made my stomach rumble. With a smile for the hostess, I stepped into the dining room, spotting Carlotta sipping iced jasmine tea at a table by the windows. I crossed the nearly empty restaurant and sank into a chair across from her.

"Tea please," I said, smiling at the waitress who stopped briefly at our table.

"How's working with Wade?" Carlotta stirred the half-full glass of tea I was sure she'd already sweetened.

I briefly filled her in on the last two days, including our morning sexcapade, which got me a laugh but didn't address the reason she'd asked me to dinner.

"Wait 'til Lanie finds out you're after her Super Ho title!"

We gave each other a conspiratorial smile, then stopped long enough to order dinner: Lemon Pepper Shrimp for me and Orange Chicken for her, with a side of egg rolls to share.

"What's up?" I asked after our waitress disappeared again.

"I'm gonna quit my job."

"So I guess the boss's nephew thing didn't go too well?"

"He asked me out," she said with a soft laugh.

My girly-sense said there was more to the story, so I probed a bit while adding sugar to my own tea. "And? What does that have to do with quitting your job?"

"He asked me out after I fucked him on his desk," she said with another small laugh. If I didn't know better I'd swear she was blushing.

"You *fucked* the Geek Meister?"

"Geek Meister had it goin' on."

"No way!" I laughed, then sobered as another thought hit me. "He didn't threaten to tell the boss, did he?"

"Worse!"

Frankly, I couldn't imagine anything worse than Chambers, her boss, finding out. We both sat back as the waitress delivered our eggrolls, and I took two, dousing them with soy sauce. "How worse?"

Carlotta paused in the middle of spooning duck sauce onto her plate. "He sent me flowers—at work."

"Oh shit." Like me, she found herself in the unenviable position of working under, and with, a bunch of men. "How much hell did you catch?"

"It was an all-day event, girl. Hell, they called while I was there today wanting to know how *they* could get flowers."

"You had to go back?" I stared at her in shock, then dropped my eggroll when it started to burn my fingers. "Ouch!" Licking my scorched fingertips, I waited on her reply.

"Yeah. He was cute," she added with a shrug.

"Didja screw him again, Carlotta?" I asked with a sigh.

"No!" She took a bite of her eggroll, then continued. "I have to go finish up on Thursday."

"Carlotta!"

"I'm just gonna finish the job and have one for the road."

"The way to a man's heart might be through his stomach but the way into your pants is via the florist."

"Sue me, they were nice flowers. Geek Meister has good taste. I don't know why you're getting all worked up. I'm giving notice on Friday and then I won't be seeing Devon anymore."

"Devon?" I arched an eyebrow and waited.

"Geek Meister does have a real name."

"Be careful, girl."

"You're the one who has a date with a co-worker tomorrow night."

"I know, I know." A date was probably a bad idea, but that didn't stop me from wanting to see him, or sleep with him, again.

7

An evening breeze pressed the skirt of my yellow paisley halter dress against my legs as Wade and I crossed the parking lot of Houston's premiere gentleman's entertainment club. The Doll Palace would never qualify as a Southern belle. She was more of a Yankee carpetbagger-type mansion lit up like Christmas.

I quirked an eyebrow at him as I stepped inside. "Wade, in case you haven't noticed, this is a strip club." Our dinner date had gone off without a hitch so far. In fact he'd been a perfect gentleman all evening, but I could see now why he'd been so secretive about this evening's plans. As dates went this one was definitely different.

"They have pool tables." Grinning, he rested a hand at the small of my back and guided me toward the cover-charge girl. *I* got in for free. "And this is the classiest strip joint in the whole state, which means the chances of us getting caught together are slim to none."

"It better be, as much as she charged you to walk in here. You bring all your dates here?" Inside the Doll Palace, some country singer was going on and on about picking wildflowers while up on stage a busty blonde pranced around in a thong and a cowboy hat.

"Only the special ones."

When Wade asked me out on a date, I never imagined he'd take me to a strip joint, albeit one that was the epitome of swanky. The place was busier than I'd expected for a Thursday night, but judging from the amount of suits and ties, Wade was right. No one from work would be caught dead in here.

We found a table near a side stage, and Wade pulled out a chair for me, then practically sat in my lap, draping an arm around my shoulder. I listened as he ordered us beer but couldn't seem to take my eyes off the woman on stage drawing a figure eight with the cheeks of her ass.

"Think you could do that?" Wade asked with a laugh.

Pursing my lips, I watched for a few more minutes. Her caramel-colored skin shone under the lights and when she turned around I didn't miss the proud, challenging thrust of her chin or the slightly narrowed eyes she appraised the crowd with. She reminded me of some Indian Priestess—Mayan maybe; I wasn't up on my lost civilizations, but she was hot.

"I could do that."

"But would you?"

"I didn't go to college for four years to strip for a living." I yelled to make myself heard above the music. "And besides, my steel-toed boots are a hell of a lot more comfortable than what she's wearing."

The four-inch come-fuck-me heels practically made me wince. But I could see why she wore them. They probably added an extra cup to her firm, dark-tipped breasts and a curve to the globes of her full bottom. She had nice tits, full and natural looking. But then most of the women in here were exceptional.

"Want me to buy you a lap dance?" He leaned over and slipped a hand up my skirt.

I squeezed my thighs together and gave him a long hard

look, then took in the Mayan cutie cupping her breasts with long red-tipped fingers and licking lips that matched. "How about *I* buy *you* one?"

"How about you give me one?" His hand slid a little higher, and I smiled at the tingle of excitement between my thighs.

"Right here?" I waved a hand at the high-class crowd, at the busty redhead who'd taken the last girl's place on the small stage two tables in front of us.

"They won't say anything. Just pretend it's the VIP lounge at Jimmy Z's."

"How *did* you get in that lounge?" I sipped my beer, needing a little false courage for what I was about to do. The thought of climbing on his lap with an audience made my blood flow a little—a lot—faster. I'd done more than my fair share of wild and crazy things but this . . . this was a new one, and I liked it.

"Gimme a lap dance and I'll tell you," he coaxed with a sly grin.

Smiling, I stood and straddled his lap and lifted my skirt out of the way so my thong and the bare cheeks of my ass rested against the rough denim crotch of his jeans. A waitress with a tray full of beer walked by, her pace slowing as she returned my smile. I wrapped my arms around Wade's neck and winked at the guys at the next table. The slender, well-fed duo—a blond with a crew cut and lots of well-developed muscles, and a preppy-looking brunet—watched in fascination. I never took my eyes off our audience, even as Wade's hands slipped under my skirt and cupped my ass. My panties grew damper and my clit swelled at Wade's strong fingers and the constant friction on my pussy lips, but I refused to let myself speed up. Refused to let myself just hurry and finish it because my climax was imminent.

Wade's lips were on my neck and he was saying something, but I couldn't figure out what. All I could do was focus on his hands, the finger slipping under the thin string of my thong to tease the tender, nerve-filled skin. Then he slid one finger inside me and I bit back a moan, licked my lips and checked to see if our audience had grown. The waitress who'd winked at me earlier now stood at the bar, watching while she chattered with the female bartender. If anything, my nipples grew harder at the few appreciative smiles I caught.

That finger slid in and out of me as I rode it, never going deep enough, never hard enough or big enough, while Wade smiled at me in a way that made my insides quiver and quicken. I slid down as far I could go and my thighs clenched his hips. "I want you," I mouthed, knowing he'd understand.

"I think that's enough for you, little girl." He gently withdrew his finger.

The absence of his finger was almost painful and incredibly frustrating and I sagged against him. "Damnit, Wade!"

"Payback's a bitch, darlin'."

I sucked in a deep breath of smoke-tinged air and let it out slowly. "So that was for Jimmy Z's?" I asked, pushing myself upright on his lap and reaching for my beer.

Nodding, he squeezed my thigh. "My college roommate is part owner."

"So, if you went to college, how come you're a drywall foreman?"

"No more talking. Let's get out of here."

"Do you have another college roommate who owns part of the Doll Palace?" I asked once we'd reached the parking lot.

"No," he laughed, hitting the alarm button for his truck. "Panties nice and wet?"

"I hope you plan on finishing what you started!" My panties were beyond wet and I ached. The silk top of my dress rubbed my bare nipples, making matters worse.

He opened the door and I slid in, suddenly aware of how

much I didn't know about Wade. "Well?" I asked once he'd joined me. "Did you drop out?"

"Nope." He backed out and headed for the road.

"Just *nope*?" Now it was my turn to laugh. I crossed my legs and hugged myself, doing my best to will some of the ache away.

"I got an associate's degree and decided that was enough for me."

We silently traveled the highway for a while until the truck's air-conditioning, and my goosebumps, forced me to speak. "Can you turn that down some?" I asked, pointing at the control knobs on the dash. He did with a grin and a glance at my chest.

"Thought it might cool ya down some."

"Very funny." I frowned at the laughter in his voice, then asked him another question that had been bugging me. "If you hadn't caught me at Jimmy Z's, would you have asked me out?"

"I thought about it . . . that day I came by your house."

We pulled onto my dark, quiet street, lit with splashes of paleness from the occasional streetlights. Neither of us spoke again until Wade pulled into the driveway beside my truck and killed the engine.

"I had a nice time."

"We're not through." I slid out of the truck to the sound of his chuckle in my ears. The warm night air quickly took away the air-conditioner's chill as I crossed from the driveway to the sidewalk, Wade on my heels. We barely made it to the door before he had his hand under my skirt again and his fingers under the thin strap of my thong.

"A wedgie is not the way to win me over," I said, yanking my keys out of my purse and finally locating the right one. My shaking hands didn't help matters at all.

"Maybe this is," he murmured huskily. His fingers trailed across my butt cheeks and down my thighs, distracting me even more from the door lock that refused to cooperate with my determined attempts to get it open, get Wade inside, and get naked. I gave one last rattle of frustration and rested my forehead against the door with a chuckle of frustration.

"Problems?" Wade whispered in my hair. His hands were busy elsewhere, pushing my thong off my hips until it was tangled around my feet.

"I can't get the damn door open." I dropped my purse.

Wade lifted the skirt of my dress and smoothed a hand over my belly while slowly grinding his crotch against me in a way that made me want to bend over and just submit. The twenty-minute drive home hadn't quenched my appetite for him at all.

Turning, I peeked over his shoulder at the quiet, dark neighborhood, then stepped out of the thong and yanked my dress over my head, dropping it beside my purse. "What happened to the old-fashioned guy who needed a bed?"

With a chuckle, he untucked his shirt and unzipped his jeans, pushing them down just enough to free his cock. "I was afraid I'd scare you off."

"I kissed a woman in a bar and you were afraid you'd scare me off?" Snorting with laughter, I wrapped my fingers around his erection and rubbed my thumb across the tip. It came away damp. My eyes on Wade, I licked my thumb, savoring the taste of his pre-cum on my tongue.

"Turn around."

"No." Giving him a saucy grin in the dim light, I leaned against the door and lifted my right leg, waiting for him to take it.

He did, moving closer so his cock was pressed against the cradle of my hips. "Your hand's in the way."

"I know," I said, giving his cock a firm stroke.

He grabbed my wrist and pushed it away, then guided himself inside me. Sighing, I relaxed against the door as he filled me, pumping into me with smooth, even strokes. The sound of an oversized pickup truck caught my attention and I wrapped my arms around his neck, watching from the safety of my recessed porch as it eased up the street with no clue that not far from where they passed a couple were fucking like rabbits. Laughing softly at the fact that Wade never even stopped, I sank my teeth into his neck, sucking at the warm, slightly salty skin.

"Harder," I ordered, slipping an arm under his and grabbing a firm butt cheek.

He obliged with a grunt, thrusting nearly hard enough to make my teeth rattle, and suddenly we were all business, fighting for our release. Fighting for it not to end. Fucking like a couple of back-alley dogs, we took turns nipping at each other.

Like I said, nothing was sacred. Wade kept me pinned to the door with one hand while the other one roamed free, down the length of my leg and back up again, leaving heat trails in its wake. He caught a tight, hard nipple between his fingers and rudely pinched it as his hips never stopped. Neither did mine.

We were both straining for our climax, until all it took was one last hard stroke, and the one leg I had on the ground buckled. I clung to him as the force of my orgasm left me breathless, and only the chunk of flesh I'd nearly taken out of his shoulder saved me from the whole neighborhood hearing what a tramp I was.

8

"I think I pulled a muscle last night," I murmured in reply to the kiss Wade pressed on my neck before he rolled out of bed.

"Come take a shower with me and I'll massage it," he offered.

"You go ahead." I threw back the covers and rolled over, smiling appreciatively at the sight of his bare ass disappearing into the bathroom. After a slow stretch, I gave my leg an experimental flex and forced myself up. I grabbed my robe from a nearby chair before hollering, "I'll start the coffee."

A few minutes later we traded places, sorta. I stepped into the steam-filled bathroom for a shower while Wade dressed and sipped at the cup of coffee I'd left sitting on the dresser for him.

On sore legs I stood letting warm water run down me, while I soaped my hair and thought. A dangerous thing for any woman, especially after a night like last night. I couldn't even begin to contemplate what a real relationship with Wade would mean for our jobs. Someone would have to leave Dolan Industries. And just then, I wasn't even sure I wanted a relationship. What I *was* sure of was that I liked his company in and *out* of bed. Wade had become more than just a fuck, but then I'd probably known that all along. A lover, maybe? Not a boyfriend. That implied too much control, and holidays and families; things that tended to complicate relationships even more. I shuddered and added body wash to the sponge, then winced as I bent over to wash my feet and legs.

"You gonna stay in there all day?"

Leaning against the wall, I peered up at Wade through the water streaming down my face. "I just got in."

"Want me to fix us something to eat?" he offered with a tender smile.

Oh dear. Maybe I'm just imagining things. I blinked to clear the water from my eyes and shook my head no. "You don't have to wait on me or anything, I'll just grab something on the way to work."

"Suit yourself." He disappeared from view, and with a sigh of relief, I reached for the conditioner. "I guess you don't want a ride to work, either, huh?"

"No, thanks." The bottle slipped from my hand and landed in the bottom of the shower with a loud splat. I frowned down at it while slowly untangling my hair. "See you later," I blurted out, unsure if it was a question or a comment.

By the time I stepped out of the shower Wade was gone and my house was silent as a tomb. Sighing in frustration, I sipped at a lukewarm cup of coffee and stared at myself in the dresser mirror. I didn't have time to think about what to do with Wade now.

After drying my hair and pulling it up with a clip, I limped through the bedroom, babying my sore leg as I dressed in old Levi's, a sports bra, and a tank top, then covered everything up with a short-sleeved work shirt.

While a bagel toasted I packed a lunch and filled my thermos with iced tea, grabbing a couple extra bottles of water for later in the afternoon. I slathered my breakfast with cream cheese, then collapsed into a kitchen chair with a fresh cup of coffee, refusing to think about how tired I was. Or how much I didn't want to go out tonight. Or how I was going to make it through the day dead on my feet. At least Wade had to work tonight. I snorted into my cup, then quickly finished my breakfast and headed out the door before I was late.

Other than stopping to talk drywall progress during the afternoon break, we didn't speak until it was nearly my quitting time. And surprisingly he didn't give off any of those bristly angry-man vibes like he'd done on Tuesday.

"At this rate, y'all might finish up tomorrow." I slid onto the tailgate of his truck and swung my legs. Fatigue weighed me down nearly as much as the heat and humidity did. Hal stood on the steps of the construction trailer watching us.

"I don't think I'm gonna make it," Wade murmured with a tired sigh. "But we should finish hanging the sheetrock tomorrow."

We both laughed softly. Thankfully, no one was within hearing distance.

"If you do, I'll cook dinner Sunday to celebrate."

"Fuck that, we're going out."

"I thought we were staying in?"

"How about a movie and popcorn instead?"

"How about you rent movies and bring them over?"

"I've got a great porno collection."

Snorting softly, I slipped off the tailgate and smoothed my jeans down with my hands.

"We need to talk . . . about this morning," he added before I could say anything.

"Yeah, we do."

"How late's your crew working tonight?" Hal stepped off

the porch and headed our way, reminding me that I had no business flirting with Wade on the clock.

Then again, I had no business fooling around with him in the first place.

"'Til the sun's gone—eight or so."

"I need to get going," I said, "but remember, I'll have my pager on if y'all need anything."

"Will do," Wade said with a nod.

"I'm sure he'll holler if he needs anything," Hal muttered snidely.

Ignoring him, I headed for the trailer to get my stuff and call it a day. By the time I stepped back outside, Hal's truck was gone. Apparently he'd slipped out early to get his nightly beer fix.

Wade motioned me over to the building's entrance. From inside I could hear the nail guns going nonstop as his men worked to finish up. "Behave yourself tonight. No seducing men in the VIP lounge."

"Just because I took you home doesn't mean I take home every man I meet."

"I did wonder."

"You aren't going to get all jealous and clingy on me, are you?" The words were out of my mouth before I could stop them, but I didn't appreciate him questioning my morals. Those were mine to live or die by, not his.

"Should I?"

"Remember when I said you weren't worth my job? I wasn't kidding, and this week I came this close"—I held my thumb and forefinger together just inches from his nose—"to losing my job."

"Don't blame me because you've got an exhibitionist streak."

"I'm not, but I don't think this is going to work. I'm sorry."

And I truly was sorry. I liked Wade, a lot. Regret at my decision weighed me down, but I didn't see where we had any other choice.

He sighed and offered up a last-ditch save. "No more sex at work, I swear."

"I don't know if that's enough for me." I needed my job more than I needed him. If I had no job, I had nothing. Going back to Washington State, home, with my tail between my legs, was not an option.

"Is it the blue-collar thing?" He offered me a smile that could only be called sad, and for a minute I softened.

"No, silly. The whole point of going to Jimmy's is about being around men who don't resent us because they have to take orders from us."

"So what do you want?"

Famous last words. "I think, in this case, what I want and what I'm gonna have aren't the same thing. I want you to be my lover; I just don't see how that's possible."

9

As soon as I got out of the parking lot, I pulled out my cell phone and hit AUTO DIAL for Carlotta.

"H'lo?" She sounded like she'd been crying. Not very Carlotta-like at all!

"Girl, are you okay?"

"I'm fine," she said, sniffling.

I pulled the phone away and stared at it before putting it to my ear again. "Meet me for dinner at Casa Grande, and call Lanie, pretty please." I hung up, not waiting for a response and forced myself to focus on the heavy Friday rush-hour traffic.

I pulled into my driveway and killed the truck's engine, then sat there listening to the soft tick of the engine cooling. I eased out of the truck and inside the house, grabbed myself a beer, and headed for the bath. Unlike last week, this one was a quick utilitarian shave and wash with no time or desire for playing. I was even more tired than I'd been last Friday. And if I stayed in the tub too long, there was a good chance I'd doze off.

I'd barely dried myself off when a knock at the door had me groaning in frustration.

"Hello, hello!" two voices chorused from the entryway. Either Carlotta or Lanie had used her key. "We brought wine and pizza!"

"Are we staying in?" I stuck my head into the hall while tying my robe at my waist.

"You look like shit!" Carlotta pursed her lips and frowned at me.

"Can I cancel tonight?" I asked hopefully.

"No!" Lanie wagged a finger at me.

"How the hell did y'all get cleaned up so fast, and don't you have a date tonight, Lanie?"

"I quit my job!" Carlotta shook the pizza box with a triumphant grin.

"And she shanghaied me out from under a Volvo! I had two mechanics quit this week," Lanie added with a scowl.

"Let me get dressed." I turned back toward my bedroom, not at all surprised when Carlotta followed with the pizza. My stomach rumbled as the spicy scent of tomato sauce filled the bedroom.

By the time Lanie reappeared, carrying paper plates and cups for the wine, I'd finished drying myself off and had slipped into some underwear. Eyeing the both of them clad in jeans, I pulled my second-best pair of Seven jeans off a hanger and shimmied into them, then dove back in for a shirt, yanking a chocolate brown crotcheted halter top over my head.

"So, I dumped Wade and you quit your job." I collapsed on the bed across from the both of them and fished a piece of veggie pizza out of the box. "I thought you were just going to give notice?"

"I was." Carlotta handed me a paper cup half-full of wine. Her smile didn't do much to hide the tight lines of tension around her eyes. "But Chambers lit into me and I let him have it. Now I have a two-week vacation before I start my new job."

"And you didn't say anything to us because?" Lanie asked from her position at my feet.

"I was afraid it wouldn't pan out. It's for a company that works with new home builders doing wiring for communications, home theaters, and security systems. High-dollar homes with high-dollar pay."

"Like there's any such thing as a cheap home in Houston," I said with a grin. "I'm proud of you for leaving that shit factory behind. So what about the Geek Meister?"

"At least he won't be sending me flowers at work anymore," Carlotta said.

"You didn't tell him you quit?" I reached for the bottle of wine and topped off my cup.

"Nope, now what's this about you dumping Wade?"

"Yeah, and hurry up. I've got a date," Lanie said.

"Bitch!" Laughing, I kicked her and nearly sent her sprawling on the floor. "What the hell are you gonna do with that Suit you picked up last Sunday?"

"Fuck his brains out, I hope. Can't have you taking my title of Queen Ho, now can I?"

While we polished off the last of the pizza and the cheap merlot, I filled them in on my conversation with Wade.

"Toldja so!" Lanie lifted her cup, and for just a moment, I considered kicking her off the bed on purpose.

By the time we arrived at Jimmy Z's, the merlot and chitchat had done their job: dragged my ass off the ceiling. We made our way through the crowded bar accompanied by the sound of Moby. I offered up a grateful smile to Brian, who'd left a small cardboard "Reserved" sign on our table. He knew us too well, appearing at our table with the first round of drinks before we'd even settled in.

"You're late, ladies," he scolded with a good-natured smile that even Lanie couldn't fail to return.

I double-checked to make sure my pager was attached to my pocket, then took a sip of my Woo Woo, letting the cold, fruity drink slide down my throat and land somewhere near my toes. Before I'd even gotten settled in or had a chance to check out the crowd, I found myself led out onto the dance floor by a swarthy hunk in a brightly striped Ralph Lauren shirt. He gave octopuses a bad name, and I quickly lost him in the crowd after spotting the blonde I'd danced with last weekend. I slipped up to her with a smile. "I had to ditch a creep!"

"No prob!" She raised her beer bottle and slipped an arm around my waist. "I'm Cherise, by the way."

"Lexi! Can I buy you a drink? Since you sorta rescued me."

After a stop at the bar, we headed back to the table with the girls. Cherise, it turns out, was bisexual like Queen Ho Lanie. Not that being bisexual made Lanie a ho: I attributed that to an old-school Irish father and four older brothers.

My pager went off in the middle of laughing my ass off to an especially bad joke Carlotta had dared to share with us. I jumped as it buzzed against my hip bone then unclipped it, frowning in the dim bar light. The readout listed Wade's number with 911 after it. I considered ignoring it, figuring he just wanted to talk, then thought better of it. I held up my pager. "I'll be back!"

The girls nodded and I slid off my stool, purse in hand as I headed for the ladies' room, where I'd at least be able to hear. The door had no sooner closed behind me than my cell phone started ringing. "What happened?"

"A small accident, but I think you need to be here," Wade replied.

Rolling my eyes at the girl standing beside me fixing her lipstick, I said, "How small?"

"Remember those skateboarders?"

"Shit!" How could I forget them?

"About the time we were closing down for the night I heard screams. We didn't hear them out there, Lexi, because of the nail guns and Ramon's radio."

"It's okay! How bad is it?"

"Just a broken leg—I think. I left Ramon in charge of closing up, and I'm following the ambulance to Memorial."

"Call Dolan; I'll meet you there!"

"Hal said not to."

"You called Hal?" I silently swore, then swore again as I caught my reflection in the mirror. Moussed and sprayed hair, dark eyeliner, and killer brown lips to match my brown halter top.

"He's the Job Supervisor, Lexi!"

"Fuck Hal! Call Dolan, or better yet, call Junior. I'll be there as soon as I can."

Memorial Hospital was close enough to the club that I didn't get much of a chance to worry how I was dressed or how I was going to deal with Hal as I zipped down the 610 loop.

I frowned at Hal's Ford as I crossed the parking lot in three-inch Jimmy Choos, preparing myself for the worst. Inside the ER was controlled chaos. I gave Wade's name to the nurse at the desk, and she motioned to a hallway on her left while giving me a once-over. *It's Friday night lady, sue me!* Spending the night in the ER hadn't been in my plans when I left the house.

I had no trouble spotting Wade still covered in sheetrock dust and plaster, or Hal, looming over him with a finger in his face. From behind a curtain I could hear soft moaning and voices, some giving orders while others fretted. "How's the kid? Did we get ahold of his parents?"

Apparently my strident voice did the trick, distracting Hal from whatever he'd been chewing Wade out about.

"Well lookie you! Dolan's bitch. He with ya?" The smell of

beer was strong, and I had serious doubts about the wisdom of Hal having driven here. He smelled as if the only place he needed to drive was between his sheets at home for a long sleep-it-off.

"If you have a problem with me or the instructions I gave Wade, you can take it up with me when you're sober." I stopped as far away as I could manage, smiling to myself as Wade stepped out of the line of fire. No way was he getting between two supervisors having a turf war and that's just what this was. "Now"—I turned to Wade—"how's the kid?"

"It's definitely a broken leg. His parents got here right before you did—"

"You didn't have any business calling Junior." Hal gave my shoulder a firm nudge, demanding my attention.

"I had all the business in the world—"

"We all know how much you like telling men what to do. Bossy-ass bitch." Hal leered at me. An ugly sight even at the best of times, but I refused to back down and propped my hands on my hips, stepping closer despite my protesting stomach.

"*I* do my job. And part of my job is keeping the Senior Project Manager apprised of safety problems."

"They don't want safety; they want results—"

"That's what you think." By this time we were shouting while Wade hovered somewhere nearby.

"That's what I know."

"The only reason Dolan promoted you is 'cause you got balls on your chest instead between your legs where they belong." He grabbed his own and gave 'em a shake for emphasis.

"You're just pissed 'cause deep down inside you know I'll make Project Manager while you'll spend the rest of your days supervising a crew." I stuck my finger in the middle of his chest for emphasis. "And *I* get the job done."

From behind me I heard Wade snicker, but I didn't dare look at him or I'd bust out laughing.

"What the hell's that supposed to mean?

"It means you couldn't get the job done if it came with directions written in single-syllable words." I gave him a scornful once-over. "You're an incompetent drunk, and Dolan should have fired you a hell of a long time ago. Probably only keeps you around—"

Hal lunged, his meaty paw landing somewhere in the vicinity of my chest with enough force to take me down in my three-inch heels. Suddenly Wade *was* there between us, spinning me safely out of the way and helping me stay on my feet while two EMTs who'd appeared from behind the curtained-off room kept a firm grip on Hal.

"Alex, you okay?" Junior Dolan appeared at my other side, his forehead creased with concern.

I nodded and gave him a grateful smile as Wade pulled me close enough that the heat of his body seared me through my jeans.

"Be right back," Dolan murmured.

With a grateful nod, I eased myself out of Wade's arms and gave both my ankles a test drive. But for a small twinge in one, they were fine.

"You sure you're okay?" Wade gave my arm a gentle squeeze, and in return, I gave him a reassuring smile and another nod of my head.

"I'm fine. Thanks!"

Wade slowly shook his head. "I don't know who was more scared, me or him. That kid was just lying on the ground squalling like a baby. I know he took at least ten years off my life. I'm real sorry I ruined your evening, Alex."

Wincing at the reference to Alex, I eased myself down into a chair. "Don't worry about it. I'm just glad you called."

I'd no sooner gotten comfortable than an angry redhead came flying out of the cubicle, her tall and tanned counterpart hard on her heels.

"What's the kid's name?" I hissed.

"Jeremy."

Nodding, I stood up and crossed the small space, reaching them about the same time Junior did.

"How's your son? How's Jeremy?" we asked, stumbling over each other.

"How's your insurance?" the obviously fuming redhead countered. Hell, she was practically foaming at the mouth. "First thing tomorrow morning we're calling our lawyers!"

"I can assure you, that won't be necessary," Junior said. "We'll cover his medical bills."

"From where I'm standing, it *is* necessary," Tall and Tanned countered. "Our son could have died on that construction site!"

"We understand that, sir, and we understand you have every right to be upset."

"Damn right we do!"

"But consider this." I forced myself to speak up despite worry for Jeremy, which they'd never addressed, and my boiling anger. "Your son and his friends were warned more than once to stay out of our construction site."

"So now it's our fault?" Jeremy's mother's face almost matched her hair.

"Of course she's not saying it's your fault." Junior rested a calming hand on my shoulder as if he knew just how angry I was.

"Of course it's not *your* fault!" I said. "Though I do wonder where you were the four times I warned your son and his friends to leave our construction site. All documented, I might add, and with witnesses."

"Are you threatening us?" the father demanded.

"No sir. We'll be happy to cover your son's medical expenses, but if you sue Dolan Industries, those four warnings and the flooding the site experienced last weekend, that I did report to the police, will all come into play. Your son and his two friends will be required to testify, and if it comes out that those boys are responsible for causing *thousands* of dollars in damages, there could be criminal charges filed against them." I smiled serenely and let my words hang in the air between all of us, pleased when the redhead deflated and her husband followed suit.

Finally the doctor emerged, announcing that someone from orthopedics would be down to take Jeremy upstairs and cast his leg. Junior assured the doctor that Dolan would cover the medical bills, and, satisfied, Dr. Reaves left to attend other patients, leaving Jeremy in the care of his parents, who disappeared back inside the cubicle with tails tucked between their legs.

Turning, I smiled at Junior and held out my arms. "Anything else?"

"I am so glad you were here," he said softly.

"You can go on home, Junior." I felt funny calling him Junior when he was at least ten years older than me. "I'll stay and take care of the hospital paperwork."

Junior turned to Wade. "You'll stay with her and do a report on what happened, and then follow her home in case Hal shows up. I don't think he will, but I fired him and he's liable to try and take it out on you."

"I will *definitely* see her home and make sure everything's okay." Wade draped an arm around my waist and gave me a squeeze.

While I walked down to the cafeteria for coffee, Wade called his guys to make sure they'd secured the site. They'd come in early and we'd do their reports on the accident. Looks like I'd end up working tomorrow whether I wanted to or not. By the time I got back, Wade had found a seat and stolen a pad of legal paper from somewhere.

"You okay?" I fell into the chair beside him and handed him a Styrofoam cup. He looked like hell.

"Yeah." He accepted the cup with a smile. "Sorry again for ruining your evening."

"You didn't ruin my night. To be honest, it's been a long week and I didn't really want to go out."

A nurse appeared and handed me a ream of insurance forms to fill out. Luckily I knew most of it by heart, and what I didn't know she assured me I could return tomorrow.

"You were right," Wade said once she'd gone.

"About?" I propped the clipboard on my knee and started filling in all the little boxes.

"Us. This was a bad idea."

"More like 'good idea, bad timing.' "

10

By the time we left the hospital we'd somehow come to a silent understanding that Wade was staying the night at my house. I'm not sure how it happened, and I'm not sure I cared. I wasn't quite ready to let go of him yet.

Inside the house I dropped my keys and purse on the hall table and turned to face him. "Is this good timing or bad?"

He wrapped his arms around me and covered my lips with his, his tongue performing a sensual exploration of my mouth that I felt in the pit of my stomach. Heat radiated outward, pooling between my thighs and making my knees weak. I came up for air and took his hand, leading him down the dimly lit hallway to my bedroom, where we silently stripped each other and fell on the bed, all hands and tongues as we found the spots we knew turned each other on: Wade's extra-sensitive nipples, the base of my spine he trailed his fingers across, the wet heat between my thighs, which I spread, silently begging him to fuck me.

More than anything I wanted to feel him inside me. I stretched out on my back and reached for his cock, running a finger across the tip and licking his precum off with a smile. The silk quilt cooled my fevered skin and made my nipples stand straight up in the chilly room.

"Don't tease me." I reached between my own thighs and stroked myself, sighing with pleasure at my wetness, at the feel of my clit swelling under my fingers.

He swatted my hand away and buried his face between my thighs, lapping and suckling at my clit until I wanted to scream. Until his mouth and my hips settled into a rhythm that I knew would only satisfy me temporarily. My hips arched off the bed, while overhead the fan spun, feathering my overheated skin with a cool, lazy caress.

While Wade's tongue teased and tormented, my hands skimmed across my rib cage to pinch my nipples. Little darts of pleasure zinged to the clit he was worrying with his teeth, and my heavy breathing and sharp moans filled the air as I came.

He settled between my thighs and stroked me with his cock before finally sliding home with a satisfied grunt. I grinned up at him, still working to catch my breath.

"You do realize"—he pulled out and slid home again—"we just did this last night."

"Nope, you didn't go down on me last night." I locked his hips between my legs and wrapped my arms around his shoulders.

"There is that." A groan rumbled deep in his chest as he sank into me again, his face tense with concentration.

I urged him on, meeting every thrust and watching intently as his control deserted him in a climax that left him clinging to me.

The sun burning through my eyelids woke me up the next morning. Wade was gone, but I had no clue when he'd left, and I'd overslept. I didn't even have time to think about *why* he'd left. I had a ton of paperwork to do.

I pulled into the parking lot of the construction site mid-morning and slid out of the truck with two dozen donuts and a cup of coffee. The site was eerily quiet but for the rhythmic sound of the nail guns, the occasional burst of male laughter, and a radio playing Cuban music from somewhere inside the building. Stepping out of the mid-morning heat, I slipped my sunglasses off with a free finger and looked around.

Despite having to work a Saturday, and the previous night's accident, things were going well, judging from the smiles on their faces. One by one the nail guns stopped, and Carter, a tall, skinny redhead, took the donuts from me with a grateful smile.

"Thanks, boss lady."

"If you want, I can open up the trailer and make coffee," I offered.

"I've got a cooler full of soda in the back of my truck." Wade gave me a tired smile.

Two of the guys took off to get the cooler while the rest grabbed donuts and found a place to sit.

"You not eating?" Wade asked.

I shook my head and took another sip of my coffee. "I ate earlier. Guys, I'll need to talk to everyone who was here last night; shouldn't take more than a few minutes apiece."

They all nodded, then Carter spoke up, asking the question that was apparently on all their minds. "Who's taking over now that Hal's gone?"

A few guys clinked their soda cans together in a toast. Guess I wasn't the only one happy about Hal leaving.

"I'm sure Junior will let us know as soon as possible."

Nodding, Wade said, "Come on. I'll show you what we've got done."

I followed him, while carrying on an internal debate. Ask why he left, or no? What was he thinking behind those cool green eyes? Because they didn't reveal a thing.

"We should be done around one or two."

"Need an extra hand?"

"Couldn't hurt," he said with a smile that left me still curious.

As soon as I finished up my paperwork, I grabbed the hard hat out of the front of my truck and spent the rest of the morning holding sheetrock in place while Wade nailed it to the two-by-fours. Just when I didn't think my shirt could soak up another drop of sweat, the nail guns around us stopped. I turned and stifled a groan at the sight of Jerry Dolan standing at the building's entrance.

"I need to see you." Dolan gave me a once-over, unaware that the bottom had just fallen out of my stomach at his terse tone.

I motioned for Carter to come take my place and followed Dolan outside where the muggy air only seemed to make my shirt wetter. Holding it away from my body, I gave it a good shake to cool my midriff.

Wade and I were busted. I knew it. And there was no way to warn him. It'd only confirm what Dolan obviously suspected. I couldn't afford to lose my job. I had a house payment. Not to mention Dolan could get me blackballed from working construction anywhere in Texas. Fuck a duck.

I'd acted carelessly and I had to suffer the consequences all on my own. There'd be time to commiserate with Carlotta and Lanie later tonight. After I cleaned out my desk.

I followed him to his Navigator, my stomach a tight knot from nerves and too much coffee, scolding myself and Wade in my head for screwing at work. That had to be it. Hal had to have heard us and retaliated by telling Dolan. It wasn't any less than I deserved. Swallowing the lump in my throat, I slid my sunglasses over my eyes to shield them from the bright afternoon sunlight. Dolan's Navigator sat parked next to Wade's truck. He motioned to the passenger side door, and on heavy feet, I climbed in.

"Care for a cigar?" he asked once the doors were shut and the Navigator was started, so that frosty cold air filled the vehicle.

I'm about to be fired and . . . "No thank you, sir."

"I would have been here earlier but I had a meeting over golf. I hate golf. In the good old days you just went out and built something. Now you gotta schmooze and grease palms to get anything done. Houston used to be a lady. Now she's just a *whore*."

I winced at the word *whore*, despite the fact that he never took his eyes off the half-finished building across the way. "What's this about, sir?" I asked, wishing he'd just get it over with so I could go home and throw up. Then go get drunk with the girls.

"I like you, Alex. I really do, but I'll be honest. I had my reservations when Junior hired a woman. You've proven me wrong more than once."

"Thank you," I murmured. "I appreciate that."

"I know there's no love lost between you and Hal and I wouldn't have put you on the same crew if I'd had a choice . . . It's a moot point now anyway," he added with a chuckle.

Fear gave way to mystification and I frowned, trying to figure out what in the hell he was talking about.

"Sometimes my position requires me to go places that . . . to be frank, my wife would kill me if she found out about. Places like The Doll Palace."

Even as my own cheeks burned in embarrassment, he was kind enough to keep his focus on the scenery outside the SUV.

"I see," I said after I swallowed the lump in my throat.

"So, it was you."

I slowly crossed my legs and folded my hands in my lap as if needing some sort of modesty. "Yes, sir."

"I almost didn't believe it." He chuckled again.

Snorting softly, I bit my lip and squeezed my eyes shut, not sure whether I wanted to die from embarrassment or howl with laughter.

"Wade's crew almost done with the sheetrock?"

"Yes, sir." I nodded slowly, wondering at the change of topic. "We've got most of it up and they should be done with the tape and bed by Thursday or so."

"As soon as Wade's crew is finished, I've got a new job for them. Next Monday a different drywall crew will come out to drop in the ceiling tiles. Make sure you're ready for them. And I'll have Junior see that you two don't land on the same project again. Which shouldn't be too hard since his isn't the company's only drywall crew, and you'll be stuck here at the site for a while. I'm putting you in charge."

Dumbfounded at the quick turn of events, I mumbled my thanks, then turned and frowned at him. "You are?"

"Junior says you're plenty capable . . . and he'll take the heat if you screw up—which he doesn't think you'll do."

"I won't. Thank you. I won't, sir." My nausea turned to giddy bubbles as I pulled the door handle.

"My wife's having a dinner party tonight, and I need to get going before she gets in a tizzy and fires the housekeeper."

With a nod, I made to step out of the truck.

"Alex," he said, stopping me, "from now on be careful what you do, where you do it, and who you do it with."

"I will, sir."

On shaky legs, I walked back to the building and gave Wade a huge grin. Peeking over my shoulder to assure myself Dolan was gone, I did a little dance over to Wade, my arms raised in the air and fisted in triumph, and all the guys slowly stopped working.

Wade stood, hands propped on his hips, watching me. "Well?"

"Say hello to your new Job Supervisor, guys!"

I accepted their cheers and congratulations while silently breathing a sigh of relief. I couldn't even bring myself to think about how close I'd come to losing my job.

Wade had called it nearly right. We were done by 2:15 and the guys were gone by 2:30. Then it was just the two of us, making sure everything was where it was supposed to be. My shoulders were screaming, and all I wanted was a long, hot soak in the tub with the jets pounding my back and shoulders.

"How come you left this morning?" I asked as we crossed the parking lot to my truck.

"I figured it was best. I needed to be here early, but you didn't."

"Is that the only reason?"

"You're a grumpy-ass in the mornings." He opened the truck door for me.

"So you noticed." Grinning, I slid past him and into the truck.

Wade's only reply was a snort.

"What are you doing for dinner?" I asked.

Crossing his arms, he leaned against the truck's door. "I thought 'our timing was off'?"

"It's my prerogative to change my mind. Besides, apparently we weren't the only ones at The Doll Palace the other night. Dolan also gave us a green light to date." Reaching out, I snagged his T-shirt between my fingers and tugged him closer, meeting his lips halfway for a warm, sweaty kiss. "Sooo, you go home, get cleaned up and meet me at my place with some Italian and those pornos you mentioned, and we'll celebrate. Deal?"

"Deal."

Epilogue

We'd had an adventurous week, to say the least, so Sunday with the girls was almost anticlimactic. Carlotta looked much more relaxed, and Lanie's smile, as we took our seats in the crowded restaurant, was positively triumphant.

Guess she got her "Suit."

"Dish it." I sat back with my legs crossed and sipped my mimosa, needing the fortification after another night short on sleep.

"He had the most amazing apartment—"

Carlotta interrupted Lanie's gushing with a wave of her hand. "We don't want to hear about his damn apartment. We want to know how he was in bed."

"Guess she didn't leave him passed out on the floor with whiskey dick." I snickered and winked at Carlotta.

Our subsequent giggles and bad behavior earned us more than a few frowns from the Sunday crowd. Too bad. I wasn't feeling terribly "good" today.

"He had the most amazing silk sheets." She opened the

menu and pretended to study it. "I'm gonna have to get me some."

I snatched the menu out of her hand. "Screw the sheets, *rate him*!"

"Five stars," she muttered, frowning at both Carlotta and me. "I can see this is gonna be a fun breakfast."

"Sorry, I'm beat."

"We did it on his balcony too." She rolled her eyes and grinned.

Before we could comment on her five stars, we were forced to stop and order breakfast.

Lanie arched one eyebrow, while from my other side, Carlotta groaned softly. "What the hell happened to you Friday night?"

With a sigh, I smoothed the starched napkin in my lap, then proceeded to fill them in.

"I can't believe you got busted in a strip joint," Lanie said with a laugh.

"You know, now I almost think Dolan was as afraid I'd seen him as he was that he'd seen me. I hear his wife's a bit of a hard-ass. A real sweetheart but very old-school."

"I can't believe you *went* to a strip joint! I mean, if it were Lanie, I could definitely see it. Especially on amateur night," Carlotta added with a wicked grin. "Then again, I *have* seen it on amateur night. So you and Wade patched everything up?"

"Yup. What about you? Get lucky Friday night?"

"No," she drawled, focusing her eyes somewhere near the ceiling, "but there was Thursday afternoon!"

Giggling, I forked a bite of honeydew. "Was that your farewell fuck? No, don't answer that. You like him, don't you, Carlotta? You *like* the Geek Meister?!"

Leaning over, Carlotta covered her mouth with her hand and whispered, "He's got a big dick."

"Lanie," I sighed, "better watch it, she's after your title."

"Ain't nobody takin' my title. By the way, I'm out this afternoon. I need to catch up on some paperwork."

"I need to catch up on some sleep," I said with a nod.

"I need to catch up on my sex."

I arched an eyebrow at Carlotta. "With Devon the Geek you swore off?"

She cut off a bite of her omelet and popped it into her mouth with a nod. "After Lanie ditched me Friday night, Cherise and I went to this swinger's club. Guess who was there?"

"Fuck sleep." I laughed, setting my fork down. "I wanna hear about this."

Lanie

1

The minute I spotted Robert Clayton the Fourth cutting a swath through Jimmy Z's Friday night crowd, all of me perked up. Every man I met was a new opportunity, each one presenting limitless possibilities, and Robert was no exception. An opportunity for what? Marriage? *No way.* Even at thirty-four I considered myself too young to settle down with just one person. The thought of only having sex with the same man—no, *person*—for the rest of my life bored me near to tears.

Which brought us to sex. *Definitely.*

And conquest? *Abso-freakin'-lutely.*

With a wiggle of my hips, I winked at Carlotta, who sat across from me, and sat up straighter on the polished chrome bar stool. Rubbing my lips together to freshen my lipstick, I gave him another once-over and assured myself he was as good looking as I remembered. Not just tall and handsome, but clean cut and clean shaven, with well-defined, patrician features. An arrow-straight nose, square jaw, sharp cheekbones. Even his blond hair was perfect. Only the cleft in his chin kept him from being *too* perfect.

He was a blue-collar girl's wet dream—at least in the looks department. The rest remained to be seen. And after the week I'd had, being forced to fire two mechanics, I definitely needed more than a wet dream to keep me company tonight.

"Is he here?" Carlotta, who knew better than to turn around, leaned forward and flicked a sheaf of blonde curls over her shoulder.

In deference to the loud music, I gave her a tiny wink and discreetly wiggled a bit more as Robert stopped at our tiny table. My nipples, hard with excitement, chafed against my lacy bra. Leaning over the stool beside me, I brushed my lips against his cheek. He smelled like musk with just a hint of something sharp and citrusy.

"Lanie, you look . . ." His words trailed off, eaten by the loud music as he gave me a once-over, his eyes traveling across my face and down my chest to land somewhere in the vicinity of the cleavage I was flashing him.

My favorite pink sweater came with ruffled edges and only two tiny buttons and didn't have much more material than a bikini top. I loved it, and it went perfectly with pink sandals and my favorite pair of Lucky jeans. *Lucky.*

I bit back a laugh and patted the bar stool beside me. "I was wondering if you'd show up."

"My mother." He shrugged, giving me an apologetic grin.

I couldn't decide whether he got points for taking care of Mom or if I should deduct them for being a mama's boy. After all, he'd been having brunch with his mother when we met the previous Sunday.

"I wouldn't have dreamed of standing you up," he added, claiming the stool next to me. "What are you drinking?"

"Dirty martini!" Smiling, I raised my glass to him, then drained the last of it.

With a nod, he motioned to Brian, the waiter, and ordered

me another as well as a gin and tonic for himself. *Points for buying me a drink without being asked.*

My night was definitely looking up. I slowly licked my lips and murmured a thank-you, ignoring the fact that he couldn't hear me over the music. He was incredibly polite as I introduced him to Carlotta. I guess he didn't know what to make of her. With her long, honey-blond curls, chocolate eyes, and year-round tan, she was, in a word, arresting—but then, so were Lexi and I. And what we wanted, we usually got.

"How was work?" Robert asked me.

"Awful! I don't even want to talk about it!" I waved the subject off with a frown. My blue-collar career was none of his white-collar business.

Brian gave us a hard, cool look when he returned with our drinks and took Robert's credit card. Some men (like Brian) didn't know when to let go. Just because I'd slept with him a couple of times didn't mean I wanted to spend the rest of my life with a waiter who was eight years younger than me.

"Do you dance?" I asked Robert.

Robert leaned back and peered down at the crowded dance floor below us. "Not really."

"So how was your week? What is it you do again?" I waved good-bye to Carlotta and Cherise, who appeared at her side and dragged her off. Apparently they'd decided to go hunt down their own Friday night pickups. *How quickly could I drag him out of the bar?*

Before I knew it, I found myself listening to Robert's life story. Apparently conversation wasn't his forte. I blinked as he mentioned his age, focusing back in on the conversation. "You're thirty-nine?"

"Is that a problem?"

"I usually date men younger than me, but for you . . ." I leaned into him, pressing my tit against his arm while I trailed my fingers up his thigh. "I'll make an exception."

He glanced down at his leg and then back up at me. "You're an interesting woman. I know . . . I know it's rude to ask your age, but I'm going to anyway." The chuckle that followed was endearingly shy.

"Just a couple of years younger than you. Let's get out of here." I wasn't here to talk; I was here to get laid.

Grabbing my purse, I slipped off my stool and headed for the door, wading through the thick crowd and up a short flight of stairs to the main bar area. If he were really interested, he'd follow. And if he didn't, I'd find a replacement.

I didn't stop until I'd pushed through the bar's black and chrome doors. Stepping into the swampy evening heat, I turned and gave him my flirtiest smile, pressing myself against the hard, lean length of him. "Didn't you say you lived close?"

"This way." He rested a hand at the small of my back and we wound our way through the evening foot traffic.

My titties bounced and my pussy ached with each rub of my jeans, and I smiled to myself at the appreciative glances I caught. Robert, on the other hand, was incredibly quiet, his hand clammy against my back as we walked.

His apartment was located three blocks away, on the top floor of The Bentley. Trust me when I say it more than made up for his quiet manner. He led me through the apartment's small marble foyer to the living room, where a spotlight shone down on a pale gray leather couch and slate and iron tables. Fluidly sculpted, flawless candlesticks and a bowl on the table gleamed dully in the dim light. They were classic Nambé.

"Would you like a drink?" he asked from behind me. His voice was a soft rumble.

"Sure . . . anything's fine."

A flick of a hidden switch from behind me revealed even paler gray walls with an enormous abstract painting taking up almost an entire wall. The man had taste, and to be frank, the sight of so much money in one small space turned me on a hell of a lot more than his conversational abilities. A view of the Houston skyline was visible through the balcony located off the formal dining area. A shiny ebony table stood in stark relief to the multicolored lights.

While Robert got our drinks, I headed for the balcony, the expensive area rugs cushioning the click of my heels. Sliding the door open, I stepped outside, welcoming the cool breeze that drifted up my sweater. The tiny balcony was as austere as the apartment, with only a single chair and table. Guess Robert wasn't a plant person.

The night breeze carried away the humidity that had been almost stifling down on the street, and I pulled my hair up and stretched, sighing in appreciation. Robert appeared at my side a few minutes later and pressed a cut-crystal glass of amber-colored liquid into my hand. "Scotch. It's all I have, except for gin, and I didn't take you for the straight-gin-drinking type."

I laughed and sipped, letting the smoky drink scorch a path through me while I contemplated the possibility of fucking him right out here on his balcony. The idea appealed to me—a lot.

"So, Robert, can I call you Rob, or is that a no-no?" Slipping my purse off my shoulder, I tossed it onto the nearby chair, then leaned against the wrought-iron railing. My fingertips slid across my belly and under the edge of my sweater, cool against the heat of my skin.

"No one's ever called me Rob." He licked his lips and took a long drink of his scotch, his eyes focused on my hand.

I let it drift lower, enjoying the light touch of my fingers on my skin as they dipped into the waistband of my hip-hugger jeans. My thumb teased the ring in my belly button. "I must confess, you don't look like a Rob, but Robert is such a . . . mouthful." With another soft laugh, I sipped my drink and then stepped closer. While I calculated how fast I could get him naked, another part of my brain, the detached analytical side, wondered if he'd back away; if he knew how to have fun; if he had any hobbies. I frowned slightly, distracted by my train of thought, as I untucked his expensive polo shirt with my free hand. "What do you like to do for fun?"

"Golf." He drained his glass and I took it from him, setting both on the table, before turning back to face him. Suddenly, my fingers itched to rumple his perfect, dark blond hair. Instead, I unbuttoned my top, purring as a stiff breeze tickled my bare nipples.

"Golf?" I stepped closer and reached for the waistband of his pants. "Doesn't sound like a hell of a lot of fun."

"I suppose not to some people." His Adam's apple bobbed. "It takes a lot of skill and an intense amount of concentration, though, and I like that. Have you ever played?"

"I play all the time."

His eyebrow twitched at the rasp of his pants being unzipped and he licked his lips. I palmed the thick, hard length of his erection, smiling at the realization that I could barely get my fingers around it. *And let me just stress the length part.* The man was well endowed, even if he was a bit of a stiff. Biting my lip, I reached for his shirt, barely managing to pull it over his head.

"What are you doing, Lanie?"

"I'm gonna fuck you, Robert. Would you like that?" I pushed my hair back off my face with my free hand, tucking it behind my ear.

"I do have a bed . . . inside."

"I'd rather fuck you right here." I tossed his shirt over my shoulder, smiling wickedly at the thought of a stiff breeze carrying it off.

"What if someone sees us?"

"Like who?" I held up my hands and made a show of looking around. All the apartments on this side of the building were dark or quiet or both. Only a three-quarter moon, hidden by the occasional cloud, watched us. *And the man in the moon wasn't talking.*

A tweak of my nipples sent a spike of need straight to my clit. It swelled, chafing against the confines of denim and my thong. I tuned Robert out, focusing on myself, my own pleasure. Licking my thumbs, I flicked them against my nipples and smiled, my lower lip caught between my teeth. My blood flowed faster as I glanced up at Robert, waiting to see what he'd do.

He didn't disappoint, stepping closer and shoving my hand out of the way. Leaning over, he drew as much of my tit as possible into his mouth, then pulled back till only the nipple itself was caught between his lips. He suckled hard and my back arched reflexively. Releasing my nipple, he licked a trail up my chest to my neck, focusing on the tender spot behind my ear and earning a moan of appreciation. "You really want me to . . . fuck you . . . out here?"

I almost laughed out loud at the way he stumbled over the word *fuck*. He was an innocent. A babe in the woods. Maybe not with women but with women like *me*, he didn't have a clue. Though he would before the night was over.

Toeing off my shoes, I unsnapped my jeans and gave him a little push. He stood back, rubbing his erection through his plain white briefs as I slid my jeans off my hips and turned to dig a condom out of my purse. I kicked my jeans out of the way and positioned the chair in the middle of the balcony, then motioned him closer with a crooked finger and a smile the devil himself would have appreciated.

Robert came willingly, as if *no* never entered his mind. Carlotta, who danced between submissive and dominant men, would like him, and the thought of both of us doing him made my juices overflow the tiny thong. It'd been a long time since we'd had a threesome.

"Take off your pants, then lose the briefs."

Robert was a sight to behold naked with moonlight bouncing off his lightly tanned skin, his chest smooth and sculpted but for a small patch of hair between his pecs and the pale fuzzy ribbon that ran from just under his belly button to the thick patch of curls between his thighs. His cock was a column of marble, jutting out at an angle from his belly. My mouth watered, and for just a minute I debated giving him a blow job, but that was reserved for special occasions.

Licking my lips, I motioned for him to sit and tore the condom package open, expertly rolling it over his erection. He sat with legs spread, an expectant look on his face as his hands trailed lightly up the backs of my thighs. His unexpectedly passive nature was beginning to wear on me.

"Don't move." I cupped my pussy and gave it a firm squeeze. Assuring myself I'd have what I wanted soon enough, I slipped my thong off and straddled his lap. My hair tickled my back in a soft caress while the hair on his legs tickled the backs of my thighs. I was a bundle of nerve endings as I leaned in so my tits were pressed against his lightly defined pecs, and I traced his lip with the tip of my tongue. I was pleasantly surprised when he caught it between his teeth and sucked it into his mouth. His hands slid up across the small of my back and gave my waist a squeeze before gliding back down and cupping the cheeks of my ass. He rubbed the most delicious circles that grew smaller and smaller while the tips of his fingers tickled the crack of my ass. If he was a good boy, and stuck around a while, I might even let him have that. Again, a special treat.

Moaning into his mouth, I arched my back, urging his fingers lower. He followed my silent command, his fingers teasing the sensitive edges of my swollen pussy while our tongues played, gliding lightly against each other.

"Feels good," I whispered against his lips. A shiver danced

up my spine at a stiff breeze and I pushed my hair off my face. "Touch me. Touch my pussy."

He did, his chest heaving underneath me. Smiling at the two-fingered invasion, I licked my way up his neck while my free hand delved between us and cupped his balls. They were full and heavy with cum.

"Like that?" I asked, rolling them in my fingers.

"Oh yeah," he moaned loudly, his head drifting back ever so slightly, offering up tender skin. The urge to sink my teeth into his neck, to push him, to crack his reserve, was almost unbearable. We were two bodies in motion with a very definite agenda, but Robert's lack of action frustrated me. Never mind that I could get what I wanted with or without him. I felt no remorse at the thought of just leaving him behind, in a completely sexual sense. I'd get mine.

"I like your fingers in me." They were thick and long, but not as long as his dick that bobbed against his belly. I nipped and sucked at his neck in a frenzy of need as his fingers pushed me closer and closer to my climax. "Stop!"

He did, instantly, his fingers still buried deep inside me. The walls of my pussy pulsated around him, anxious for release. "Feel that?"

Swallowing, he rasped out a "Yes," his eyes dark and painful, filled with his own needs and frustrations. But which button would push him over the edge?

"Lick your fingers."

He watched me for a minute before wetting his lips and sliding his fingers from my pussy. He ran his tongue up first one finger, then the other. Before he could stick both in his mouth and clean them off completely, I joined him, flicking my tongue across his knuckles, all the way up to his fingernails, where our tongues met. I licked the salty, slightly sweet flavor off my lips, then his. Our cleaning turned into a highly charged erotic kiss with both of us suddenly fighting for control.

Robert grasped the cheeks of my ass and lifted me up, impaling me on him with a grunt of satisfaction. In retaliation, I refused to move, just sat there slowly squeezing him with my pussy.

"Say it."

"Say what?" he panted.

"Fuck me, Lanie. Say it." I cupped his head in my hands, letting my fingers slide through his hair as I focused on his incredibly handsome face only inches from mine. Handsome but lost in a way I didn't feel like contemplating.

"Fuck me, Lanie . . . please."

I leaned back, as if I had all the time in the world, and arched my hips until only the very tip of him was still inside me before sliding back down with an appreciative moan. "I like your dick."

I rode him, in complete control of everything: him, me, timing, pressure, position. Underneath me, he stayed tense, pulling me close and latching onto one nipple, burying his face in my breasts and sucking at both intermittently. "Fuck me," he insisted, sinking his teeth into one hard tip. His grip on me tightened, leaving me breathless. "Fuck me harder, Lanie."

I did, impaling myself on him while maintaining the same steady pace. His face, buried in my chest, stifled his moans, but the wind carried mine away. "Bite it, bite 'em. Bite my nipples. Hard."

I fisted my hand in his hair, making a point to mess it up, and tightened my grip until I knew it had to hurt, but he never protested, just clamped down on one stiff point with increasing pressure that sent little sparks of electricity to my cunt. Leaning back, I took him with me and used my feet for leverage so I could ride him harder, so his dick rubbed against my G-spot. Head thrown back, I moaned loudly as my orgasm ripped through me; Robert gripped my hips and kept them moving, pushing me up and down in a rhythm that suited him until his own climax hit.

Below us, a door slid open, and I wondered how much his neighbor might have heard. Tension eased from my back as a post-coital lethargy hit me, and I held him to me, watching him in detached fascination. The almost pained look men get at climax had always mystified me, and no man had ever been able to explain it to me. Releasing me, he sagged against the chair, his eyes closed and features relaxed enough to make him look much younger than thirty-nine.

Finally he stood with a deep sigh and carried me back inside, through the living and dining areas to his bedroom. He leaned over so I could pull back the down coverlet, then laid me on the bed.

"I'll be right back."

As I slid under the silky soft white sheets and stretched out, I heard the sound of a faucet being turned on in the bathroom.

Okay so he hadn't been so bad, but we'd have to see what round two brought.

2

I parked at the very edge of my parents' curved driveway in case it became necessary to make a quick escape. Lack of sleep after my night with Robert, who hadn't turned out to be a complete dud, made the day ahead of me even more painful.

With my sunglasses firmly in place, I slid out of my Toyota Prius and took a deep, steadying breath. The air tasted like sunshine and freshly cut grass. Everything looked so peaceful. *I assure you, it's all an illusion.*

I hadn't even made it in the door and already I was a ball of tension, all my defenses on high alert. Ma insisted I wasn't a complete woman until I'd known the glories of marriage (hmmpf) and giving birth (ick), while Dad insisted I was just abnormal, an abomination and a failure as a daughter. If I were a masochist, a trip "home" would qualify as a wet dream.

Even though I'd followed in Dad's footsteps and become a mechanic, I'd done the unthinkable and not followed him and my three oldest brothers into the family business. Instead, I'd struck out on my own, determined to be successful in my own right. And I was now forced to endure the constant teasing of my brothers—except for Jackie, that is. He was the only sibling who had managed to bring more shame on the good family name than I had.

I rubbed my lips together, and forced my feet, in a demure pair of Sketchers slip-ons, to move. Ma's azaleas bloomed a sharp, brilliant pink on either side of the steps. Some sadist had wrapped brightly colored ribbons around the beige porch posts. As if Jackie were coming home from the war or something and not recently sprung from the Texas Penal System.

Why was he getting a party if he'd just gotten out of jail? Because Ma lived in a constant state of denial, sure that some day I'd "get my act together and settle down with some nice man" and "little Jackie would mend his wicked ways."

From the backyard came the screams of a gaggle of nieces and nephews, courtesy of my brothers. They were all good Irish Catholic boys who'd married young and procreated beyond my mother's wildest dreams. Between the three of them, there were ten, with a set of twins on the way. Idiots.

With a groan, I turned back to the Prius for the fruit salad I'd forgotten—fruit salad being the only thing Ma would let me bring. Obviously she didn't think I could cook. How she thought I ate, living on my own, I had no clue, but like I said: state of denial.

"Going somewhere?" came a voice from the corner of the house. Standing beside a rosebush devoid of blooms was Jackie himself, dressed in jeans and a faded T-shirt. The sun created a halo around his closely cropped chestnut hair. At five foot nine, he was small, the smallest of all my brothers, and wiry, but good looking in a way that contrasted sharply with Robert, The Suit, whom I'd left snoring in his king-size bed early this morning.

"I forgot something." I waved my keys at him. Pulling the door open, I grabbed the oversized plastic bowl from the back seat and backed out, nearly dropping the bowl as Jackie appeared at my elbow. I hadn't never heard him approach.

"Can I carry that?"

"Sure." I shoved it into his arms and gave him a brief, hard hug. "Welcome home." Maybe if he took it into the house I could escape an interrogation from Ma on my love life. Okay, maybe "put it off" was more accurate, because I guarantee you by the time the day was done, she'd get her maternal claws into me. "Nice tattoo."

Jackie snorted. "Ma had a fit; spent five minutes trying to wash it off."

I peered closer at the prison tattoo that circled his wrist, while thinking of the butterfly hidden under my shirt and my pierced belly button. The one-inch-wide intricate Celtic knot work must have taken days if not weeks to finish, considering the limited supplies in prison. "You're lucky you didn't get an infection."

"Ma said the same thing."

With a laugh, I followed him toward the house, taking a left at the steps.

"No way, uh-uh, get over here!"

Turning, I gave him my most pitiable look. "Don't make me go in there."

"She gave me an earful on you last night. You do know you're going to hell if you don't push a kid out soon, don't you?"

Snorting in frustration, I reluctantly turned and followed him inside. "Damn near twelve grandchildren and she's still not satisfied. So, how's it feel to be a free man?"

"Showering has never been so much fun."

Despite the lack of humor in his voice, I couldn't resist a small chuckle. I didn't even want to think about the meaning behind his words, though. Instead, I silently closed the door behind him. Maybe his jail experience had been the making of him. He sure looked a lot older than thirty-one.

"A word of warning from your jailbird brother: I think they're setting you up," he mumbled.

I sighed, shoulders briefly slumping under the weight of his words. The last guy they'd set me up with had been so slick the kids could have used him for a Slip 'n Slide. "I guess we could just run away."

"I already tried that. It didn't work."

Eyeing the pile of purses hanging from the coat rack, I clung a little tighter to mine, a reminder of an easy escape as I trailed down the shadowy hallway behind Jackie. Even barbecuing meat couldn't override the squeaky tang of Murphy's Oil Soap mixed with Pledge.

In the back of the house, the kitchen was a hub of activity, complete with a box fan sitting on the table. It vibrated and made so much noise the women had to shout to be heard. Ma stood at the counter, mashing potatoes (thank God they weren't turnips. I hate turnips) while sister-in-law #2 pushed the screen door open with her hip and stepped outside with a relish tray in each hand.

"Hey Melanie!" Polly (aka #3) stopped filling glasses with ice and made to lift her gargantuan baby belly out of the kitchen chair, but I waved her down.

"Damn girl, you better not let anyone get near you with any sharp objects! You might pop."

Jackie barked with laughter while Ma, who never even bothered to turn and face me, started scolding. The faded red bun on her head shook while she mashed, poured milk, and scolded some more, but #3 just smiled and rubbed her belly.

"Did you make extra?" Polly asked me.

"I always make extra for you, sweet thing." Leaning down, I kissed her forehead and gave her a hug. No sense asking where #1 was. The nature queen, aka Esmeralda, was probably sitting outside with her Birkenstocks propped on a footstool and a baby latched onto her breast. "What can I do to help?"

"Get that fruit salad into the fridge before it spoils and we all end up with botulism!" Ma turned around and shook her whisk at me, the perpetual frown lodged between delicately arched eyebrows just as it had been for as long as I could remember.

"I already did, Ma." Jackie collapsed in a chair across from Polly and stretched his legs out in front of him.

"You"—she aimed her whisk at him, then pointed it toward the door—"get out of my kitchen. You know the rules."

We all knew the rule: *No men in the kitchen while the womenfolk cooked.*

"And besides," she muttered, turning back to the poor, defenseless potatoes, "you need some sun."

I frowned at the flower pattern on Ma's blouse, then at Polly, who pursed her lips and kept her eyes on the bag of ice her hand was jammed inside of, while I weighed my options. Inside: *Ma's nagging.* Outside: *Available Single Man of unknown and highly dubious merit waiting to meet me.*

One last glance at Ma convinced me to take my chances. Grabbing up a tray of cups, I followed Jackie outside and set it on the long picnic table tucked under the kitchen window. A plastic tablecloth covered with hideous pink cabbage roses flapped cheerfully in the afternoon breeze, obviously much happier to be here than I was. Or maybe it was mocking me.

At the very edge of the porch a monster-size grill sat oozing smoke. My stomach rumbled, while around me, mayhem reigned. Some idiot had turned two sprinklers on and the kids ran through it screaming while Esmeralda sat nursing a fat, black-headed baby. With her was Karen, toweling off her youngest daughter while scolding her for dripping on her expensive designer shorts.

Dad held court near the grill, smoking a cigar (something he's not allowed to do inside) and cutting up with my brothers, all clones of him that varied only slightly, and the aforementioned Available Single Man.

The stranger, with his dark curly hair, chocolate eyes, and five o'clock shadow, fell somewhere between white-collar smooth and my wild Irish family. Though technically my hair was the same chestnut brown as Jackie's, it was currently dyed an arresting shade of eggplant.

"Mel, come say hello," Dad barked.

Oh dear God, save me now.

Never mind that I owned my own business; as neither a brood mare nor a stallion, I fit at neither table, so I ambled over, but didn't sit, choosing to lean on the back of Jackie's chair instead.

"Lanie, do you remember Jeff Cash?" My brother, Grant, smirked up at me.

"Nice to see you again." Despite his casual outward appearance, Jeff Cash oozed Southern Male Charm. Of course I remembered him, vaguely. He and Grant had been running buddies back in high school. He'd had more money than us and a father who could, and had, gotten him out of all sorts of trouble.

You couldn't grow up with four brothers and *not* learn a thing or two about men. I gave him another once-over. The once crisp khaki shorts, the expensive, yet well-broken-in running shoes, and an equally expensive but tasteful watch at his wrist. He was definitely a step above the last guy they'd persecuted me with.

"Your dad says you own your own business down there in Houston," Jeff said.

As if Tomball was a world away (though in some ways, it was). As if Dad didn't have a huge chunk of the garage market sewn up in and all around Houston. As if I was the competition. As if it was no big deal that I owned my own business, like it was a hobby or something.

"She caters to *women.*" Grant, brother #2, snorted and shook his head, while Jeff emitted what sounded suspiciously like an embarrassed chuckle.

I hated him. Grant, not Jeff. The jury was still out on Jeff, and I didn't see them coming back in anytime soon. He was deliciously hot with a very pretty smile. But there was no way in hell I could date a friend of my brother's; and if you're wondering why not, think, "asking for trouble."

Inside the house a timer buzzed, and Dad lumbered out of his seat, looming over me as he passed by to tend to the brisket.

"Did you turn the meat, Pop?" Ma yelled through the open kitchen window.

"Yes, dear!"

I snorted, and under my fingers, Jackie's shoulders shook. Dad's words weren't exactly loving, despite the endearment.

"So Mel, how's business?" Grant asked, while Jeff kept checking me out, his face open and friendly but inscrutable—if that was even possible.

"Booming," I said, loud enough to be heard over my brother's snickers.

"That's good." Dad patted me on the shoulder as he maneuvered past me again. "Because Jackie here needs a job."

"I see," I countered carefully, while quickly assessing the position Dad had just put me in . . . and my choices.

"I can find my own job," Jackie insisted.

"Doing what?" a sneering Clay asked beside him.

My fingers itched to reach out and smack his head. Jackie might be a bit of a loser, but Clay had no business being mean to him. I did it anyway, smiling as my fingers connected with his scalp and he winced. He turned and gave me a nasty look.

"Mind yourself," I whispered.

"Dyke," he mouthed.

"Far from it, asshat."

Jackie started laughing again and turned to look up at me. "You don't have to give me a job, sis. My parole officer will help me."

Giving Jackie a job was apparently the other reason I was here. Dad wouldn't give him a job because he was ashamed—as ashamed as Ma, in his own way—so he'd thought to pawn Jackie off on me. Fine. So be it. We outcasts had to stick together.

Nodding, I crossed my arms. "I'll give ya a job, but you get no preferential treatment."

"He needs a place to stay," Dad said, reclaiming his seat. He refused to meet my eyes, a sure sign of his discomfort.

Shit! "There's an apartment above the garage he can use. Anything else?"

Dad's ruddy complexion turned even redder.

"His parole officer thanks you." Clay ducked when I made to backhand him again.

What the fuck had I just signed on for? Jackie wouldn't be the first ex-con I'd hired, so I knew how the whole parole officer thing worked. It was a total pain in the ass. However, I'd spent the last seven or eight years distancing myself from my family and building a life on my own terms that made *me* happy. It wasn't a matter of shame, but self-preservation. I was living a dual life. One that, up to now, I'd had no problem keeping separate. There was Hardworking Lanie, who endured the occasional family get-togethers, and then there was Party-Girl Lanie, who took great pleasure in spending her weekends in white-collar bars and sleeping with whoever caught her eye. I hadn't quite figured out how I was going to manage the two with Jackie around, but I'd better find a way fast.

The Bite-Me-in-the-Ass potential had risen exponentially.

"We'll spend Monday cleaning up the apartment. I'll spot

you two grand to get it in working order and take it out of your pay." *Take that, Dad.*

"Why can't he just stay with you?" Grant stood and fetched himself a glass of ice, filling it with tea from the jug Polly had brought out while we'd been talking.

"I'm sure he doesn't want his style cramped any more than I do mine."

If anything, the afternoon only got worse. At dinner the men stayed at their own table. The women were stuck at the longer table at the other end of the patio with a bunch of dripping wet, fussy kids to tend. And me? I sat with my plate on my knee and my back to the wall, where I could watch for ambushers, just like in *Gunsmoke*.

"Mel." Ma turned and pointed her spork at me. She had a really bad habit of pointing at things. "Jeff's an investment banker."

"That's nice." I shoved another sporkful of mashed potatoes into my mouth. The creamy, buttery potatoes almost made me weep for joy. Ma might like to point at things but she could also cook.

"Keep eating like that and you'll run to fat."

I turned and frowned at Clay, then caught Jeff's eye. He sat silently laughing beside Dad.

"She won't get fat," Ma countered. "She never cooks."

"I do so!"

"So Mel, how do you find time to cook with a business to run?" Jeff asked.

"How do *you* find time to cook? Being a bachelor and all."

"I cheat," he said with a nod. "I have a housekeeper."

My face melted into the second genuine smile I'd managed all afternoon. "Maybe that's what I need to do."

"Maybe," Ma interrupted, "you should think about settling down. You're not getting any younger."

"Ma! I've got a business to run and you've already got more grandkids than Noah!"

"Mel!" Ma reached out and jabbed my leg with her spork.

In retaliation, I shoved my half-full plate right on top of a relish tray and jumped up. "Stop poking me! And stop trying to manage my life, and Jackie's life too, for Pete's sake! There's more to life than having babies. What did you think I was gonna do with a business degree? Work for Dad?"

"That'll be enough, Melanie Jean!" Dad scowled at me.

I scowled right back, and then focused my attention back on Jeff. "Did they warn you about me? Did they tell you what a mouthy bit—?"

"Melanie!" Dad lurched to his feet, knocking his chair over in the process.

"The next time you think about setting me up, do us all a favor and just don't." I hated myself for letting Dad and Ma push my buttons. I should have just kept my mouth shut, played it cool. I took a long, hard look at my family, at the scared faces of my nieces and nephews, and felt ashamed, and I hated myself for that even more. Finally, I focused on Dad. "And the next time you need a favor just save us all some trouble and pick up the damn phone."

I turned to leave, cutting through the house to get my purse and keys, and slammed the front door with bone-jarring force. The sight of Jackie leaning against my car slowed me down.

"You really did it now," he said, shaking his head.

"My life; my rules." I sagged next to him, against the side of my car.

He nodded slowly, the twinkle gone from his eyes. "You don't have to give me a job. I know Dad put you on the spot back there."

Sighing, I kicked at the gravel driveway before looking back up at him. "We outcasts have to stick together."

3

Heads turned as Carlotta, Lexi, and I trailed after our hostess through the thick, Sunday post-church crowd at Baroque. Middle-aged men stared covetously while their female counterparts watched in disapproval and maybe a touch of jealousy.

The place definitely lived up to its name, with an ornate water fountain in the middle of the restaurant and white and gilt decor. Every time I walked in I felt like a little girl playing dress up. Like any minute I'd get caught and sent to my room. Never mind that I'd dug out my favorite: a bold red Theory skirt, denim slingbacks, and a sleeveless cashmere sweater.

Poor Lexi just looked tired and pale under her freckles, with faint circles beneath her eyes, and the demure, cream silk halter dress didn't help. Carlotta had gone all out in an embroidered Joystick tunic and turquoise linen pants. I felt a twinge of guilt for dumping her Friday night, but she was a big girl and she'd had Cherise to keep her company.

We'd no sooner gotten comfortable than our server appeared and passed out mimosas for all of us. After yesterday, I needed it. I took a long drink, letting it tickle its way down my throat.

"Dish it." Lexi sat back with her legs crossed and sipped her drink.

Blinking, I swallowed my mouthful of champagne and orange juice and shook my head slightly at her abrupt demand for details. "Robert had the most amazing apartment," I teased.

Carlotta interrupted my gushing with a wave of her hand. "We don't want to hear about his damn apartment. We want to know how he was in bed."

"Guess she didn't leave him passed out on the floor with whiskey dick." Lexi snickered and winked at Carlotta.

I briefly squeezed my eyes shut at the reminder of last week's horrendous pickup, who had indeed suffered an incredible case of whiskey dick—in other words, he'd drunk so much he couldn't finish the job, then he'd passed out on me. Well, not *on* me. On his living room floor where I'd left him.

At the next table an elderly man scowled at us. In return, I winked at him and hooked a stray lock of hair behind my ear. "He had the most amazing silk sheets." I opened the menu and pretended to study it. "I'm gonna have to get me some."

Lexi snatched the menu from my hand and held it out of reach. "Screw the sheets, *rate him*!"

"Five stars," I muttered, giving them both a pitiful look. "I can see this is gonna be a fun breakfast."

"Sorry, honey," Lexi sighed, looking apologetic, "I'm beat."

"No sweat." I waved it off. "We did it on his balcony too." I rolled my eyes and grinned, knowing they'd get a kick out of that. I didn't mean to be so naughty. I just couldn't help myself. And Robert had brought out the worst in me; his stuffiness made me want to push every button he had.

We stopped chatting long enough to order breakfast, then I turned to Lexi, who'd disappeared shortly before Robert had shown up. "What the hell happened to you Friday night?"

I sipped my drink and nibbled at a plate of fresh fruit while she filled us in, laughing softly to myself at the thought of her boss catching her at the Doll Palace (Houston's *hottest* strip club). "I can't believe you got busted in a strip joint."

"You know, now I almost think Dolan was as afraid that I'd seen him as he was that he'd seen me. I hear his wife's a bit of a hard-ass. A real sweetheart but very old school."

"She sounds like my mom," I muttered.

"I can't believe you *went* to a strip joint! I mean, if it were Lanie, I could definitely see it . . . especially on amateur night," Carlotta added with a wicked grin. "Then again, I *have* seen it on amateur night. So you and Wade patched everything up?"

"Yup. What about you? Get lucky Friday night?"

"No," she drawled, focusing her eyes somewhere near the ceiling, "but there was Thursday afternoon!"

Lexi giggled and forked up a bite of honeydew. "Was that your farewell fuck, Carlotta? No, don't answer that. You like him, don't you? You *like* the Geek Meister?!"

Leaning over, Carlotta covered her mouth with her hand and said in her best stage whisper, "He's got a big dick."

"Lanie," Lexi sighed, "better watch it, she's after your title."

"Ain't nobody takin' my title. By the way, I'm out this afternoon. I need to catch up on some paperwork."

"I need to catch up on some sleep," Lexi said with a nod.

"I need to catch up on my sex."

Lexi arched an eyebrow at Carlotta while I snorted softly to myself. "With Devon the Geek?"

Nodding, Carlotta cut off a bite of her omelet and popped it into her mouth. "After Lanie ditched me Friday night, Cherise and I went to this new swingers' club. Guess who was there?"

"Fuck sleep." Lexi laughed, setting her fork down. "I wanna hear about this."

"So do I! The paperwork can wait."

Carlotta, being Carlotta, spent breakfast dropping broad

hints and teasing us, insisting we had to wait until we left to get all the (very) dirty details.

"Since you didn't get lucky *Friday* night . . ." Grinning in the face of her smirk, I slid the tray with the check in it her way. "I guess I better get it in gear. I don't wanna be at this all day."

"Ew, I just remembered. You had to go to your parents' yesterday." Lexi stood up and slung her purse over her shoulder while Carlotta fished some cash from her wallet.

Curling my lip was the most appropriate response I could come up with in reference to my family. "My brother starts work for me tomorrow."

"Is this a bad thing?" Carlotta asked over her shoulder.

"Well, I guess it means no sex at work." I snickered, following her out. "But I suppose it'll be okay. It'll just be weird having family so close."

"I thought you hated your family?" Lexi stopped walking long enough to frown in confusion at me over the top of what looked like brand-new sunglasses.

"I do. When did you get new sunglasses?" I asked, reaching for them.

"Like them?" She stepped back and wiggled them before resting them on her nose. "Gucci, bitch."

I peered at Carlotta and said, "Ten bucks says she loses them inside of a week."

Lexi had a sunglass fetish made worse by the fact that the more expensive the glasses, the faster she lost or broke them. Carlotta and I high-fived each other in agreement.

I trailed after Carlotta to her 4Runner. "If you could have seen the way they treated Jackie—it made me sick! Denial is Ma's crack of choice and Dad, he's just as bad. You know what really sucks?" I plowed on, not bothering to wait for an answer. "If he'd just called me up and *asked* me, I probably would have said yes, but he had to humiliate Jackie in front of the family and Grant's friend. . . . It was just wrong."

"Holding out on us, Lanie?" Lexi asked, giving me a nudge with her elbow.

"Nope. There was nothing to mention. He's my brother's old friend from high school. I could see that: Jeff, I'm bisexual. Please don't tell my brother." Once they stopped laughing, I continued. "So anyway—"

"If he wants a construction job, I might be able to get him one at Dolan," Lexi offered softly.

"I appreciate it! I'll tell him if this doesn't work out, but I think it will. I hope it does. The more I think about having him around, the better it sounds."

"He's an ex-con?" Carlotta opened up the back of the SUV and leaned against the cargo area.

"He's my brother." Carlotta and I frowned at each other. "Now, about Devon . . ."

We spent the next few minutes getting the dirty-skinny on Carlotta and her Geek Meister's wild, er, dominant side, discovered during their Saturday night date.

"Felt up in a Cuban restaurant," Lexi said with a slow shake of her head.

"Gives new meaning to the phrase 'Latin Rhythm.' "

4

Jackie was waiting for me when I pulled into the parking lot Monday morning. I slid out of the Bronco, a large vanilla latte in one hand and a battered leather briefcase crammed full of paperwork in the other.

"Nice sign," he said, sliding off the hood of the Pinto that Dad had stuck him with.

"Thanks." The sign sat at the top of a pole on the edge of the parking lot. A fuzzy baby chick with hot pink sunglasses and high heels pointed one wing at the words "Chick's Garage," which were spelled out in big pink and white letters. All of it was superimposed on the prettiest pale yellow background and trimmed in hot pink the same color as the sunglasses. I'd created the ubercute logo just to piss Dad off; then it had grown on me. Hell, the building's cinderblock exterior was even pink, the doorway of the glassed-in waiting area flanked on both sides by huge buckets filled with whatever "in season" greenery bloomed pink flowers.

"So how was it?" *After I left.*

"Mom thinks you're a lesbian." He popped open the trunk

and then peered at me from around the back of the car. "Not that she actually said the word *lesbian*." We snickered at each other as he shouldered two overstuffed tote bags. "I really appreciate this, Lanie, and I won't let you down."

"You mind yourself, Jackie. No bullshit. You got any issue with taking orders from me, we need to hash them out before the rest of the crew gets here." I shoved my key in the heavy metal door and unlocked it, not bothering to wait for a reply. The minute we stepped inside, the unique and questionably aromatic combination of grease and dirt greeted us.

"I got no problems taking orders from you," Jackie said once I'd disengaged the alarm.

After hitting the panel of light switches, I turned to face him in the ugly glare of fluorescent lights. "I fired two mechanics last week who said the same thing when I hired them."

"Well, unlike them, I don't have much choice."

"You made your choices, Jackie Ray Daniels," I said softly while hoping like hell I didn't sound like Ma or worse, Dad.

"I know, and I'll pay for it for the rest of my life."

"Maybe, maybe not, but for the record, I'm not here to judge you." I motioned for him to follow me and walked the length of the shop, my crepe-soled boots relatively quiet on the concrete floor. "Though I do have to ask, why'd you do it, Jackie?"

"I dunno. I've had ten years to think about it, but I still don't know."

Squinting slightly as my eyes adjusted to the much brighter light in my office, I dropped my briefcase beside my desk and went to make coffee. Jackie slumped in a ratty grease-covered chair across from me, toeing the bags at his feet. All his worldly goods.

"I knew I was gonna get caught. Maybe I *wanted* to get caught. Maybe I robbed that store for the same reason you're here and not working for Dad." He quirked an eyebrow and gave me a crooked, knowing grin. That's when I noticed his left eyetooth was missing.

In some perverse way, he was probably right about me and Dad, and I leaned against the ancient credenza, snorting with laughter while the coffeepot behind me began to perk. "That's fine and dandy, but I'll tell you what. You can keep on paying for it or move on. Don't let him and prison be all you define or measure your life by. Do you actually believe Dad would have let me work for him? Outside of the office, that is?"

"No, but he loaned you the money for this." Jackie waved his arms, indicating the garage.

" 'Cause he didn't want people talking. And I paid back every cent—*with interest*. You know the first thing he asked me when he saw this place? 'When you gonna paint it?' You should have seen the look on his face when I said I already had."

The coffeepot made sucking sounds that signaled it was almost done, and the smell of fresh-brewed coffee mingled with garage perfume. Turning, I filled a cup and handed it to him while trying to figure out how to word the proposal I'd been thinking about since I'd left my parents' house Saturday afternoon. I reached for my own cup on the desk and took a sip, buying myself some time. "You don't really want to be a mechanic, do you, Jackie Ray?"

"No more than you wanna be married."

He was right, damnit. Snorting softly, I briefly squeezed my eyes shut and pinched the bridge of my nose. "I just don't see what the big freakin' deal is." I held up my hand to forestall whatever he'd been about to say and pinned him down to the chair with a narrow-eyed gaze. "I need help and you need a job, but you don't wanna be a grease monkey, so how about this. You take care of the front counter and help me with the paperwork and minor bookkeeping. This ain't no mercy job either. Whether Dad and company like it or not, I've got more business than I can handle."

"Deal," he said, his bright blue eyes twinkling.

At that moment he reminded me of Dad more than I'd ever admit to, and I took another sip of my rapidly cooling latte to cover my twinge of discomfort.

"Good, now let's go look at your new digs." Leaning over, I grabbed one of his bags with my free hand.

The stairs just outside of my office led to the upper level. One side held open shelves of parts, old and new, as well as an assortment of junk left behind by the previous owner. The other was the tiny apartment that had been the former owner's home away from home while his divorce went through.

"It's not much, but it's a start." I pushed open the door and winced. I hadn't been up here in months, usually limiting myself to cleaning and dusting a couple of times a year. The efficiency wasn't that little, just very sparsely decorated. A mini-kitchen with an electric stove, a rickety dinette table and a window that looked out over the front parking lot took up one end of the room. At the other end sat a sofa and coffee table circa 1960-something, complete with an oversized, braided rug in blues and greens, and a screen that hid a queen-size bed. "Bathroom's in the bedroom."

"At least I won't have to walk downstairs in the middle of the night if I have to pee." With a laugh, Jackie dropped his bag by the door and I followed suit.

"I guess it looks pretty grim." I looked around the tiny apartment, wishing there were more to it. But it hadn't bothered me to live here the first year I was in business and I figured it wouldn't bother Jackie. "But it's not forever."

"It's a palace compared to my previous home."

And it probably was.

Once the rest of the crew showed up, I introduced Jackie around and handed out work assignments, then I excused both of us with a fictional parts-running errand. We headed out to Target and anywhere else we could think of. I wanted to make damn sure he had food and other essentials he needed, including a new mattress and box springs. If Jackie failed, it wouldn't be because I hadn't tried to help him—though I refused to look too closely at why it was suddenly so important to me that he *not* fail.

By the time we got back to the garage, the fans were waging a losing war against the heat and climbing humidity, and all four bay doors were wide open. I slipped into my office long enough to yank a pink uniform shirt over my T-shirt and tuck it into my jeans. Outside, the persistent whine of air tools mingled with the sound of Led Zeppelin, but I spent another hour in the tiny yellow-and-white lounge area, showing Jackie how to fill out work orders and file them on the board just outside the door.

No sooner had I unscrewed the drip pan on a Mercedes than my cell phone rang. While oil the color of pitch and nearly as thick slowly began to drain, I snatched up a rag from the top of my toolbox and gingerly picked up the phone, frowning at the unfamiliar number. To answer, or not to answer?

"Hello." I stuck a finger in my other ear so I could hear over the garage noise.

"Lanie?"

Shit on a stick! "Robert, hi!" I took off for my office at the fastest walk I could manage.

"I haven't heard from you."

Because I'd completely forgotten to call him. "I've been busy."

"Where are you?"

"At work," I huffed, closing the door behind me. "What's up?"

"What's that noise?" he asked with a nervous laugh.

I dropped into my chair and propped my feet on the cluttered desk, staring at the water-stained ceiling tiles and debating the wisdom of seeing Robert Clayton the Fourth again. "*That* is the sound of money being made—"

His voice dropped to almost a whisper as he added, "I *really* want to see you again."

With a roll of my eyes I sank a little lower on the stool and debated how to answer. "Look Robert, I don't think we should see each other again."

"What have you done to me?" he whispered.

"I haven't done anything."

"Yeah you have. I can't get a damn thing done at work. All I can think about is—"

"Fucking me?"

"Do you have to be so—"

"Blunt?"

"Right."

"I rest my case. Good-bye, Robert." As I replaced the phone in the cradle, a twinge of regret at how harsh I'd been dug at me. A very small twinge. I knew exactly what Robert wanted, another walk on the wild side, but he'd have to look elsewhere for it. Despite the fact he'd been a decent lay, I'd had to work too hard for it, and well, I wasn't normally one for giving second chances. Jackie being the exception to that rule.

I swung my legs off the desk and spun around in the chair, only to jump out of my skin at a knock on the window. A perplexed-looking Jackie stood on the other side, watching me.

With a soft groan, I stuck my head out the door to see what he wanted. "Everything going okay?"

"Yeah . . . I just saw you take off and thought maybe something was wrong."

"Personal call." Smothering a groan, I forced my lips to curve into an easy smile. "I need to get back to work, and so do you."

Back outside, I removed the oil filter with a low, short groan of frustration. No wonder the oil that had drained out had been so thick and slow. It looked like it should have been changed about six thousand miles ago. Once the oil filter was replaced, I quickly finished the job.

In the welcome cool of the waiting area I finished filling out my ticket and handed it to Jackie. "Mrs. Peters, you're good for another three thousand miles. Don't wait so long to come in next time."

"Thank you." Smiling, she clutched her tiny black-and-white shitzu to her and stood up. At least she had the grace to blush.

"I'll back it out while Jackie rings you up. And I'll see you in two thousand miles to change that transmission fluid."

Once Mrs. Peters was on her way I went and checked on the rest of my crew. Linda was the only female mechanic working for me, and cute, in a tomboyish way. Of the three mechanics I'd hired in the last month, she was the only newbie left.

She stood on a footstool, her head under the hood of a two-year-old Lincoln Navigator. The owner, a Mrs. Caitlyn Dupree, had taken it in to the dealership three times for the same problem, only to have her claims that there was something wrong dismissed by the mechanic when he couldn't pinpoint a problem. When she'd complained at a luncheon, another client of mine had referred her to us. Stories like Mrs. Dupree's were the reason Chick's Garage had more business than we could handle. Women were tired of getting ripped off, or worse, laughed at by male mechanics who thought they knew better—something I'd seen my own father's mechanics do countless times while I was growing up.

I tapped the side of the hood to catch Linda's attention, then reached up to tighten my ponytail. Even this early in the afternoon the heat and humidity were making things uncomfortable. "You about done?"

"Yeah," she grunted. "So what's the deal with the new guy?"

"What do you mean?" I couldn't hold back a smile.

"He's cute. Is he single? And where'd you find him?" She stood and stretched to work the kinks out of her back.

"Through a friend, yeah he's single, and yeah he's cute." *Yes,*

I can say my brother's cute in a completely unbiased, sisterly way.

"You got dibs on him?"

"No, but you know better than to mess around with any of the guys." I arched an eyebrow in warning and headed over to Julio, who was working on a birthday present for another client's husband. In bay two the engine of a '68 Camaro hung from a winch.

"How's it going?"

Julio dropped his arms at his sides, his slight shoulders sagging, and shook his head while cursing in Spanish. Some things are universal.

"Need an extra hand?"

Julio shook his head and grinned, the smile lines in his face accentuated by a hint of the grime that permeated everything, including our skin, and waved me away. I went with a good-natured laugh. Last on my stop was John, currently the only other ex-con on the job, working on an ancient but pristine Cadillac.

"Get that new carburetor in?"

"Yeah." He stood up, resting his hands on the front framework. "But it still failed the emissions test. Old bag oughta buy a new car."

"Just make it work." With a frown, I turned and headed to the board outside the office for my next ticket, a car that couldn't seem to stop overheating and probably needed a new water pump.

And that's how the rest of the day went. I had no time to think about Robert or tomorrow or even when I'd get to shower, which, God willing, would be soon.

Only the pizza Jackie and I had for dinner had kept me going. By the time I parked my Bronco next to the Prius and climbed out, it was nearly ten.

In the laundry area, I stripped down to my panties and threw my clothes in the washer before pouring myself a glass of wine. The sink was empty and the house smelled like Pledge and Lysol. The maid service, a bimonthly treat, had come today. Which meant clean dishes and clean sheets. *There was a God.*

I was tired, but wired and not ready for sleep. The wine and a long hot shower helped considerably. I refilled my glass and stepped out onto the back patio wearing only my towel.

The kidney-shaped pool gleamed like black ink under a nearly full moon, and except for the occasional bark of a dog, the entire neighborhood was quiet. Dropping my towel in a chair, I crossed the pavement to the edge of the pool and climbed in, sighing as cool water washed over every naked inch of me. A dozen laps unworked the last of the knots the day had created. With a sigh of satisfaction I stood up and smoothed my long, wet hair back from my face and stretched my arms above my head, smiling as my nipples puckered in the chill brought on by the water and a slight breeze.

I ran my fingers across my chest and over the stiff peaks, then did it again. A tingle of awareness trickled down between my thighs. After slowly spinning around to again check that the neighbors' houses were all dark, I walked to the steps and sat, legs propped wide so that water tickled my pussy. I touched myself, caressing my thighs under the water and trailing my fingertips to the edge of my pussy lips.

My cunt clenched, demanding more, but it was too soon. Instead I massaged the edges, then let my fingers trail up across my stomach to my tits. They were covered in goose bumps, pale in the moonlight. Grasping my nipples between my fingers, I squeezed as hard as I could stand and rolled them between my fingers, watching myself and getting more excited by the minute. I slid lower in the water and rested my head at the edge of the pool, pushing my hips up out of the water and bobbing up and down so it swished against me, lapping at my pussy. My fingers continued their roll and tweak, until I ached with the need to stroke my clit, to climax; until all I could think about was having something big and really hard inside me.

I thrust my hips upward again and held them just above the water's surface. Squeezing my bottom, I pulled the skin covering my mound tight and gently patted my swollen lips, only stopping when an orgasm became imminent. All it would take was a few strokes of my fingers, but I wasn't ready to finish yet. Leaping out of the pool, I grabbed my towel where I'd dropped it earlier and quickly dried myself off before stepping through the glass sliding door into the chilly air of my bedroom. From the bottom drawer of my nightstand I retrieved my favorite toy—nine inches of slightly curved jelly material sculpted to look like a real dick, that would vibrate at my whim—and covered it with a thin layer of lube.

Back on the porch, I covered the chaise with my damp towel and lay back, spreading my legs as wide as possible. For just a minute I lay there with my eyes closed, enjoying the feel of the soft night breeze on my skin, teasing me, before dipping the dildo between my thighs and spreading my juices around. My lips curved into a smile as it came into contact with my swollen clit. Not yet.

I slowly pushed it inside me, letting my hungry cunt draw it up, and gave myself a few slow, experimental strokes, relaxing as my pussy adjusted to the invasion. *Nice.* With a flick of the dial, the vibrator hummed softly inside me. I arched my hips upward so I could watch it glide in and out of me while slowly increasing the speed of my thrusts and the vibration until my climax was imminent. Then it was there, rolling through me so my hips convulsed and my pussy greedily sucked at the vibrator I continued to thrust inside of me, until I was completely satisfied.

With a sigh, I shut it off and stretched out, closing my legs tightly until the aftershocks faded and I'd caught my breath.

Too bad I'd blown Robert off. I could have called him and let him listen.

5

The phone ringing jerked me out of a deep sleep. About the time I realized it was Jackie on the other end, my eyes focused on the clock. I'd overslept, and not a little. The clock flashed 8:00 AM in big, bold, accusing letters.

The garage's parking lot was full, and a flatbed tow truck with a Mercedes 300SL convertible sat parked in front of bay two. I parked next to Jackie's Pinto and entered through the waiting area so I could check up on him. Poor Jackie was red-faced in obvious frustration as an older woman in designer jeans, with her silver hair cut in a pixie to frame her face, frantically chattered at him—yes, *at*.

Three women, in stages of amusement and frustration that ranged from "I just got here" to "Is it done yet," watched, while the hum of a talk show on TV provided background noise. I gave them all a warm smile as I slipped behind the counter and squeezed Jackie's arm reassuringly.

Both he and Ms. Pixie Cut visibly relaxed at the sight of me. "Oh good. A woman . . ."

"Yes ma'am." I smiled while tracking the black Infiniti that had pulled into the lot. "But Jackie's more than capable of handling whatever you need."

"My car"—she pointed out the safety glass toward the tow truck with her car—"*he* says you can't get to it today." Sighing, she gingerly rested her hands on the countertop and leaned forward. "My son . . . told me to get it looked at, or trade it in, and I forgot. I didn't forget to trade it in; I forgot to get it looked at."

Her words hung between us as we gave each other a look of complete female sympathy.

"Do we know what's wrong with it?" I asked, glancing up at Jackie. If it needed a new set of spark plugs that was one thing, but . . .

"A transmission."

Oh shit. "My apologies ma'am. I'm afraid Jackie's right," I said with a little grimace. Outside a tall, incredibly handsome man dressed in a navy suit slid out of the Infiniti. The car was sweet, the suit looked custom tailored, the sunglasses were Armani, and the man was Jeff Cash. Licking my lips, I pressed on while wondering what the hell he was doing here. "A transmission is more than a couple-hour job. For that matter, I'll probably have to contact the Mercedes dealership for parts." And if they didn't have a transmission, one would have to be ordered. Add water; insert headache.

"How long?" she asked, wide eyed and breathless as the door swung open behind her.

"What year is it?" I looked out the window again, trying to gauge the car's age. The Mercedes was a pristine 1990-something Roadster.

"Mom, Jackie, Mel," Jeff said, slipping his sunglasses off his nose.

"Jeff!"

Mom?

"The car? How old is it?" I asked, looking from Jeff to his mother and back. Jesus, he even smelled expensive.

" '91. My husband bought it for an anniversary present. Jeff says I should just get a new one, but then, the boy doesn't have a sentimental bone in his body."

Biting my lip at her dramatic pronouncement of her son, I glanced at Jeff, who just shrugged.

"She's right. I don't. So what's the prognosis?"

"I'm afraid they can't fix the car today." She looked the tiniest bit shamefaced while Jeff gave her an "I-told-you-so" look.

"The best I can do is call a rental place . . . or we can have you towed to the Mercedes dealership."

"Absolutely not!" they chorused.

Mrs. Cash's lips were compressed into a grim line. "I want *you* to fix it. Jeff said you were the best. And my friend Margaret agreed."

I smiled while my insides quaked. Jeff had sent her to me. And if I didn't miss my mark, her friend Margaret was a Houston blue blood who'd had similar complaints about getting her Jaguar fixed at a dealership earlier this year. Word of mouth had definitely been my friend. But . . . Jeff?

I pulled Jackie over by the sleeve and handed her over to him. "Jackie will take down all your information. I'll call you by six and give you an update. How's that?"

She gave me a brilliant smile. "Perfect."

I watched Jeff and his mother leave, watched him help her into her car, and wondered how much of a mama's boy *he* was.

With the matter settled, I grabbed a clean uniform shirt. By the time I reached the bays, Mrs. Cash's Mercedes had been unloaded and the tow truck was gone. I'd just slid behind the wheel when Jackie appeared at the car door.

"You doing okay?" I smiled up at him.

He nodded. "Thanks for in there. I thought she was gonna go all socialite on me."

I laughed. "She's a nice lady . . . just stressed over her car. You did good. Mostly they just want to be treated like they have a brain. You'd be surprised the number of times I've heard stuff like 'I told my husband . . .' You get all settled in?"

"Yeah . . . are *you* okay?"

"I'm fine, why?"

"I just kind of expected you to be here this morning is all." He stuffed his hands in his jeans pockets.

"Well, I sure as hell didn't expect to oversleep like that," I said, laughing. "Knock off around five and we can go over the daily wrap-up stuff again, then we can go grab a burger."

"Sounds good. I bet your accountant's a woman, huh?" He laughed but I could see the unspoken question in his eyes.

I was single at thirty-four because I chose to be, and my sex life, especially my bisexuality, weren't things I planned on sharing with my family anytime soon. Not even with Jackie, my fellow misfit. With a wave, I sent him back inside.

The Mercedes struggled to go into reverse, and forward was no better. I put it in park and slid out, calling for John to come give me a hand. He'd have to anyway, since he was the German car expert. Together we got it pushed into the bay, then stood conferring with arms crossed.

"I'm gonna go call the dealership," I said, "and if they have the transmission we need, I'll send Jackie for it in my Bronco."

"I can start on it tomorrow," John said.

"Good. Mrs. Cash is really wigging out. We need to try and get it out as soon as possible. What are you working on now?"

"Replacing the head gaskets on that Acura." He pulled his ball cap off and swiped his arm across his forehead.

"I can come help, or just take over if you want. We have anything else waiting?"

"Couple oil changes." He smirked, and I shook my head. Between putting out fires, answering phones, and running for parts, the only thing I had time for anymore was maintenance:

oil changes, transmission flushes, belts, and of course, paperwork. Hopefully all that would change with Jackie around.

The phone call didn't take long, and Dan, the parts manager, assured me they had what I needed. I dug my keys out and headed for the waiting area.

"I need you to go get that transmission." I held the keys out to Jackie.

"Where'm I going?" He took them with a grin, obviously glad to get out from behind the counter for a while.

"The Mercedes dealership on 45 north, just past the airport. You know where that's at?"

"Does Texas grow barbecue?" he quipped. With a laugh, he slipped past me and headed out the door.

"Just ask for Dan!"

I spent the rest of the afternoon helping John with the head gaskets and running back and forth to catch the phone and cash out customers. We got his Acura out of the way, and Linda's Explorer. I didn't really worry about Jackie until the second hour. A quick call to Dan assured me that Jackie had gotten the part and left, so all I could do was wait and fret and pester the hell out of John until my cell phone finally rang. I frowned at the readout on my caller ID. "Hello?"

"Sis." Even though I could barely hear his voice over all the background noise, I knew it was Jackie.

"Shit! What the hell happened?" With the phone wedged between my ear and shoulder, I grabbed a clean rag off of John's toolbox and started scrubbing at my grime-covered hands.

"I got stopped for speeding."

"And they arrested you?"

"Technically, no. But they're holding me until you come down here and verify that the truck and transmission are yours."

"I'm on my way." I hung up tossing the rag down with a grunt of frustration. "John, lock up."

"Everything okay?"

The concern in his eyes slowed me down enough to tamp down my anger. Crossing over to the Acura, I leaned against the front bumper and spoke so only he would hear me. As if anyone else would or could over the sound of air-driven tools. "Jackie's an ex-con, and he got picked up for speeding. Apparently they think he stole my truck so I've got to go get him."

"You know—"

"Don't start!" I gave him a warning look, despite the twinkle in his eyes.

"For all you act like a bitch sometimes, you got a good heart."

In lieu of a response, I gave him a long, hard scowl before turning toward my office.

The police substation was controlled chaos in shades of black and white—checkered floors, black chairs and white walls. Either someone had a sick sense of humor, or they'd gotten a great deal on the tile and decided to run with it. I ignored it all and made a beeline for the main desk. "I need to pick up my brother."

After giving my grease-stained appearance a hard once-over, the desk sergeant asked for my brother's name, then barked at me to have a seat. Except there wasn't an empty seat to be found. Both benches—yeah, all two of them—were full, and I was covered in grease and dirt. More than one appraising glance was thrown my way from officers who passed by, and none of them were friendly.

Finally, a young patrol officer came and escorted me through a beehive of desks to his, where Jackie sat handcuffed to a chair. He looked sheepish and more than a little embarrassed. Instantly, I felt awful for him. As many ex-cons as I'd had work for me, you'd think I'd remember how tough the police and parole officers could be on them. I guess when it came to Jackie, it'd slipped my mind.

"Why is my brother here?" I asked, waving at Jackie.

"Your brother is being held until we can verify ownership of the vehicle."

"Officer"—I glanced at his nametag—"Reeves, I am the owner of the vehicle *and* the transmission in the back, which I needed to put into a Mercedes this afternoon." Southern charm was obviously not my forte.

A smirk on his face, Officer Reeves looked me up and down as if he couldn't imagine *why* I'd need a Mercedes transmission. "Did you bring any proof?"

Sighing in frustration, I reminded myself that despite my lack of charm, venting on this cop wouldn't do Jackie or me any good. "Y'all didn't run the registration? I mean, we do have the same last name."

"Sis," Jackie hissed.

I bit my lip before I landed Jackie in even more hot water and fished my wallet and driver's license out of my tiny leather purse. "You can compare the name to the name on the registration."

"That'll work." The idea apparently hadn't occurred to him.

Numbnuts. My foot bobbed up and down while he tapped at the keyboard in front of him with excruciating slowness.

At last he looked up at me, as if he was seeing me for the first time. "You know you have grease on your face, Miss Daniels?"

"I own a garage."

His face immediately split into an amused grin. "Really?"

Such an original concept, huh? "Really," I said as matter-of-factly as I could.

"Are you that Chick's Garage lady that was on TV a couple years back?" a female officer asked from his other side.

"That would be me, and my brother Jackie *works* for me. So

can you please take off his cuffs now?" I asked, focusing on the cop holding my license and my brother hostage.

Officer Reeves nodded and fished the handcuff keys out.

"By the way, where's my truck?" I asked.

Jackie rubbed his wrist, refusing to meet my eyes. The hesitant look on Reeves' face said it all. He really didn't feel up to tangling with me. Trust me, the feeling was mutual. "Where do I have to go to pick it up?"

He dug in his desk drawer and pulled a pad out, ripping off a piece of paper with the address and phone number to the impound yard printed on it.

Jackie looked beaten. Not physically but emotionally, and I felt terrible for him. If Dad found out he'd been picked up, even if it wasn't his fault, it would be another nail in the family coffin for Jackie.

We flew across Houston with two by sixty A/C if we were lucky—two windows and sixty miles an hour, as long as the dense late-afternoon traffic didn't stop us. We didn't speak again until we reached the impound yard.

"I'm sorry," he said as he pulled the Pinto into the impound yard.

"It's not your fault. Now let's get my Bronco. John needs that transmission when he comes in tomorrow morning."

A bit of haggling and my American Express card got me the Bronco in no time, though I was $120 poorer for my trouble. While we waited for them to bring it out, Jackie said, "You can take it out of my pay."

"Bullshit! Jackie Ray, quit being like this!"

"How am I supposed to be?" He scowled down at me. "I have to report to my parole officer tomorrow, for fuck's sake, and he's gonna chew my ass out!"

"Want me to write you a note?" I grinned up at him, hoping my flip tone would bring him down, and it seemed to work.

"No," he said, laughing. He ran a hand through his short hair.

"How about that hamburger, then?" Just then my phone rang, and with a roll of my eyes, I answered it. "Yo!"

"Hey Chiquita!"

I smiled at the sound of Carlotta's voice. A huge-ass margarita and her ear to bend for a while would go over really well about now.

"Where the hell you been?"

"Working my ass off. Let's do dinner tomorrow." I waved my thanks to the yard guy who climbed out of my newly sprung vehicle, then peeked through the side window, happy to see the transmission was still in the back and looked fine.

"Can't. What about tonight?"

Was Jackie up to company? Hell, it'd probably cheer him up. "No Chinese, and my brother's eating with us."

"Oh boy, after all this time she's introducing me to family," Carlotta said with a laugh.

"Shut up and behave yourself. Jackie's a nice boy."

A chuckling Jackie punched me in the arm and mouthed, "I'm not a boy."

"Is this the one that was in—"

"Yeah. You wanna have dinner with us, or not?"

"Rusty's work for you?"

Rusty's was a very low-key hamburger place. "Perfect. I haven't had a chance to clean up."

"And they sure as hell won't care," she added, chuckling.

"Fine, we'll see you in about thirty minutes."

"You need to take off?" Jackie asked once I'd hung up.

"No way. I asked you to dinner, and Carlotta wants to meet you."

"Carlotta, huh? Sounds exotic." He gave me his usual—cheeky grin—and I smiled back.

"She's a handful," I warned.

He laughed again. "You know how long it's been since I've been on a date?"

"Let alone gotten laid?"

"I never bent over in the shower."

I winced slightly. "No more butt jokes."

"Sorry, my socialization skills have suffered. The guys in the yard, they weren't much on formalities."

"With that smart mouth of yours, it's a wonder you didn't get your ass kicked, regularly."

We pulled into the crowded parking lot at Rusty's, an oversized cabin surrounded by a huge deck where you could sit outside, eat crab legs and burgers, and drink beer.

I climbed out and shrugged off my grease-stained work shirt, happy to see there were only a few stains on my tank top. "Carlotta's already here."

Jackie nervously ran his fingers through his hair. "How do you know?"

"That's her 4Runner." I motioned to the shiny black SUV parked next to me.

I slid out of the Bronco and waited for Jackie to join me, anxious to see his reaction to Carlotta. She was, in a word, stunning—even dressed in jeans and a T-shirt like she was now. Underneath the soft, worn cotton, her nipples stood at attention, an amazing feat in the late afternoon heat. She wore her long hair loose, blonde curls reaching the middle of her back. I slipped up beside her and pulled her close for a hug, then turned and introduced Jackie. She promptly brushed her full lips against his cheek and batted her eyelashes at him. And Jackie? His eyes lit up like a Christmas tree.

"I think you've rendered him speechless."

"He's a cute one." Dimples creased her cheeks as she gave him a final once-over.

All three of us voted for the patio, and we settled ourselves around a round table with beers and an order of cheese fries to start off with.

"How's the vacation going?" I asked Carlotta.

"It's . . . nice," she said, obviously unwilling to elaborate.

The hesitation in her voice wasn't a good sign. Maybe I could get her to meet me at my house after dinner. I had a feeling we needed to talk. I knew *I* needed to talk, and I could use the company. I nudged the platter of cheese-covered fries in Jackie's direction.

"Eat!" I sipped my beer, happy to feel myself decompress after another very long day.

"You sound like Ma."

"Hey, fuck you."

"There are worse things in the world than being told you sound like your mama," Carlotta said, sticking an elbow in my side.

"You haven't met my mother." I frowned at her from under my eyelashes.

"This is very true." Jackie shook his head while helping himself to more fries. "So, Carlotta, do you have a man?"

"Uh, yeah. Well, sort of." Nodding, she sipped her beer.

Oh, we definitely needed to talk. "I thought it was—"

"Excuse me! Don't wave my business around in front of your brother!"

"I can leave." He looked from Carlotta to me and back at her.

"No," we both barked, causing the waitress who'd approached to take our order to stop dead in her tracks before covering the last few steps to our table.

Once she'd left, Jackie seemed to visibly relax, even flirting with Carlotta a bit. As if the fact that she was taken, and his sister's best friend, somehow made her safe. There were worse ways for him to get his feet wet. And Carlotta didn't seem to mind, so why should I?

Outside the restaurant we parted ways, waving good–bye to Jackie. I turned to Carlotta. "Follow me home?"

"Right behind you, love."

Twenty minutes later I pulled into the driveway, parking the Bronco in the garage. Between the grime of a day's work and the heat and humidity, I really, *really* needed a shower. In the kitchen, I pulled a bottle of wine from the fridge and then went and unlocked the front door for Carlotta. She stepped inside, slamming the door behind her and leaning against it, one hand dramatically clutching her stomach. "I'm so full! And you look as shitty as I feel."

"Lemme get cleaned up. Wine's on the counter."

"I'll pour."

I stayed in the shower until the smell of grease and dirt was chased away by cucumber melon body wash and the water had begun to cool.

By the time I joined Carlotta on the living room floor, she'd found the bag of Hershey's Kisses I stashed in my cookie jar, popped popcorn, and slipped a movie into the DVD player.

"Braid my hair, please?" I asked

"Come on, baby." She spread her legs and patted the spot between them.

Setting my glass of wine down, I positioned myself between her thighs, my back to her. "So, you wanna go first, or should I? What'd you put in anyway?"

"*Underworld.*" She eased herself off the floor, perching on the edge of the couch as she gently towel-dried my hair. "I don't even know where to begin. Devon has . . . turned out to be different than I expected."

"Different how?"

She silently combed my hair smooth, then divided off a section in the front before she answered me. "He's too close, and I can't seem to stop him. I'm not sure I want to, and that scares me."

"Is that a bad scared or a good scared?" On screen the previews started to play. Her fingers were soothing, relaxing me as she slowly but deftly braided my damp hair.

"I'm not sure, and I think that's what worries me." Laughing, she paused long enough to sip her wine. "Who would have ever thought a geek like him would turn out to be such a surprise."

"Oh. My!" I laughed and tilted my head back to look at her, then rolled my eyes when she just grinned at me. "So you're diggin' this submissive thing?"

"Against my better judgment, yes. Now, sit up." She gave my head a gentle push. "What's up with The Suit? You did give him five stars Sunday at brunch."

"Kicked him to the curb." I finally pushed PLAY, tired of listening to the intro music repeat itself. "But guess who came into the shop today?" Digging a couple Hershey's Kisses out of the bowl beside me, I unwrapped them, handing one to Carlotta and popping the second into my mouth.

"Hmmm," she muttered around her mouthful of chocolate. "Your brother's friend?"

"How the hell did you know?" My head dipped only to jerk upright at the sharp pain that traveled up my scalp. Carlotta still had hold of my hair.

"Easy enough to figure out since he's the only other man you've mentioned lately." She gave my head another tug.

"I forgot to call Mrs. Cash."

"Who?"

Before I could answer, I needed more chocolate. "Jeff's mom! I was supposed to call her about her car this afternoon but when Jackie got picked up it sorta slipped my mind."

"Relax, I'm sure she'll understand. And if not, I'm sure Jeff could make her understand," she said, laughing.

"You know Jeff's off limits."

"Well, maybe he shouldn't be?"

"Yeah, right. My brother finds out I'm boinking one of his friends and tells the whole family. Then I catch hell for being a slut. We're Catholic after all."

"Don't talk to me about Catholic. I know all about it. And I get the picture."

Jeff was *definitely* off limits.

6

Jackie was sitting outside, squatting beside the building smoking, when I pulled up the next morning.

"I didn't know you smoked."

"Prison," he said, holding up what was left of his cigarette.

"Just don't throw your butts on my pretty grass."

"Okay."

He put out his cigarette and followed me inside. The television in the waiting room and all the bay lights were already on and the little coffeepot I kept for customers was full of hot coffee.

"Jeff Cash left three messages on the answering machine."

"Triple shit!" I turned to face Jackie, sagging slightly in defeat. "I remembered when I got home last night."

"Want me to call him?"

"No." I held out my hand for the pink slip of paper he was holding and went to use the phone in my office. After slugging back a huge mouthful of my latte for fortification, I released a deep, shaky breath and dialed Jeff Cash's work number, navigating through the receptionist, and finally, past his secretary.

"This is Jeff." His husky baritone voice traveled across the phone line and put a smile on my face.

Maybe I should invest with him. I almost couldn't talk past the snicker that threatened to choke me.

"Hello?"

"Hi, it's Mel Daniels."

"Mel! How are you?"

"Fine. Good." My quick little white lie about a problem getting the part soothed him considerably, and he assured me he'd handle his mom.

"Thanks for sending her in."

"I just wish she'd come earlier."

"She's a sweet lady." I leaned back in my chair and sipped my latte.

"How's that bucket of bolts?"

"We at Chick's Garage prefer the word 'classic,' and that bucket of bolts is a Mercedes. It'll probably still run after we're all dead."

His laughter filled my ear, and I chuckled.

"Duly noted. How the hell did a cupcake like you get stuck with a nickname like Mel?"

"Four brothers." Now it was my turn to laugh. "And I can cook, but Mom's never forgiven me for taking shop instead of home ec . . . and I'm not a cupcake."

"Surely I can call you something besides Mel."

"If I tell you my super-secret nickname, you can never, ever, on penalty of death, tell Grant or any of my brothers."

"Never?"

"You do and you'll die a horrible death," I good-naturedly threatened.

"You tell me, and I'll take you to dinner."

"That's not necessary, Jeff." *But hey babe, whatever floats your boat!*

"I know, but maybe I want to."

I knew I was in big trouble when I found myself picturing the smile on his face. "Listen—"

"Just say, 'Yes, Jeff.' "

"Why should I?"

" 'Cause I can guarantee you a good time."

Player. Jeff was a player. But I liked and appreciated his directness. "Lanie, my super-secret nickname is Lanie, and I have standing plans." That, for once, I sort of regretted. Smiling, I tucked a stray hair behind my ear and swished the last drops of latte around in the cup before pitching it into the trash can.

Jeff laughed. "Lanie . . . I like it. Now, about Friday."

"There's a lot you don't know about me," I warned, discretion warring with interest.

"There's a lot I'd like to know about you. Anyway, whatever happens at Jeffy's place stays at Jeffy's place. Though in this case, it'd have to be your place. I've got a temporary roommate."

"Uh-oh." I frowned down at the clutter on my desktop.

"Yeah, a friend. His marriage is breaking up. Like I said, it's temporary."

"What makes you think anything's gonna happen at my place?" I asked, grinning to myself.

"A guy can dream, can't he?"

I gave in. I couldn't help myself. He made me laugh. "Jimmy Z's, second level. Look for the table by the south stairs that leads to the dance floor, with three hot chicks." With one last smile I hung up, yanked a work shirt from the closet and my keys off my desk. Once my Bronco was backed into the first bay, John and I unloaded the transmission.

"Think we can finish this up by tomorrow afternoon?"

"I can do that." John leaned against the Mercedes with his arms crossed over his chest. "I see you got Jackie all straightened around."

"Just a dumb misunderstanding. You need some help? I can pull Linda in or help you myself."

After I got John all squared away, I went back up front to run the desk for Jackie, who'd gone to see his parole officer.

Linda came and propped her butt on a nearby stool during her morning break. "Where'd Jackie go?"

"Why are you so nosy?" Sighing, I held up a hand in apology. "I'm sorry. It's been a long, shitty day."

"No sweat." She slid off the stool at the sight of the Pinto pulling into the lot and stood watching him. He looked sullen, so I didn't press him for details about how it had gone.

"Morning, Jackie." Before he could return her greeting, she turned and headed for the swinging door. "Guess I better get back to work."

Her hips swung as she crossed the garage and ducked under the hood of the Tahoe she was working on. He caught my eye and I smiled. As far as I was concerned he had a green light to do as he saw fit. Never mind that I officially frowned on fraternization; getting laid would probably do Jackie a world of good.

7

John and I worked late into the night finishing up, and I was on the phone with Mrs. Cash's housekeeper first thing Thursday morning. Apparently, Jeff's mom suffered from migraines, but arrangements would be made to get the car picked up.

I had my head under the hood of an Audi A6, replacing the starter, when Jackie came out to tell me Jeff Cash had arrived. With a sigh, I grabbed a rag and wiped my hands before following him inside. My pace slowed and I cautiously stepped behind the counter. Surely he was smart enough not to say anything in front of Jackie about our Friday-night plans.

"Well, hello again, Mr. Cash."

"Jeff. Remember? And hi, yourself." His hazel eyes twinkled just like they had the first time we'd met, and the top two buttons of his dress shirt were unbuttoned to reveal a teasing glimpse of chest hair.

"Here's the bill." Jackie slid the ticket over, forcefully bumping my elbow. His voice reminded me that I needed to behave myself.

"Jeff," I corrected with a smile. "I'll go pull the car out for you while you fork over your hard-earned money to Jackie here." One last pat on Jackie's shoulder and I turned to pluck the keys from the board.

"My pleasure," was the last thing I heard before I stepped out the door and let it swing shut behind me.

Jeff stood on the curb, his jacket slung over his shoulders. The sleeves of his shirt were rolled up to just below his elbow, and his hair was a messy riot of chocolaty curls. He was as casual as Robert was uptight, reminding me more of an unrepentant fallen angel than any sort of cherub.

I slid out from behind the wheel and leaned against the car door. "She's all yours."

He slowly circled the car as if he had all the time in the world. As if he were a man who never rushed—at anything.

Despite the sunglasses, I had the feeling that he was checking me out in all my sweaty, grease-stained glory as he trapped me between the car and him.

"We changed the oil too. Tell your mom I need to see her at 3,000 and 5,000 miles from now on, and if she has any problems at all, she should call me."

"I'll tell her. Maybe next time she'll listen to me." With a shake of his head, he leaned against the car and held out his hand. "I appreciate it."

I held out my hands palm up and shrugged. "They're clean but . . ."

He took my hand and held it in both of his.

"Good. See you Friday?"

I laughed but before I could answer, he continued. "By the way, I'm supposed to invite you to Mom's on Sunday. She's having a party and she'd like to you to come, so she can thank you personally."

"I uh . . . I have brunch with friends every Sunday."

"Party doesn't start until four. I could pick you up," he offered, attempting to charm me with a smile.

"I don't always drive that old truck; I have a nice car."

"That isn't what I meant."

"Sorry," I whispered, feeling chastised.

"So, you in?"

"Sure." I smiled at him and turned to go.

I headed back into the garage and the Audi, pausing long enough to give Jackie a cocky wave. It wasn't an invitation to join me, but he did anyway.

"You sure were out there a long time." He propped his arms on the top of the car door, a concerned look on his face.

"Jackie!" I warned, one eyebrow quirked. "He invited me to his mom's house on Sunday—*per her.*" I leaned against the Audi and gave him a tired look.

"She, uh . . . she's pretty high class, huh?" He shuddered.

"You get used to it after a while."

"Hard to believe her son is a friend of Grant's."

We stood there grinning in companionable silence until Julio yelled at us from over in bay three to get back to work. With a good-natured wave, Jackie headed inside, but not before throwing what sounded like a Spanish insult over his shoulder at Julio, who just laughed.

Friday came and not a moment too soon. My cell phone had been blessedly silent, at least where Robert was concerned, and for that I was grateful. However, Lexi, Carlotta, and I stayed in touch constantly.

I spent the morning doing payroll and the afternoon teaching Jackie the last of my bookkeeping system.

"So, you going to Mrs. Cash's on Sunday?"

"I told him I would, but I don't know." I ran a hand through my hair and leaned back in the chair. I'd spent more time than I cared the previous night asking myself the same question.

"Oh come on. How bad could it be?"

"As bad as Sunday dinner with the family?"

"No way. Nothing's that bad. I think you should go. It'd be good for business."

"Listen to you!" I laughed. "And besides, it's complicated."

"How complicated could it be?"

I leaned forward and rested my elbows on the desk so I wouldn't have to look at him. "I'm supposed to meet up with Jeff tonight."

"No wonder you were out there with him for so long yesterday. Not like a date or anything though?" He sounded truly concerned, brotherly concerned in a way I'd gotten unused to in the last eight years.

"Yeah, and he's Grant's friend. I can't believe I'm discussing men with you."

"Better than John, I suppose." He pointed outside to where John was cursing under the hood of a BMW.

"This is true. Though John is quite the ladies' man. Maybe he could give you some tips," I added with a laugh.

"Very funny. So what's the problem with Jeff, besides the fact he's Grant's friend?"

"Isn't that problem enough? He says he won't say anything but—"

"But you're afraid Grant will find out."

"And do you know what happens if Dad and Ma get wind of me seeing someone they approve of? Of someone they"—I shuddered—"like?"

"You're back in the fold." He held out both hands, palms up. "The golden girl."

"I don't want to be the golden girl," I hissed. My fingers clutched at the edge of the desk in protest.

"Clay . . . called," he said, suddenly red-faced and unable to meet my eyes.

"Clay?" I frowned in confusion. "Clay never calls. No one does. Hell, Dad's secretary called about last Saturday." I sat up a little straighter as understanding dawned. "What did you tell him, Jackie?"

"Nothing. I swear to God, Mel, not a damn thing." This time he met my eyes. "I would never betray you."

Guilt nibbled at me, at that first doubt over having sharing my business with Jackie. "I believe you," I assured him and myself.

"He was asking about you, about working here, how business was. He asked about your personal life too. I told him I didn't know anything other than you hadn't lied about how busy you were. Otherwise, I just played dumb as much as I could."

My shoulders sagged on a sigh. "Clay is Dad's stool pigeon."

"I remember," he said softly. Even when we were kids, Clay had been the first to tattle, eager to earn a pat on the head or whatever other attention Dad would dole out.

"Dad's fishing." We stared at each other—both of us, I'm sure, wondering exactly what Dad was fishing for. "I'll take care of it."

"So, tell me about Jeff."

I rolled my eyes and shook my head. "He's just a guy."

"You can do better than that."

"Tell me about Linda. I hear you two have a date tomorrow night." Linda had accosted me, giddy as a teenager, the minute I'd come in the door this morning.

"She's just a chick."

I laughed again. "Better not let her hear you say that."

"Maybe you should lighten up on Jeff. Give him a chance. Don't hold his bad taste in friends against him." We both laughed. Grant was a pretentious blowhard.

"It's not that I don't want to give him a chance; it's just that I don't have relationships. And how can I not have a relationship with Jeff of all people?"

"You . . . then what do you do, sis?" He leaned forward in the ratty blue chair, elbows propped on his knees.

"I have flings," I quipped, though I wasn't really kidding.

"Like . . . one-night stands?"

"All short term," I said with a nod. "Which makes Jeff's bite-me-in-the-ass potential pretty damn high, but I like him, damnit! Why am I telling you all this?"

"Because I'm a better listener than John?" he quipped back.

"I'm not a sharer," I confessed, almost to myself. "I share with Lexi and Carlotta; I don't share with anyone else."

"Maybe you should."

"I just did—with you. What else do you want?" My sarcasm wasn't lost on him.

"Fair enough." Raising his hands in surrender, he stood up to leave.

"So, Linda . . . I wanna see her smiling when she comes in on Monday."

"I'll do my best," he said, giving me a tiny salute.

8

I climbed out of my Prius and smoothed the wrinkles from my little black Kay Unger dress. The valet at Jimmy Z's handed me my ticket, his eyes bouncing from my cleavage to my legs. *God, it felt good to get out of jeans and steel-toed boots!*

Nearby laughter caught my attention, and then all I could do was laugh, too. Standing on the sidewalk, teeming with early evening foot traffic, was Carlotta—also dressed in black.

Arm in arm we stepped inside the bar with a smile for Rudy, the bouncer. Searching the crowded bar for Jeff would be nearly impossible. He'd just have to find me.

"How'd the rest of your week go?" Carlotta practically had to shout to be heard over Alicia Keys.

"Better. Where's Devon?" I replied with a grin. "He was supposed to come get my seal of approval."

"He can't make it."

"Trouble in paradise?"

She shook her head, her features hardening. "Let's just say I fucked up." Crossing the crowded bar to the lower level where our regular table was, we chatted despite the loud music. She pointed out a couple of prospects that only made me pull an icky face.

"Slim pickings for you, chick."

No shit! Thank God I had Jeff to look forward to, if he showed. "Maybe it's time we found a new bar. As far as Jimmy's goes it seems like if I haven't fucked it, I don't want it."

"I suppose if you get desperate enough, there's always Brian." Her grin was positively evil as she pointed to where Brian stood chatting with Lexi and Cherise.

"How did that ho beat us here?"

"Brian works here—"

"I meant Lexi!" I nudged her in the side with my elbow.

"I don't know, but I think Cherise is after your man."

Cherise's blonde curls shook as she leaned forward, offering Brian a gander at the valley between her full breasts, and laughed at something he said.

"You know," I said, pulling Carlotta closer, "she's got nice tits."

Carlotta laughed and shook her head, giving my waist a squeeze. "Maybe what you need is a change of taste."

"Maybe!" The idea had merit. "Speaking of a change of taste"—I quirked a brow at her as we took our seats—"Jeff is supposed to meet me up here."

"The usual, ladies?" Brian interrupted with a grin that made my hands itch to slap him. *Brat.*

"First round's on me." I slid my credit card out of my purse, handing it to him as I claimed the stool next to Cherise with a smile.

"You should be nicer to him," Carlotta said after he'd left. "Someday he's going to spit in your drink."

We both scrunched up our faces at each other. She did have a good point.

"What's this?" Lexi asked, leaning over the table.

Laughing, I filled her and Cherise in.

Lexi grinned at me over the top of her martini glass before taking a sip and setting it back down. "He's a nice kid. Doesn't seem like his speed."

"Never judge a book by its cover," Cherise said, flashing me a toothy grin. The girl had a serious clothes thing going on, with pink lipstick and a hot pink halter dress that dipped in a scooped neckline between her breasts. Then again, she'd been wearing pink the first night we met too. I couldn't seem to stop staring at her cleavage, and I was dying to know if her shoes were pink too, but refused to look under the table.

Lips pursed, I glanced at Carlotta out of the corner of my eye. She nodded the tiniest bit. Maybe a change of pace was what I needed and besides, what Jeff didn't know wouldn't hurt him. Did I worry that maybe Cherise wasn't bi, or wasn't interested? Not really. I figured if she wasn't she'd let me know. No harm; no foul. But she'd checked out Lexi with the same interest she'd given Brian, so I was pretty sure she swung both ways. "Honey, you wanna dance?"

She nodded, and I drained half of my apple martini before sliding off the bar stool and leading her down to the dance floor crowded with sweaty people bumping and grinding to something with really heavy bass. We quickly worked up a sweat, and I smiled, pleased, when she pulled me close, her hand sliding up the back of my bare leg, her eyes glued to my lips. None of the couples around us even noticed, and if they had, I wouldn't have cared. Thank God I'd worn something short and loose.

At the feel of another body behind me and hands on my ass, I turned and smiled, pleased to see Carlotta had joined us. Only the thin silky material of her black halter top separated her breasts from the bare skin of my back. Her hands joined Cherise's on my legs. I was in heaven, every inch of me itching for more. My eyes drifted low as I wrapped one arm around Cherise's neck and reached behind me with the other to cup the smooth round globe of Carlotta's ass. She had a thong on and so did I, and her hand was under my dress.

Then Cherise's lips were on my neck. My head tilted back and my lips curved into a smile of delight as I stared up at the whirling multicolored lights overhead, all thoughts of Jeff temporarily forgotten. Her warm wet tongue flicked at my earlobe while her fingers skimmed up my sides and across my stomach, up to my braless tits barely contained by the stretchy black material. Laughing, she nipped my earlobe and backed up about a foot to dance by herself. Her hard-nippled tits jiggled under the silky pink material as she lifted her skirt and shook to some funky mix of blues, reggae, and a bit of Santana thrown in for good measure.

I turned and gave Carlotta an open-mouthed kiss. Another little test for Cherise. Every inch of me was damp with sweat while my pussy was tender and swollen, aching to be touched.

"Damnit, I'm horny," I said with a chuckle.

Carlotta laughed. "I can tell."

Cherise moved up behind me, her hands under my skirt and in my panties while our hips ground in sync. Only a few inches separated us from Carlotta, who kept dancing and watching, a sly grin of what could only be called enjoyment on her face. Cherise forced me to move with her, her hand massaging my mound. Finally, she slipped her fingers between the slick folds to strum my clit. I bit my lip as blood rushed to my pelvis and my clit swelled under the attention of her skilled fingers.

"You like?"

I nodded and licked my dry lips, turning my head to answer her when I spotted Jeff no more than three feet away and moving in for the kill. Cherise must have felt the slight change. She tightened her grip on the inside of my thigh.

Thinking was not an option right now.

I hadn't meant for him to see me like this. My heart raced, warring between titillation and panic. A deep breath pumped much-needed oxygen to my panic-stricken heart and brought me down a little.

Then again, maybe I had meant for Jeff to see me like this.

At this point, Jeff had no idea what was going on or where Cherise's hands were. Judging by the grin on his handsome face, he certainly didn't have a problem with us dancing together. Well, at least he thought we were dancing. I had about five seconds to make her stop—or not. Instead of stopping her, I slipped a hand inside my dress and cupped my tit, worrying the nipple with my fingers. He stopped dead in his tracks and gave Cherise and me a once-over before closing the last few feet between us.

I made eye contact with Carlotta and then glanced pointedly at Jeff, hoping she'd catch the hint. She disappeared with a tiny wave but not before giving Jeff a nudge in our direction. Grinning, he complied, and for a few heartbeats, we stood there staring at one another while he took in the picture we must have presented: both of us in short, skimpy dresses and high heels and both of us with our hands inside my dress.

"Don't stop on my account." Grinning, he ran his hands through his hair, mussing it even more, and moved closer so he was dancing with Cherise and me.

But did he have a clue what she was really doing under my skirt? She made to draw her hands back but I covered them with mine and stopped her with a glance over my shoulder. As much as I wanted Jeff, I had apparently made my choice. *He'd just have to take me as I am.*

He took it all in, never batting an eye. My limbs turned to jelly at the thought of climaxing right here in front of all these people—some of whom were probably doing the same thing—and more importantly, in front of him. Licking my lips, I drew my hand out from under my dress and pulled him close, clutching the sides of his crisp black dress shirt and letting Cherise's fingers do their job. I relaxed against her in spite of the ever-increasing tightness in my belly. Then Jeff's lips were on my neck, drifting lower, nuzzling my cleavage, his five-o'clock shadow scraping my skin while his warm wet tongue made me ache. The heat of him pressed against me seared my skin.

"Having a good time?" he asked. He was so close now, he had to know what was going on.

All I could do was nod as my hips rolled faster and faster against the insistent friction of Cherise's fingers. I was so hot I couldn't breathe, but a warm firm masculine hand cupped the bare cheeks of my ass, holding me upright as my legs shook, nearly giving way underneath me. All I could think of was getting my clothes off and rubbing every inch of myself against Jeff, against Cherise, I didn't care.

I threw my head back and grabbed her chin so we could kiss, our tongues sliding warm and smooth against each other. The rough friction of Jeff's shirt against my chest sent little darts of pleasure through me. He was talking, but I couldn't make out the words. I was focused on one thing: the climax I was hurtling toward.

Moaning in Cherise's mouth, I finally came up for air, pleasantly surprised to see Jeff lean down and take my place. I watched them kiss, caught between them, the erotic play of their tongues teasing me and pushing me toward my release until I bucked against her fingers with the force of it, biting my lip so I didn't moan as the DJ changed songs.

Jeff's purr reverberated against my chest as he watched me come, his brown eyes sleepy-looking and a smile on those beautiful lips of his.

The crowd no longer registered as I sagged between them, hot, sweaty, and satiated. And Cherise, naughty as she was, slipped her hand from my panties and licked her fingers, a smile on her face.

Weak-kneed, I turned and hooked a finger in the material

gathered between her breasts and pulled her closer. We were nearly nose to nose, studying each other, weighing the possibilities.

I slid my hand across a smooth expanse of chest and cupped her by the neck, pulling her face to mine until only a hairsbreadth separated our lips, then thanked her with a kiss.

9

Cherise went down on me in the kitchen while Jeff watched.

We'd caravanned to my house and stumbled inside like a bunch of teenagers having a party while the parentals were out of town.

As casually as possible I'd warned Jeff (yes, again) about squealing to my brother; he, in turn, had informed me that squealing on me meant squealing on himself too. Then, in the middle of a discussion over the merits of a midnight swim, Cherise had lifted her dress over her head and tossed it onto the kitchen table.

Cherise had amazing tits. Heavy, pale globes crowned with puffy deep-pink tips. My question about the authenticity of her amazing rack got a laugh from Jeff.

"I'm glad you asked, 'cause I'da gotten slapped for that." He untucked his dress shirt and yanked it off. "You just gonna stand there?" He pointedly looked me up and down.

In lieu of a reply I backed Cherise up against the cabinets and kissed her, teasing her mouth with my tongue while I pushed her thong off and caressed the bare curves of her hips.

But for the hot pink shoes and matching toenails, she was buck naked. I squeezed her ass, spreading her cheeks and tickling her crack while she fumbled with the tiny zipper at my waist. Finally Jeff moved in and did the deed for her, pushing my dress off my shoulders. His light touch sent a shiver down my spine.

I leaned over and wiggled against the crotch of his jeans, pleased when he obliged my silent request, thrusting his denim-covered erection against my bare skin. The occasional, and not so accidental, contact with my hungry little pussy only made me want more.

And of course, this put Cherise's tits at eye level. I wasn't about to ignore the treat in front of me. I buried my face between them, stroking the tips until they were hard pebbles under my fingertips and her skin was covered with goose bumps.

"Stand up." She gently fisted her hand in my hair and pulled me upright, licking her full lips. Dressed in nothing but my three-inch heels, I let her lead me to the kitchen table, where she pushed me down and sat her naked self in a chair. I kicked off my shoes and spread my legs wide, propping my heels on the table.

My bottom rose off the table at the first warm slide of Cherise's tongue on my pussy. I looked down at her, her blond head buried between my thighs while she expertly lapped at me. Jeff stood a few feet away watching, his erection protruding from the top of his blue briefs. He ambled closer, stroking himself through the soft cotton material. I desperately wanted to help him but needed both hands to hold myself up and fuck Cherise's very talented tongue. Jeff moved in closer and pushed her hair out of the way so he could watch, pausing long enough to press a tender kiss to her cheek and the inside of my thigh. I met her stroke for stroke, shivering and smiling to myself at the feel of her tongue pressed against my ass. While he watched, Jeff fondled one of her tits.

Cherise took multitasking to a whole new level. She held my

pussy open with one hand and continued to eat me out while she used her other hand to jack Jeff off, pausing long enough to lick away the tiny drop of precum that appeared.

"We could take this in the bedroom," I gasped.

With one last hard suck of my clit, Cherise stood up and offered me her hand. I climbed down, leaning forward to lick the taste of me off her lips, then I gave Jeff a taste, straight from my mouth to his.

In the bedroom we threw the comforter and top sheet off the king-sized bed and dived in with Jeff in the middle. I straddled his stomach and reached for Cherise, running a hand across her belly.

"She's pretty," I said, smiling up at him.

"You both are."

I leaned over and sucked at her nipple, letting it go with a loud pop that made us both giggle.

"Go on," he said with a nod. "You know you want her."

"I want you too."

"I know," he said, waggling his eyebrows. "I can wait."

"Condoms are in the top drawer." I pointed to the nightstand. "Toys are in the bottom," I added, chuckling.

I stretched out on top of a smiling Cherise, undulating against every soft inch of her and tracing her lips with my tongue before I deepened the kiss. Men just don't kiss like women do. It's a unique experience, much softer but just as possessive. Hip to hip and breast to breast, we wiggled against each other. The smooth slide of soft female skin on skin left me breathless and aching.

Jeff's hands stroked and teased the both of us while our tongues played against each other. At the tickle of his hair against my bottom, I tucked my knees up under me. Cherise moaned in my mouth and spread her legs. I came up for air long enough to take a peek down. Jeff had his head buried between her legs as well as one finger inside of me.

She squealed and giggled and whispered how good he was, then with a smile asked me what I wanted. I dug out a bottle of lube and a long thin vibrator with an egg-shaped head, coated it real good, and handed it to her with a soft "pretty please," before joining Jeff.

"Are you having fun?" I whispered, rubbing at his ear. I winced slightly at one slippery finger probing in my ass, then relaxed and let Cherise do her job.

He stopped in mid-lick and grinned up at me just as Cherise replaced her finger with the thick head of the vibrator. I caught my lower lip between my teeth, forcing myself to breathe while she slid it deeper. She slowly drew it out, until only the bulbous head was left, and turned it on. The walls of my cunt pulsated at the nearby vibrations around the two fingers she'd slipped inside me.

I held her open for him, her lips rudely pulled back to expose her swollen, pink clit. It stuck up, demanding attention, and I couldn't resist drawing it into my mouth and sucking at the sweet, tender skin until Jeff nudged me out of the way.

She moaned and fucked me harder, until we were both in such a frenzy she pulled the vibrator out and replaced it with her mouth. Moaning harshly, I rested my head against her thigh, inhaling the sweet scent of her sex and the sight of Jeff working furiously to make her come. Her hips arched up off the bed, her ass clenched with her impending climax and I joined Jeff, both of us licking her clit while she convulsed under us, humming her pleasure against my pussy. Finally, she collapsed against the sheets, her heavy breathing drifting across my skin.

Jeff sat up on his knees, his cock already sheathed with a condom. "How do you want it?"

Smiling, I flipped over and stretched out on my back, legs spread, and sighed in anticipation. He positioned himself between my legs and stroked me with his cock, spreading my juices all around before thrusting inside. I couldn't hold back a moan of pleasure.

Cherise lay curled upon her side, a satiated smile on her own face as she snuggled closer. "Feel good?" she whispered.

"Real good." I giggled.

"I wanna watch him fuck you."

I nodded, and she pushed herself upright, propping her chin on one of my knees. She licked her fingers and dipped them between my thighs, stroking my clit as Jeff pumped into me, sliding home with a smack that made me squeal. He leaned toward her and caught her full pink lips with his, and I relaxed deep into the bedsheets, enjoying the show. Cherise smacked his ass with a tiny naughty grin and went back to watching him and murmuring words of encouragement. I closed my eyes and moaned softly, biting my lip. Lifting my legs, I rested them against Jeff's shoulders and trapped Cherise's fingers on my clit.

The sound of skin slapping skin and Jeff's own groans of pleasure filled the room. I arched my hips off the bed, digging my heels into his shoulders for leverage, so he could get deeper. He picked up the pace and growled at me to hurry. I wasn't one for disappointing a man.

I relaxed and let loose all the tension I'd been holding onto so tightly, howling my pleasure and arching my back as I rode out the waves of my climax, with Jeff following shortly behind me. He spread my legs and collapsed in a sweaty, gasping heap on top of me with a strangled chuckle.

"I should have let your brother drag me to dinner sooner."

We dozed, the three of us snuggled together under my soft down comforter, and then I got to watch Jeff go a round with Cherise only to fall into a deep sleep brought on from complete sexual satisfaction.

I snuck out of bed early and whipped up a breakfast casserole: eggs, bacon, cheese, chives, and Bisquick. While it baked, I took a swim, letting the cool water loosen kinked-up muscles. That's where Cherise found me. She'd washed off the last remnants of the previous night's makeup and pulled her hair back in a scrunchie. She slid into the pool beside me.

"Whatcha cookin'?"

"Breakfast." I gave her a cheeky grin. "I'm starved. Please tell me you're not one of those bitches who don't eat." I stood up and stretched, smoothing my wet hair off my face.

"Girl, please! If I didn't eat, my tits would deflate."

Snorting with laughter, I splashed her with water, which of course resulted in a fight that woke Jeff up. He stood at the edge of the pool wearing unbuttoned jeans that clung precariously to his hips. His hair was rumpled, he had sleep lines on his face, and the beginnings of a beard graced his jaw.

We were lucky we hadn't caught the attention of any of my neighbors. We stood in the pool, topless with arms wrapped around each other, and gave him our most innocent smiles.

"Go back to bed," I ordered good-naturedly. Apparently, Jeff wasn't a morning person.

"Sure y'all don't mind?" he asked, his eyes still bleary with sleep.

We both waved him off but not before flicking some water at him. Cherise and I stayed in the pool until the timer I'd set on the patio table went off. "Let's eat."

One last hurried kiss and I hustled out of the water with her hard on my heels. In the kitchen, the smell of eggs, bacon, and cheese made my stomach rumble as I dried off and pulled the casserole out of the oven.

I loaned Cherise a T-shirt and some shorts, which, of course, required a trip into the bedroom. Jeff lay sprawled out on his stomach, his snoring muffled by the pillow he'd covered his head with. Damn, he was cute!

We made fresh coffee, barely able to wait for the casserole to cool before we cut into it and heaped our plates full.

"So, lemme get this straight." Cherise plopped down on a bar stool and sprinkled her breakfast with salt. "Lexi is straight. Which is a waste, if you ask me."

"She's been known to play but she *definitely* prefers men." Grinning, I added cream to my coffee and slowly stirred.

"Carlotta is bi, too, but prefers men—and *you*." She gave me a wicked grin and popped a bite of egg and bacon in her mouth.

"I don't discriminate."

"What about Jeff?" She forked a steaming bite of eggs and blew on it.

"I don't think he's bi," I said, snickering into my cup.

She giggled. "You two are an item."

"We barely know each other!" I dug into my breakfast, unwilling to look at what happened next in terms of Jeff.

"You know each other better than you think." There was no laughter in her eyes, just a serious intensity that made me wonder if we hadn't all underestimated her.

Snorting, I asked if she was psychic.

She shook her head, lips pursed. "I just know."

"If you start in about kids and shit, I'll kick your ass," I said, pointing my fork at her.

"You don't look like the kid type."

"I have ten nieces and nephews and two on the way. Believe me, the folks ain't hurting."

"But you worry . . ."

I nodded slowly. "My family isn't close. Dating Jeff is gonna be complicated—"

"You'll figure it out—and don't hold your family against him."

By the time Jeff finally graced me with his presence, Cherise was long gone and almost all my laundry was done.

"Hungry?"

He slowly nodded and rubbed his belly. "My goddamn phone wouldn't quit ringing."

"Mmm, your roommate?" In the kitchen, I fixed him a plate and slid it into the microwave to warm it up.

"Yeah. He was supposed to move out this weekend but his girlfriend dumped him." He shook his head and accepted the coffee I'd poured him. "She's actually his mistress, but that sounds so old-school."

"I'll say." I slid his plate across the counter to him and took a seat at one of the bar stools.

"So, what are you doing the rest of the day? You like crab legs? I know this great seafood place."

My lips twisted in a grimace. "Jeff, I really like you . . . and you're a damn good lay . . ."

He stopped, the fork halfway to his mouth, his eyes darkening and narrowing.

"Cherise and Jackie say I shouldn't hold Grant against you—"

"They'd be right," he said and took a bite. "Why do you worry so much about what Grant thinks? He's not any more perfect than you are. For that matter, neither is your dad. Clay's the only one toeing the line with his woman 'cause Polly'd beat his ass if he didn't."

I blinked in surprise, trying to process his words. "I didn't realize you knew my family that well."

"I'm your dad's investment counselor. I know a hell of a lot more than I should, and unlike a lawyer, I'm not sworn to attorney-client privilege or anything like that."

"Coffee," I quietly offered, stunned and still at a loss for words.

"Please."

Staring, I turned his news over in my head while he continued to eat, then opted to tell him about Clay's fishing expedition. "It's not so much that I care what they think about me or anything, but they have expectations that I can't meet. Expectations I gave up on meeting a long time ago. I spent eight years building a life that suits me and I'm not giving that up for them. The farther away I stay from them the better."

"So you're worried about their expectations of you."

"Yeah—No! But that doesn't mean I want to hear about it, and believe you me, I already hear plenty about it."

"What if I told you not to sweat it, that you could date me and not only would your family *never* know, but if by some odd coincidence they did find out, they wouldn't pressure you?"

"You gonna tell me how you plan on pulling a rabbit out of your jeans, Mr. Cash, or leave me wondering?"

"The guy sleeping on my couch is Grant."

If he had slapped me, he couldn't have shocked me more. "Dad's golden boy?" I squeaked, still trying to absorb his words. *Mr. Pompous Ass has been sleeping on Jeff's couch* played on a continuous loop in my head while I sat there, grinning stupidly at Jeff.

He slowly nodded while popping another bite of the casserole into his mouth.

"Um, um, would you like some more coffee?" I offered, at a loss for words but feeling the need to say *something*.

"Got any OJ?" he asked once he was done chewing.

While I poured him a glass of juice, he continued talking. "Grant goes home every night, showers, eats with Karen and the kids, and then, after they're in bed, comes and sleeps at my place."

"Why all the pretense?"

"Your mom. If she found out, she'd kill him. Or at least, nag his ass to death, and Karen absolutely, positively won't have him back."

"So, Dad knows."

"Your dad knows all, and keeps an iron grip on your brothers. He's got the dirt on Clay, Grant, and Junior, and *I've* got the dirt on him."

I'd probably burn in hell for being so overjoyed, but I'd cross that bridge when I came to it. We sat grinning at each other.

"Now," Jeff said, "about those crab legs."

"I'll buy dinner," I offered, "if you give me the dirt on my dad."

10

My conversation with Jeff had replayed itself in my head all the way to Tomball, the home of Daniels' Garage. By some miraculous twist of fate it seemed Jackie and I had escaped a fate worse than death: being beholden to Dad.

Dad and Grant might be guilty of infidelity, but apparently I had my own guilt to deal with, though it wasn't especially troubling. In my quest to distance myself from the family I'd thought was perfect, I'd forgotten that they weren't. Grant had always been a pompous ass, Clay had always been a tattletale, and while Junior might not have a (known) mistress, he was a carbon copy of Dad. Right down to being a blowhard.

I'd called my dad's assistant (who apparently doubled as his current mistress) and made sure he was working today. And his oversized Ford F250 was parked outside.

I stepped inside, past waiting customers, and took the stairs two at a time to the second floor, where the executive offices were.

Diane, a smooth-looking blonde in her early forties, watched me speed past, surprise written on her face, despite my phone call. As if she couldn't believe I'd actually shown up. The last time I'd set foot in the garage was when I'd borrowed the money from Dad.

"Is he in his office?" I never stopped for her answer, just breezed past and pushed my way inside.

Diane had apparently warned him I was coming. The stage was set with him behind his desk, and Clay a mere two feet away in a black leather office chair.

"Hey pigeon," I practically shouted my greeting with an overabundance of false cheer as I slammed the door behind me.

"Pigeon?" Clay frowned, jerking back at the sound of my voice.

"Did I interrupt something?" My voice couldn't have been sweeter if I'd swallowed a five-pound bag of sugar.

"What makes you think you interrupted something?" Clay asked, shifting in his seat.

"You both look so serious." I circled the office. It seemed big enough to take up half the upstairs, and I reminded myself that Dad once had a grungy office, tucked in the back of the garage, just like I did. "I'm surprised Grant isn't here."

"He's at home—with his family," Dad rumbled.

"Really?" Biting back a smirk, I pasted the sweetest smile I could on my lips.

"Really!" Dad leveled his gaze at me, and we had a brief stare-off before he broke contact. As if he realized that I knew he was lying.

I stepped closer, so that only the desk separated us, before plunking myself down in a chair and admiring my flip-flops. His eyes widened and something inside me swelled, desperately wanting to escape. Laughter? I didn't dare laugh at a thought so silly it made me tingle all over.

He was afraid of me.

Oh, not physically afraid I'd do him harm, but a part of him feared me. I felt big, strong, and suddenly more fearless than I ever had in my life. A glance at Clay, who wore that same hesitant, anxious expression as Dad, assured me that I was right.

"You're a liar."

"How dare you—"

"No! How dare you try to get Jackie to spy on me!"

"I did no such thing."

"You're a liar," I said, looking pointedly in Clay's direction. His face was flushed a deep red, but he stayed quiet. "Grant's living at Jeff Cash's house, and Diane out there"—I hooked a thumb toward the outer office—"is your mistress, but yet, for the last eight years you treated me like a freak, a pariah?" The calm in my voice surprised even me.

Dad was nearly white under his tan while Clay sat wide-eyed, watching us. "When the hell did you get so disrespectful?" His naturally loud voice fairly echoed off the walls as he sat scowling at me.

"You didn't think I'd hire Jackie, did you?" I countered with a shit-eating grin.

"No, I damn sure didn't—"

"And? Why did you ask me to, then?" I wanted to crow in triumph at the beaten-down look on his face. "You thought you could teach me a lesson, and Jackie, too. Kill two birds with one stone, huh?"

"Having an ex-con around could be bad for business," he said, glancing over at Clay.

"Which you'd just love. Unfortunately for you, I've had one around for years and it hasn't hurt my business a lick."

"But everyone would have known who Jackie was if I'd hired him. You were my—his—only option."

I frowned at his verbal flub. *Weenie.* "So why'd you have to put me on the spot in front of the brothers and Jeff?" I demanded, matching him scowl for scowl.

"They're not *the* brothers; they're *your* brothers—and Jeff, well, you could do a whole hell of a lot worse."

I rolled my eyes, my head dipping low to hide my disgust. "Then you turn around and call, asking Jackie about me. Why?"

"I did no such thing!" he insisted for the second time.

I could see the truth in his eyes even while he sat there, lying to me yet again. "You did, through Clay, after your plan backfired." I nodded toward my brother, who sat with a death grip on his own chair. "Or maybe that was your plan all along. Get me to hire Jackie and get Jackie to spy on me?"

If anything, he looked even more scared, as if he were grateful to have the width of his desk between us. For all his bluster and attitude, he was afraid of me. I'd been blind, but thanks to Jeff, I now saw everything so clearly. "You tried to use Jackie, yet you don't even approve of his—"

"Should I approve of my son the felon?" he roared defensively.

"So he screwed up! According to the courts, he served his time. And he might be a 'reformed' felon, but Dad, you're still an adulterer." I eased to my feet and took a few steps in Clay's direction.

"You think you're better than us?" Clay's hazel-green eyes turned stormy while his over-loud voice filled the room.

"Never, ever, did I think I was better than you, Clay," I replied, shaking a finger at him, "but Polly *is*." I waved a hand in Dad's direction. "You never respected my business. You never respected the fact that I was different. You just passed judgment on me, and on Jackie. You don't know me any better than you know him." I took a deep breath, mentally shifting gears. "Why do you think he robbed that store?"

"What?" Dad looked as if I'd asked him for a million dollars.

"You don't know, do you?" I frowned thoughtfully. "Maybe you should ask him."

"You don't respect me either," Dad bluffed, deflecting my words.

"I respect you because you're my father; I don't respect you as a man, or as a person." The dead silence that followed me on my short walk to the door was perforated by the ringing of my cell phone, and I smiled at the sight of Jeff's name on the caller ID, snapping the phone open. "Hello." My hand on the knob, I paused long enough to assure him that I was on my way. Hanging up, I turned back to face Dad one last time. "Now, if you'll excuse me, I have a date."

Carlotta

1

He wasn't the same Devon Fry I'd met a week ago. That man, the one I'd seduced and fucked on his desk while wearing nothing more than a tank top and my ankle socks, was nowhere to be found.

This man, the one sipping his drink and scanning the leather and latex crowd through those eerily calm blue eyes, was cool, confident, and reserved—not shy.

"Do you know him?" Cherise asked. When I didn't respond, she nudged me with her elbow. "Carlotta?"

I slowly nodded, turning and finally focusing on her. "He's mine."

"Duly noted." Her lips twitched and with one final, conspiratorial grin at each other we said our good-byes.

Accompanied by a classic ZZ Top tune, I wound through the thick crowd, past women in dog collars and men on leashes, while trying to figure out what it meant. Why would Devon Fry, Geek Meister, be sitting in a bar that catered to people who preferred anything but ordinary sex?

I approached slowly, losing myself in the crowd so he didn't see me, and positioned myself at the bar a few seats away. He was tall and slender. I knew for a fact he swam three days a week at the Y. He was wearing black chinos and a snug black cotton shirt that didn't even begin to do justice to the sculpted lines of his chest, or the rest of him.

Waving to the bartender, I pulled a twenty from my purse. "Tequila and OJ . . . and a drink for him." I pointed to where Devon was sitting. The bartender nodded while giving me a quick once-over, and filled my order. I kept my eyes on the mirror behind the bar, waiting to see how Devon would react.

When his head swung my way, I gave a little wave and raised my glass. He smiled, revealing deep dimples in his cheeks and pearly white teeth that contrasted sharply with his dark hair and tan.

"You're a long way from home," he said, turning to face me as I approached and looking me up and down. I stopped between his thighs, a mere twelve inches from his crotch, and gave him a once-over in return.

"I could say the same thing about you. I mean, if this were a country bar or even blues, but"—I motioned to the crowd—"these people like to hurt each other for fun."

The one thing that had always bugged me about Devon was my inability to read him despite his seemingly easygoing nature. The bar's dim lighting put me at an even bigger disadvantage.

"Let's go find a table." He stood and held out his hand. I took it, letting him wrap his long, smooth fingers around mine and lead me to a cozy section of booths near the back of the bar. "So, why are you here?"

"My girls ditched me and I was bored, so when a friend suggested we check this place out, I figured it was better than going home early and alone."

He nodded, then eased back and slipped an arm around my

shoulder. "You know what you said about hurting each other for fun? Is that what you think about the people in here?"

Wondering why he even cared, I frowned up at him. "Why else would someone let another person put a collar on them?! Collars are for dogs! How humiliating can you get?"

He nodded again, but I don't think it was a nod of agreement. What did he know that I didn't? "I'm surprised you bought me a drink after the way you lit out of there Thursday afternoon." He raised his glass in a salute before taking another sip.

My gut twisted slightly at the memory of the camera I'd found tucked away in a corner of the drop-in ceiling. "You were fun, Devon, I just don't *do* long-term. How come you slept with me?" *If you're going to get your jockeys all in a wad now?*

"You were pretty."

Snorting, I picked up my glass and took a sip of my drink.

"But you already know that. I wanted to see what you'd do if I let you."

"If *you* let *me*?" I arched an eyebrow at him, trying to hold back a laugh.

"I didn't have to sleep with you. I could have stopped you at any time." He sounded almost arrogant despite his easy grin.

"So why didn't you?"

"I haven't been with a woman in a long time. Haven't wanted to, until you." He downed the last of his drink and slid his glass across the table, then pinned me where I sat with an unexpectedly intense gaze.

Had Chambers spilled the beans about why I'd quit?

I wanted to ask why Devon hadn't been with a woman, but didn't. I waited instead, figuring he'd tell me when he was ready. And instead of speaking, he stood up and held out his hand. Again, I took it, but couldn't quite figure out why. Other than the fact I knew he wouldn't hurt a fly.

Holding hands like any normal couple, we left the packed bar and slowly walked through the steamy June evening, the sound of our footsteps lost in the busy evening foot traffic.

"I lost my wife to breast cancer two years ago."

"I'm sorry. Your uncle never told me. He didn't say much about you." *He was too busy being an asshole.*

"He said you quit."

"I was going to give notice but . . . he pissed me off." My soft laughter covered a hot twinge of anger at Chambers, and his complete and total assholishness. I wondered if Devon even had a clue what type of perv his uncle was.

"Finesse isn't one of Uncle Doug's finer points," he said with an apologetic laugh.

"No shit! Obviously you take after the other side of the family."

"Actually, he's an uncle by marriage, and the wiring job was business. Annie didn't like him either," he sighed, giving my arm a swing.

"Annie was your wife?" A logical conclusion, but I asked anyway.

"And my sub."

I laughed. I didn't mean to and immediately regretted it. *A lot.* "I'm sorry. Your 'sub'—you mean like BDSM Sub?"

Hand in hand, we slowly wound our way through the bar's dimly lit parking lot.

"Yeah. Like a BDSM Sub. It wasn't so much our life as our sex life," he explained.

"May I be rude?"

"Sure." He leaned against the hood of a dark blue Passat, his hands stuffed in his pockets.

"You just don't seem like . . . a Dom," I said, hoping I'd used the correct terminology.

He smiled, his teeth gleaming in the light. He looked . . .

charming. "Maybe that's because you don't know what a real Dom is?"

"True," I conceded with a shrug and a rueful smile.

"Would you like to find out?" His voice was subdued, persuasive.

I blinked, focusing on him as every nerve in my body went on high alert. The answer, of course, was *no*. Hell no. *Wasn't it?* "Me?"

"You." Even in the dim light there was no mistaking how serious he was. "When do you start your new job? I assume you have one."

"I do." Was this really something I wanted? Thanks to my father, I knew all about dominant men and how they could turn a woman into nothing. "I start in two weeks."

"So, what are you doing in the meantime?"

"Eating myself silly, getting a jump start on my tan, and catching up on my reading."

"What do you say we hang out?" He made it sound so simple, so easy.

"Hang out . . . like . . . how?"

He swung me around and pressed me against the car, wrapped his hands around my wrists and gently pinned them at my sides, his grip warm and firm. I caught my breath as he lowered his lips, hovering over mine. Leaning forward, I stuck my tongue out, but he pulled back, out of my reach. Chuckling, he slowly eased back in and did it again. This time I knew what he wanted and stood perfectly still, waiting to see what he'd do. I consoled myself with the fact that it wasn't *order-following*, but *waiting*. He covered my mouth and kissed me slowly, exploring every inch. Impatient, I struggled against his grip on my wrists, wanting to pull him closer, but he refused to let go. Frustrated, I jerked my head away and inhaled gulps of the steamy air.

"You interested?" He still held my wrists, giving me my first inkling of what being a sub might be like. At least, in a very small way. There was nothing painful or forced about his touch, his grip; it was just *there*. No matter how much I wriggled my wrists, he refused to let go.

"I . . . have reservations," I huffed. Not the least of which was his uncle and what he'd done to me. Then again, you couldn't pick your in-laws, and I certainly didn't blame Devon for something he'd had no part in.

"I wouldn't expect you not to. Meet me for dinner tomorrow, and we'll discuss it."

My nerves were still on high alert. My brain was numb. My legs and the rest of me were weak, and I sagged against the car, giving up the struggle to free myself.

"Dinner tomorrow," he gently prompted. "I'll pick you up."

"A date?" I whispered.

At his nod, I rattled off my address. Finally, he freed my wrists and I rubbed them even though they didn't really hurt.

"Get in."

I gave directions as he silently drove me to my car, still in Jimmy Z's parking lot three blocks over. Devon made me feel self-conscious, as if he could see right through me. It was a totally new feeling from an unexpected source. As much as I didn't like that, there was something about him that kept pulling me back. Something that made me want to take him up on his offer.

The first day we met, he'd opened his office door and stood there looking like an absentminded professor, complete with rumpled brown hair, wrinkled shirt, and glasses perched on his forehead. He'd quickly slid them down onto his nose, then taken them off and wiped them on the corner of his shirt while giving me a nervous once-over. Those eyes—those bright, penetrating blue eyes—had seemed to follow me everywhere as I started wiring his office. At lunch, I stopped and stripped for him. I still remember how that one dark eyebrow shot up under his bangs when my tool belt fell to the floor.

We'd put his desk to good use Monday and Tuesday. Wednesday he'd sent me flowers. Thursday, of course, had been D-Day. The day I'd found the camera hidden in the ceiling. I'd taken one look at Devon, struggled to regain my composure, and spent all of ten seconds debating whether he'd put it there. No way. If he had, he would have made the first move. Since Devon was the first person to ever occupy the office, and I'd made the first move, logic dictated that his uncle probably had.

Turns out, logic had been right. Early this morning, I'd confronted Chambers and left shaken but triumphant, a DVD of Devon and me doing the horizontal hanky-panky on his desk tucked safely in my purse. I hadn't said a word, not to anyone. Not even Lexi and Lanie. I was too ashamed of how I'd let things get out of hand, out of control.

So I'd quit and written Devon off as the fling he'd been. Now here he was driving me to my car and planning a date with me.

A drop of water slipped from beneath the towel wrapped around my hair and down the side of my face. I brushed it away and plucked a chocolate silk Vera Wang slip dress off the closet rack, then chose a pair of coordinating Manolo Blahnik alligator slides from the sealed box on my shoe shelf. I threw both on my bed, the dark brown dress a sharp contrast to the red, purple, and yellow cotton quilt with its whimsical embroidery.

It had been a long time since I'd been on a real date. Like pick me up, take me out to dinner, kiss me good night; that sort of stuff. After standing there digging my toes into the shag carpet and debating my selection, a glance at the clock got me moving again. Dropping my robe with a shiver, I yanked open my lingerie drawer. Matching bra and panty sets, all organized by color, ran the gamut from virginal white to sexy pink to black.

Black, definitely.

Stockings? No, not even thigh-highs.

Once my hair and makeup were done, I slipped the dress off the hanger and stepped into it. The cool silk slid against my skin as I pulled it up and twisted and turned, struggling with the tiny zipper.

I'd no sooner slid my feet into my shoes and shoved my lipstick into my purse when the doorbell rang.

Devon had arrived.

A glance in the mirror over the dresser assured me my hair was nice and fluffy and I didn't have any lipstick on my teeth.

With one last deep breath, I slowly walked down the hall. Slate-colored Berber muffled my footsteps until I got to the ceramic entryway. Then the click echoed my heartbeat as I opened the door.

"Come on in. I just need to get my keys." I sounded so calm. Calmer than I felt under his steady gaze.

I stepped back and let him pass, pleased to see he'd gone for navy khakis and a shiny bluish-purple shirt with razor-sharp creases down the sleeves. It highlighted his tan and set off his eyes.

Pushing the door closed, I stepped past him with a smile and grabbed my keys off the sofa table, where I had dropped them the night before.

He spun in a slow half-circle, taking in the distressed black furniture, cinnamon-colored couch, and bright Mexican pottery. "You like black?"

"Normally I go for more eclectic stuff but I saw this and fell in love. Bought the whole set."

"Are you nervous?"

I hated the way he changed subjects so easily, how he looked so calm as he closed the space between us. "I'd be lying if I said no."

"Would you feel any better if I promised not to tie you up tonight?" Dimples promptly creased his cheeks, assuring me that he was teasing.

Chuckling, I reached up and smoothed a hand across his shirt. It was cotton, but as silky soft as it looked. "Much."

"We talk"—he leaned closer and tucked my curls behind my ear—"and we play. If you decide you still want to do this."

2

The Cuban restaurant Devon took me to had all the ambience and charm of the multicultural neighborhood it was located in. One not very different from where I'd grown up. It was nothing more than a hole in the wall, albeit a packed one, with dim lighting, tables made for two, and cozy booths. Devon asked for a booth.

While we ate the most delicious pork roast with grilled, seasoned potatoes and steamed vegetables, he peppered me with what seemed like dozens of inane questions. And some not so inane ones.

"How many men have you been with?"

My fork slipped from my fingers and clattered to the plate. His presence next to me all through dinner had been a bit disconcerting but as my cheeks warmed with anger and a bit of embarrassment, I was thankful he couldn't see my face. I slowly finished chewing the bite of broccoli I'd just taken.

"Honesty, Carlotta."

I sipped my wine to buy myself some time before I responded. "I don't keep track. How many women have you slept with?"

"Ten . . . twelve. I've never been overly promiscuous. Now, your turn." He smiled at me, but I still couldn't seem to form an answer. No man had ever asked me something so personal, and some questions you just didn't answer.

"A lot. More than you."

"Why?" He smiled, genuinely curious, but it still irritated me.

"Why? Why did I sleep with a bunch of men? I do what I want." Now I was scowling. "You sound like my mother."

He apologized. "The most important aspect of a dom/sub relationship is trust. *Implicit trust*. I don't expect you to answer me now, Carlotta, but someday I will."

"Trust is earned." And I trusted few people. I picked up my fork and forced a bite of potatoes between my lips.

"Exactly." He sat back and pushed his plate away, draping his arm around my shoulder. "Eat."

I silently finished the last of my dinner, conscious of him watching me the whole time. Conscious of his hand on the back of my neck, rubbing slow circles into skin and muscle. His hands were smooth and uncallused but not weak. Strong in an understated way. Sort of like him.

"How does the idea of being tied up make you feel?" he murmured over the guitar music playing.

"Scared." I looked up at him, a solemn expression on my face.

"You know I would never hurt you."

"I know."

"But you have to trust me and I have to figure out what you want, what you need. To do that, you have to open up to me. If you can't, there's no point in going any farther with this." He turned just a little, enough to rest his hand on my thigh.

"How much opening up are we talking about?" My eyes slid away, drifting over the dimly lit restaurant as I thought of the DVD stashed in my nightstand.

"Don't lie to me, ever. But especially when it comes to sex. Lying then can get you hurt, and I don't want that." His hand crept higher on my leg. "What if I touched you right here with everyone watching?"

The thought of him feeling me up in the middle of the crowded restaurant created a bubble of heat in my belly that expanded with every breath I took. I glanced around while his hand slipped under the skirt of my dress. He'd chosen the tiny, dark hole in the wall restaurant for a reason.

"Spread your legs." His touch was light as he traced his way to the juncture of my thighs. "Spread your legs wider and sip your wine. I'm going to touch you. Don't come," he instructed. "Just say 'can we go now' when you've had enough. Okay?"

I shifted, sinking in my seat just a bit to accommodate his hand. "Will someone—"

"Don't talk. No talking," he whispered.

Taking reassurance in the heavy linen tablecloth and the relative seclusion of our booth, I picked up my wineglass and slowly sipped while his fingers delved under the edge of my thong.

"Satin?"

I silently smiled up at him but didn't answer. He'd told me not to talk.

He leaned down until only an inch or two separated our lips and whispered, "You can answer me."

"Yeah."

At the sound of our waitress clearing her throat my head spun around. I was sure she knew exactly where Devon's hand was. *Did I look guilty?* I felt guilty. I hated feeling guilty, but the thrill of him touching me and wondering if she knew made me even hornier.

"Do you want dessert?" Devon asked, as if he weren't cupping my freshly shaved mound under the table.

Of course I wanted dessert. I wanted *him* for dessert. I blinked up at him, then the waitress holding our empty plates, and back to him, trying to decide if he were kidding.

"We have flan with the chef's special Caramel Pineapple Sauce," the waitress offered.

"Bring us one." Devon smiled up at her. "We'll share."

"I'll be right back." With one last smile, she turned toward the kitchen, never looking back. Maybe she didn't know what we were doing.

"You'll love their flan." One finger slipped between the slick folds of my cunt.

"I haven't had flan in years," I whispered weakly. My free hand wadded the napkin in my lap. Heat spread from my belly and wetness pooled between my thighs. The last thing I wanted to do was think about flan or the spot I was going to leave on the back of my dress. "I'm gonna—" Before I could continue the waitress was back with our dessert. Once she left, I tried again. "I'm gonna—"

"I said, no talking."

This was important! "My dress," I hissed.

He pushed his finger deeper, sinking it in the wetness of my pussy, and I just couldn't bring myself to care anymore. I sighed, wishing I could close my eyes and help him, wishing he'd go faster, wishing my heart wasn't pounding so hard. The sweet scent of caramel and pineapples mixed with sex tickled my nose.

"Feed me." His finger lightly stroked my clit.

I opened my mouth to say, "You're kidding," then remembered I wasn't allowed to speak. I rested my head against his arm and leaned into him, every inch of my skin sizzling with need.

"Feel good?" he asked, returning my smile. "You can answer me."

"God, yes."

He slowly withdrew his finger until it was positioned just between my pussy lips, one eyebrow arched. "Pick up the spoon, Carlotta."

I forced my shaking hand to work, scooping up a bite of the flan and holding it out for him. He closed his mouth over it while his finger slid against my clit, circling it.

His eyes closed and he moaned softly as if he'd never tasted anything better in his life. As if he were the one getting felt up, not me. "Try some."

I struggled through feeding the both of us while he stroked me, pushing me closer and closer to the edge. My nipples strained against the confines of my bra as I drained the last of my wine.

"Can we go now?" I choked out, at the first light ripple that signaled an impending orgasm. I sighed, a soft whimpery sound, and wished I could spread my legs wider, even pinch my nipples to relieve the ache that had invaded me. The sharp clatter of my spoon against the plate did little to push back the sexual fog clouding my mind. With my free hand, I squeezed his thigh—hard—and breathed a sigh of relief at his nod.

Devon leaned in, kissing my temple as he wiped his fingers on his napkin. Looking so cool and calm he made me want to scream, he dropped a credit card on the little plastic tray the waitress had left.

I blew out a long, slow breath and clenched my thighs together while my nails cut into the palms of my hands.

"Don't come." He gave my shoulder a gentle squeeze.

I nodded my head and fisted my hands into the seat of the booth, forcing a smile to my lips for the waitress's sake, as she stopped to take Devon's credit card. Once the receipt was signed, he gave me a nudge and I stood, thankful he walked behind me, his hand at the small of my back, as we left the restaurant.

"Now what?" I turned and looked up at him. The knot in my belly loosened, the need not quite so intense now.

"Did you like that, in there?" he asked, slowly leading me across the parking lot. " 'Cause that's just a small taste of what you're in for."

The insides of my thighs were slick. I *had* liked it and told him so. "I almost waited too long." My voice shook, but in a way, I felt proud of myself. It was all about control.

He turned to face me, cupping my face between his hands and brushing his lips across mine. "You did fine . . . and practice makes perfect."

"That's a long way from whips and chains."

Even he had to chuckle at that one. "My place?" he asked.

I was surprised he asked, figuring he'd just tell me, instead. "To be honest, I'd feel more comfortable at mine."

He opened the passenger door but stopped me before I could climb in, and lifted my skirt from behind. "This isn't about you being comfortable. This is about you learning your limits." While he spoke his hand lightly traced the path of my thong between the cheeks of my ass. He didn't have to tell me not to move; the command was understood, but that didn't stop me from wishing I could. As much as I enjoyed him touching me, as much as I wanted him to touch me, there was a part of me that wished he'd stop. There was something possessive about all of it that made my stomach tight with nerves—and a tinge of fear—all over again.

"My limits?" I turned, eyeing him over my shoulder.

In response he nodded slowly while his hand squeezed that tender nerve-filled area so close to my pussy lips. "How do you feel about whips?"

I slid into the car and away from his touch. "Absolutely

not." I paused to frown up at him. Whips weren't something I wanted any misunderstandings about.

During the short drive we talked, mostly about my health, sexual and otherwise. Devon said it was important for later.

"Above everything"—he pulled into the driveway of a tidy old house, circa WW2—"you *must* trust me."

"You said that. And I thought we were going to my place."

"Limits, Carlotta." He eased the car into the garage and killed the engine. We sat there as the door slid down behind us on a slow grind. The brief click of his seatbelt unlatching was loud in the silence of the car. "I will do everything I can to earn your trust, but you have to give 100 percent. I might push your limits eventually, but I'll never cross them."

"How can you push my limits when I don't even know what they are?"

Rather than answer me, he climbed out of the car, and came around to open my door. "There's only one way to find out," he said, holding out his hand.

I was still unsure of what I was about to do, of letting Devon "push my limits" and of this whole trust thing. Letting people in gave them the ability to hurt you. But I couldn't sit here all night. Climbing out, I took Devon's hand and let him lead me to my fate.

His house was plain, more austere even than the most typical bachelor pad, but somehow different, in a way I couldn't quite put my finger on. The kitchen was illuminated by a chrome light suspended from a pole above the sink. I dropped my purse on the bar, taking a moment to caress the white Corian countertop. It felt smooth, cool, yet somehow alive. The slate floors gave way to wood in the living area, giving the space a wide-open "normal" feel that didn't mesh with what was about to happen. What *was* about to happen?

"Did you bring condoms?" Devon asked, interrupting my ruminations.

"In my purse." I turned to smile at him. "Do you need some?"

"I have some."

"Then why did you ask?" I forced myself to hold perfectly still as Devon closed the space between us. Every nerve in my body screamed for me to move, but there was no place to go as he pulled a curl straight and released it, smiling as it sprang back into place.

"Curious whether you were the prepared type. I never met a woman who took condoms to work with her," he said, referring to our work-time fling.

"They were in my purse. Like American Express."

"I like your curls." He pulled on another, then trailed his fingers from my temple across my cheek to my lips, eliciting a gentle and strangely erotic electrical sensation as we stared at each other, testing, weighing the possibilities.

"Most of my toys are still packed."

"Like what?" I couldn't seem to take my eyes off his lips. They were perfectly sculpted and surrounded with just a dusting of stubble. I stood there, willing him to kiss me.

"Whips," he hissed, "spreader bars, a suspension bar, cuffs for your ankles and wrists; things I probably won't be using on you anytime soon. "Well," he added with a grin, "I might use the whip, but I won't *whip* you with it."

"You're going to fuck me with a whip?" I frowned. The idea held little appeal.

"No, Carlotta," he chuckled, "I'm going to make love to you with it."

The thought left me mystified, but I finally got my wish. Devon leaned in, covering my mouth with his, silencing my moan as I met his tongue halfway. He reached under my dress, his hands gliding across my skin, and hooked his fingers in the waistband of my thong, pushing it off my hips. His touch, like his kiss, was sure and light and meant to tease, to entice.

I had seriously underestimated him.

I shivered against him and my nipples strained against the confines of my satin bra as he backed me against the cabinets.

He finally let me come up for air while his hands continued exploring underneath my skirt, meeting at the damp juncture of my thighs to cup my swollen lips. He never took his eyes off my face as he massaged me with one hand. My hips arched outward, instinctively seeking more, and he smiled in a way I'd never seen him smile before: sure, confident, possessive. Shivering slightly, I gave myself over to the heat building, to the wetness that made my thighs slick, and to the muscles of my abdomen that clenched, demanding more.

He held a finger covered in my juices out to me. "What do you smell?"

"Pussy." *Should I lick his finger, and if I do, will he punish me?* Somehow punishment didn't seem like punishment anymore. I ran my tongue up the length of his finger.

Devon didn't punish me. He smiled and slid his finger back in my cunt, then offered it to me again. I covered it with my mouth and slowly sucked it clean, all while keeping an eye on him.

"Spread your legs."

At that point I was so hot I would have let him fuck me on the counter. I did as he asked, kicking my panties out of the way. He slowly trailed his finger across my cheek, across my neck, and down my chest, leaving a damp trail in his wake.

Cool air tickled my pussy, but Devon made no move to touch me again, just stood watching me, his icy blue eyes now as warm as a summer sky at twilight. "You like pussy?"

With my tongue stuck to the roof of my mouth, all I could do was nod.

"Play with yourself . . . play with your pussy." The intense look in his eyes made me shiver.

"Unzip me?" I turned and showed him my back. The sound

of my dress being unzipped was harsh and loud in the silence of his little house. It was so quiet otherwise that everything seemed amplified, even the sound of my dress as it fell off my shoulders and over my hips to pool at my feet.

I turned back around and watched as he picked it up and hung it on a pantry knob. Leaning against the counter, I nervously licked my lips and looked down at myself. Not that I'd never played with myself in front of anyone before, but this was different. Because *he* was different.

My breasts overflowed my strapless bra, the skin ultrasoft under my hands. I could almost hear them slide against my skin as they moved lower across the flat plane of my belly. I repositioned myself, legs wide, hips thrust outward in a provocative pose, as I pulled the lips of my pussy apart. My cheeks warmed at the sound of wet flesh that filled the kitchen, and I glanced up at Devon.

He met my gaze with an encouraging nod and I slipped two fingers between the folds. My belly clenched, my bottom tightening, unconsciously demanding more. My head dipped, and I stroked my swollen clit while wondering what Devon was thinking. Was he turned on? Or was he laughing at me? "You like to watch?" I gasped, my eyes closed.

"I like lots of things." His soothing and almost hypnotic voice—unusually loud in the tiny kitchen, but not loud enough to cover the sound of me playing with myself—filled my ears. "Don't come, Carlotta. You can't come until I tell you to."

I nodded, moaning again. "I'm so fucking horny."

"I know."

I swear I could feel the heat of his body maybe only inches away, but again, I didn't look.

"Fuck yourself, Carlotta."

Despite my awkward standing position, I managed to get two fingers knuckle deep. It wasn't enough.

"Add another."

I did, sighing in satisfaction at the stretched feeling, though it still wasn't what I really wanted. I forced my eyes open, forced myself to look at him standing only a few feet away from me, a hot and hungry smile on his face. "I want you."

"You have to earn me, Carlotta." He ran a hand through his hair and moved closer, close enough for me to see his erection. I wasn't the only one being teased. The revelation that I was more in control than I'd thought made me blink in surprise.

"How?" My fingers slowly slid in and out of me.

"Do you want to play? Hmmm? Do you want to play with me, Carlotta?"

There was something about the way he said my name that made me want to stretch and purr like a cat. It drifted across me soft as a caress, a verbal seduction. I licked my lips and forced a soft *yes* past my thick tongue.

"I'll talk, you listen. Now nod your head like a good girl." He moved even closer, unbuttoning his shirt with each step.

I nodded.

"Stop playing with yourself, but leave your fingers where they are." His voice rolled over me like a caress. "Safety words are very important. Do you know why?"

"Limits," I moaned, my cunt pulsating around my fingers.

"That's right. Yellow means slow down, red means stop, and green is go. Now you say it."

I repeated it back to him.

"Good. For the next two weeks I'm the only person you'll play with and you'll follow my every command, understand?" He pushed my hair away from my face, his fingers tantalizingly light against my skin.

I repeated it all back to him.

"That includes no masturbating, unless I say so. You've been a very good girl so far," he purred, his lips against my ear. His hands were on my shoulders, burning into my skin, and his crotch was pressed against my hand. "Are you ready to come?"

I nodded my head, my mouth again too dry for me to speak.

"Say please, Carlotta," he whispered, so softly I almost didn't hear him.

I forced my brain to work, my tongue to lick my lips, and my vocal chords to form the right sounds. "Please."

"That's my good girl." He pressed a kiss to the top of each breast, his lips whisper-soft; then my belly; and suddenly he was between my legs, gently licking my fingers, pulling them out of me and replacing them with his own.

He pulled my clit into his mouth, increasing the pressure with each suck and stroke of his tongue until I was literally holding myself up with the counter, my knees ready to give out. I climaxed on a scream that seemed to bounce and echo through the quiet little house. My knees finally did give out and only Devon's grip on my bottom kept me upright.

"Will you fuck me now?" I smiled down at him, a sleepy satiated smile.

"Say please." He pressed a kiss to my belly button.

"Please."

In the bedroom, Devon pulled the down comforter back and instructed me to lie down. I stretched out and wriggled against the cold, crisp sheets, wishing he'd undress faster, then wondering if I should offer to help with the condom.

"Roll over," he said, once he had it in place.

One last catlike stretch and I rolled onto my knees, ass in the air. The bed shifted with his weight. I could feel him inside me already and he hadn't even touched me.

"A proper submissive pose is like this, with your head down." While he talked, he repositioned me. His touch was light and deft as he gently pushed my forehead to the mattress and adjusted my arms, palms down in front of me.

I could breathe but the tingle of fear that raced up my spine and choked me ever so slightly prevented me from turning my head to either side. Once he was apparently satisfied, Devon moved behind me and slid in. Pure satisfaction filled me, pushing my fears away. One of Devon's better attributes was his size, the other that thing he was doing with his hips, making his cock rub the ultrasensitive walls of my pussy, and right now, anything other than submission wasn't an option. I gave myself over to him and the second orgasm that shot through me. He gave me no time to recover, just drove into me harder and faster, and I yelped with each thrust. The harsh sound of his heavy breathing, and finally, a few hoarse grunts as he came, filled the air.

He collapsed, sweaty and panting on my back, then eased onto his side, dragging me with him. Escape wasn't an option either. Not that I had the energy to escape anywhere. It felt as if we'd been engaged in foreplay for hours and muscles heavy with fatigue and sexual happiness refused to let me move. My brain, too numb to think of getting up, searching for my clothes, and insisting he take me home, made the decision for me. All I could do was close my eyes.

I woke slowly, the insistent urging of my bladder forcing me to stretch and wriggle out of Devon's hold and the blanket he'd covered me with at some point in the night. The clock on the nightstand showed just after 4:00 AM, and thanks to the bathroom light he'd left on, I had no trouble getting my bearings. Pushing my hair off my face, I eased back onto my elbows and watched him sleep.

I grinned.

He looked so damn innocent. Hell, he looked innocent when he was awake, too.

Sliding out of the bed, I crossed to the bathroom and quietly closed the door behind me. I'd put myself in quite a bind.

I was stuck here at Devon's mercy. I supposed if I didn't show up for brunch tomorrow, the girls would call, but calling either one of them at four in the morning was out of the question. I focused on the pink tile wall in front of me, trying to figure out if I should make him take me home now or if that were even possible. Would he? If I asked?

When or where exactly did this slave/master thing end?

After washing my hands, I stopped to peer at myself in the medicine cabinet mirror. My hair was unruly, nothing new, my makeup smeared.

I didn't really *look* any different, but I felt different. I didn't like how Devon made me feel. He was very sweet and the sex was incomparable, but . . . I shook my head, unsure if I could handle two weeks of this.

I turned the tap on and splashed my face with cold water, then grabbed the fluffy white towel from the bar at my elbow. Briefly I debated the wisdom of wiping my face on the pristine white cotton, then muttered a soft "Fuck it," and did it anyway. It wasn't like I did his wash.

Back in the bedroom I searched for my clothes, then scrubbed at my matted hair with a soft growl of frustration. My dress and panties were still in the kitchen, where we'd left them. After assuring myself Devon was still sleeping, I tiptoed out, shutting the door behind me and blinking to adjust to the lack of light in the hallway. Using the wall as a guide, I slowly walked to where it split off. If I went straight, there was another closed door. If I turned, I'd end up back in the living room and kitchen.

Carlotta's Adventures in Wonderland, to be sure.

The more alert I got, the more I wanted to go home. With a glance over my shoulder, I went straight instead of turning and pushed the door open. The room was dark but for the moonlight slicking through the blinds and leaving horizontal slashes across a large, evil-looking device that made me think twice about exploring further. Frowning, I felt around for the light switch, and flicked it on. I blinked at the sudden brightness, then snorted softly to myself. It was hard to be intimidated by something purple even if it *was* evil looking.

I walked around it, then took a second, slower, trip, trailing a finger across the smooth surface and trying to imagine how it worked. The entire device was about five feet long and had sides that curved up sort of like wings, sort of like a gymnast's horse but with foot rests. The sides would barely reach my knees. The middle part of the device was U-shaped and had three thick rings at the end.

Two large boxes sat in the closet. I glanced at the doorway, then tiptoed over to the closet and knelt down. Around me the entire house was heavy with silence. Both boxes were open, the tape stripped back and dangling off the sides. They looked incredibly normal. Just as I leaned over and nudged one with my bare toe, the air conditioner came on. A blast of cold air from the vent overhead reminded me I was buck naked, and I shivered, suddenly feeling incredibly vulnerable. With one finger I gently pried back the box flap and peeked inside. It was full of B & D paraphernalia. Padded restraints with what looked like medical-grade buckles, chains, even a two-foot-wide bar with cuffs at each end. The other box held a wide variety of nasty-looking whips.

"See anything you like?"

At the sound of Devon's voice, I dropped the red quirt I'd picked up and fell back on my bottom, automatically shoving my legs closed. That was just a bit too vulnerable. "I want to go home now."

"Like that?" He nodded in my general direction, a sleepy smile on his face. His hair was rumpled and he looked almost cherubic but for the hard pecs and washboard abs.

Like I'd forgotten I was naked?

I held up the quirt and said, "Interesting," before tossing it back into the box.

He crossed the room and held out a hand. I eyed it, trying to imagine those long, tapered fingers using any of the paraphernalia in the box on me. The picture didn't come.

The ride home was long and quiet as we sped north across the deserted Houston highways.

As soon as he pulled into my driveway, I unhooked my seatbelt and made to get out, get away. From Devon? Or myself?

"I had a nice time," Devon said.

A nice time? "I'll call you." I shoved the door open, letting the cool early morning air waft through the car.

"Actually, I thought we could get together this afternoon." His voice, still gruff with sleep, and his hand lightly squeezing my shoulder, stopped me.

"I have brunch with the girls." And I'd be lucky to make it on time because I desperately needed more sleep as well as some time to think.

"I'll pick you up about three."

"And if I say no?"

"I thought we had a deal, Carlotta." His warm drawl took the edge off the censure in his voice.

"Make it four." I slammed the car door with a sigh, resigned to seeing Devon later today.

3

Sunday after breakfast we all stood in the parking lot of Baroque planning the rest of our day. I *had* to talk about Devon, but I had serious reservations about discussing the nitty-gritty details in the middle of a crowd fresh from a dose of God's love. Whispering and giggling about whiskey dick was one thing, but whips?

"So, I made a deal with Devon."

"Just exactly what kind of deal did you make with the Geek Meister?" Lexi asked once were through discussing Lanie's Saturday Family Fiasco.

"He, uh . . ." The beginnings of a full-blown laugh tickled me. "Apparently he has control issues." I couldn't bring myself to look at Lanie.

"Control issues?" She snickered.

"Yeah, he and his wife—"

"Whoa!" A wide-eyed Lanie spun around and stepped in front of me. She frantically waved her hands as if to stop me.

"She's dead," I quickly explained.

"Aw!" Lexi frowned in sympathy.

"They were into bondage-type stuff."

Lexi's jaw dropped the tiniest bit while her eyebrows slowly rose.

"And?" Lanie's grin was just wicked. She knew me better than anyone and already had a pretty good idea of where this was going.

"He thinks"—I glanced at both of them, knowing they were going to give me hell—"I'll make a good sub."

They both howled with laughter, and I pushed past them, only to stop at Lanie's hand on my arm.

"Did he spank you, Carlotta?" Her lips twitched and her whole body wiggled with suppressed laughter.

I couldn't resist letting a giggle of my own escape as I climbed into the back of my 4Runner. "He gets two weeks."

"To tie you—I mean try you—out." Lanie took a seat on my left.

"Ha ha! And yeah." I shrugged and then heaved a sigh of relief.

"Are you sure you want to do that?" Lexi climbed up on my other side and draped an arm around my shoulder.

"I'm not sure. He, uh . . . he scares me. Not in a *bad* scary way. It's like he knows what buttons to push. How to get to me. How to . . . to make me want this, and I don't mean just sex. It's like he knows *me*. Like I don't have any secrets. He made me say please, you guys!"

"And you liked it," Lanie said with another grin.

Grunting in frustration, I punched her in the arm. "Yeah, I did! Now be a good friend and tell me to back the hell out of this."

"Back the hell out," Lexi insisted.

"What do you want to do?" Lanie asked. "I know it's creepy, but he doesn't sound like a bad guy; just . . . perverted."

"You are no help!" We all got tickled again, much to the annoyance of a family attempting to climb into the oversized

SUV parked next to us. Once their doors were closed, I continued.

"I promised him I'd give him two weeks, but I'm seriously not sure if I can do this."

"It is only two weeks," Lanie said. "Maybe you should just go into it as a learning experience. Are you worried he'll hurt you?"

"Devon wouldn't hurt a fly."

On my other side, Lexi stayed suspiciously quiet.

"No, I'm worried I'll like it." I slid off the back of the SUV and motioned for them both to stand up, a signal our conversation was over.

With a "call me if you need anything," Lanie took off, leaving Lexi and me behind in the parking lot of Baroque. I slammed the back of the 4Runner and glanced at Lexi. The serious expression on her face brought me up short.

"I don't like this, for the record." She stood beside me, gently rubbing my arm.

I knew she meant well. "Sometimes I don't either." There was still the matter of Devon's uncle to discuss with someone, anyone but Devon himself, and as much as I loved Lanie, Lexi was the one you went to if you had a serious problem. "How tired are you?" I asked. Despite the fact I couldn't bring myself to destroy the DVD, the entire situation had begun to eat at me, and I kept wondering if, at some point down the line, it would come back to bite me in the ass.

She ran a hand through her short, wavy hair. "Not too tired, if you need to talk."

We walked to the coffee shop next door, ordered iced teas sweetened with Valencia, and claimed two cozy club chairs tucked in a corner away from the early-afternoon traffic.

"Remember when I quit on Friday?" I said, eyes on my tea. My belly clenched, nausea rising threateningly at the memory of my confrontation with Chambers.

Lexi nodded encouragingly, and I pushed on.

"The reason I got so pissed off was because I found a camera in Devon's office." At the look of shock on her face, I quickly added, "It wasn't his!"

"Oh my God, Carly!" She leaned over, practically sitting on the arm of her chair. "Why didn't you say something?!"

I slumped lower in the chair and thought about crying, but that wasn't an option. I just wasn't one for tears, in public or otherwise, but my cheeks were burning. "I was embarrassed. And besides, I took care of it."

"I don't care if you 'took care of it,' we're your friends! That's what we're here for, honey!"

"I know." I felt bad for not saying something sooner. Sighing, I rested my head on the chair's armrest.

"I can skip a nap if we need to break into his office or something," she said with a conspiratorial grin.

I grinned back. "I got it. At home, in my nightstand. I promised not to go to the police as long as he gave it to me."

"Girllll." Lexi sighed and banged her head on the armrest a couple of times for emphasis. "So what did Devon say when you told him?"

"Are you out of your mind?" I whispered harshly. The thought of telling Devon made me ill all over again. "No way in hell am I telling him."

"You sure that's a smart move?" She sipped her tea and sighed.

"Look, there is no way I'm telling him what a skeezer his uncle is!"

"Like he doesn't know? Or at least have some idea. He is family after all." She sighed, her shoulders slumping slightly before she straightened them again and looked me in the eye. "Carlotta, I don't mean to sound like a prude, but are you sure you want to go through with this . . . thing?"

"You mean with Devon?"

"Yeah. I mean, what if you get hurt?"

"Devon's a pussycat, and besides, it's just sex. How am I going to get hurt?"

"I mean physically," she hissed, wide eyed.

"He's not like that," I insisted.

"For your sake, I hope so."

"So where exactly are we going?" I crossed my legs and smoothed my hands down my jeans. The starched material was rough against my fingertips. I'd deliberately worn a loose, frilly blouse, something simple I'd be comfortable in. Devon was dressed in faded Levi's and a pale yellow polo shirt. We looked like any other ordinary couple out running Sunday errands.

But we weren't.

"We're going shopping." While he spoke, he pulled into a little strip mall near the Galleria.

The low-slung beige building, with buckets of bright spring flowers and perfectly sculpted bushes, looked like any of a hundred strip malls scattered across the greater Houston area.

"Normally, I'd say knock yourself out, but . . ." But there was no telling what shopping with Devon was going to entail.

He parked in front of a nondescript store—well, except for the latex and leather display in the window and the neon whip that curved around a sign.

"*Snap*? I'm surprised they didn't call it Leather and Lace."

Devon laughed and slid out of the car. I followed reluctantly, but I was unwilling to ask him what he planned on buying me. "I'm surprised they let places like this open on Sunday. Especially since Texas is practically the heart of the Bible Belt."

"I thought that was Mississippi," he said, holding the door open for me.

"Same difference." I took in my surroundings slowly while wishing I hadn't eaten quite so much at brunch. The store was like the boxes in Devon's closet but ten times *more*. I wasn't a prude; far from it. But the sight of so much leather and latex left me feeling squeamish, and damn it all, cranky.

"Latex?" An amused-sounding Devon motioned to the mannequin on my left. She wore elbow-length latex gloves with a matching mask and thong.

"Definitely not. You know"—I slowly turned to face him—"Southern Baptists don't have anything on Catholic guilt. What are we looking for?"

"Something for a lapsed Catholic, apparently."

"Ha ha." I gently poked Devon in the gut. Lapsed was an understatement.

"A corset, maybe."

"Beg pardon?" Listening with only half an ear, I crossed the tiny store to check out an array of collars on the wall, finally selecting a red one with an O-ring in the center. "I wonder if this has a matching leash?"

"Yes, as a matter of fact, it does."

Collar in hand, I turned, only able to blink at the woman in front of me. She held the matching leash in one hand and wore a studded apple-green collar of her own. She was pretty in an arrestingly pale way with her blonde hair in pigtails. Her pink T-shirt sported handcuffs that were stretched slightly out of proportion by her generous breasts, an odd match with olive-green cargo pants that rode low on her hips.

"Do you have any red corsets?" Devon asked.

"Follow me." She turned and I bit my lip at the round cheeks of her bottom. They filled out her cargo pants.

With a quick glance at Devon, who grinned knowingly, I followed.

"Psst."

I stopped in my tracks, afraid to turn around, but I forced my head to move. Devon stood behind me, his eyes twinkling. He pointed to a red latex minidress. It came complete with lace-up middle that started just below the waist, but looked so short I doubted it would cover the wearer's ass.

"Uh-uh." I hurt just looking at it. Shaking my head, I turned and followed the clerk to a round rack filled with a variety of corsets—more latex and leather in a variety of colors as well as some heavily embroidered satin ones.

"Red, right?" she asked.

"That's what the gentleman said. I like the satin one."

"But will he?"

Grinning, she handed me an ornate red satin corset that hooked up the front and laced up the back.

"I'm the one who has to wear it." I held the corset out in front of me, trying to imagine it on, then glanced over my shoulder, happy to note Devon still wasn't within hearing distance. "Are you . . . a sub?" I practically whispered while keeping my eyes on the corset.

"Five years now." We could have been discussing the best brand of diapers or our favorite restaurant. "That'll go great with your skin," she said.

Personally, I didn't agree. It was too bold; I needed something warmer in tone. Five years. Hell, I'd never been in a relationship longer than five months. I couldn't imagine. Wouldn't it get boring after a while?

"There's a dressing room in the back if you want to try that on. I've got to stay out here since it's just me, but I'm sure . . . your Dom?"

"Sorta." I shrugged, doing my best to look bored with the whole topic.

"Well, he's cute, and I bet he can hook you up." With one last smile, she circled around me, patting my shoulder.

I stared down that short hallway lined with swinging doors, wondering if I really wanted my "Dom" to hook me up. *Hook me up?* I held up the corset again, and pulled my lower lip between my teeth to keep from saying a word. Devon circled around in front of me and took the corset from me. From the rack beside him, he selected another, this one longer and in a warmer shade of red leather. Something that wouldn't leave my boobs hanging out.

"I can't decide if I want to get you something you can wear in public, or not." Turning, he headed for the dressing rooms.

My lower lip caught between my teeth, I followed. "In public?"

"Out on the town?" At the last room, he held open one of the swinging doors and motioned for me to step inside. "Strip to your panties."

"Why in the world do I need to strip to try on a corset?"

"Trust me. It'll be easier to try on," he coaxed, but that didn't stop me from scowling or, well, being a bad . . . sub.

"No." Arms crossed over my chest and hip cocked, I waited to see what he'd do. He propped his arms against the doorframe and slowly nodded his head.

"Don't do this, Carlotta," he said, his voice low.

"What are you going to do, spank me?" I sauntered closer, a smirk on my face.

"Maybe later, if you ask nice." His grin was positively cheeky, as if he didn't give a damn how much I misbehaved. Then he dropped his voice, and said, "And if I wanted to spank you, you'd already be over my knee."

I gave him my haughtiest, highbrowed look, the same one I reserved for Jimmy Z's less desirables who had trouble taking no for an answer. "So, how are you going to punish me because I'm not stripping?"

"Do you really want to fight me, sweetheart?" He stepped closer and, even though Devon wasn't a large man, he was tall. "Is control worth that much to you?"

The dressing room shrank in proportion to his nearness, then he dropped in a crouch and slid the brown leather Mudd sandals off my feet. "You think I'm a threat to you." From his position in front of me, he had easy access to the button and fly on my jeans and quickly undid them, pushing them down my hips. I stayed perfectly still, my arms still crossed, despite the heavy denim pulling my yellow cotton panties down so they rode low on my hips. Devon removed my jeans, then oh-so-gently fixed my panties, his smooth fingertips light on my skin. "A threat to your independence."

He uncrossed my arms and began unbuttoning my blouse. "What you fail to realize is, you're here with me because you chose to be. Not because I've forced you."

He slid the gauzy top off of me and hung it on a nearby peg, then picked up my jeans and did the same with them. "Turn around, please."

By now I knew better than to argue. He'd just turn me himself. Other than the eerie sound of classical music playing, the store was silent. Licking my lips, I turned, forcing myself to hold perfectly still as his fingers brushed against my skin while they unhooked my bra. My nipples puckered at freedom but still I didn't move or show any signs of possible embarrassment as he slid the bra down my arms and draped it over my jeans.

From a hook on the other side of the dressing room he retrieved the red satin corset and undid the front. "Lift your arms."

I did, taking my hair with them and propping them on top of my head.

His hands circled my waist, bringing the corset with it, and he hooked me up, starting at the bottom. Then, from the back, his hands untied the strings and began cinching me up.

"I can't breathe."

"Breathe through your nose." He pulled my hands from my hair, forcing me to drop them back at my sides. "You like it?"

I couldn't seem to focus on it. I was too busy focusing on him. The tiny frown between his eyebrows, the gentle slide of his fingers under the edge of the corset as he rubbed the material between his fingers. I was also aware of the corset cutting into me. "I can't breathe. Can you loosen it?"

"You won't have it on that much longer."

"I can't breathe, Devon!"

"Patience, Carlotta."

I turned and frowned at him over my shoulder.

"I don't like it," he said, shaking his head. "I'll be right back."

Then he walked out. Just left me standing there in my panties and a corset, struggling for air. I growled under my breath and turned, intent on getting out of the damn thing. By the time I'd gotten the last of the front hooks undone, Devon was back, a longer, butter-yellow leather corset in hand. I held out the red one and motioned for the yellow one, which I loved on sight, but he shook his head. Fine. I hung the corset back on its hanger while he silently watched.

"Face the mirror again."

"No." I crossed my arms under my breasts again and waited to see what he'd do.

We had a stare-down; me scowling again while he just stood there. He looked away first, backing out of the dressing room and running a hand through his hair in frustration. "Get dressed. I'll be up front."

The deal was off.

No way would he want to continue our little experiment after the stunt I'd just pulled.

And wasn't that what I wanted?

4

I settled back in the passenger seat and stared out the window until I realized that he wasn't taking me home.

"I thought you were taking me home."

"I'm not trying to break you, Carlotta, and deep down inside you know that. I'd *never* break you." He pulled into the driveway and put the car in park.

"What are we doing here, Devon?"

In the daylight hours Devon's north Houston neighborhood looked like any other. Next door, a toddler rode his Big Wheel down the sidewalk while his mom watched from a spot in the middle of her yard. The sun shone, birds sang; it was all disgustingly normal.

Devon silently slid out of the car, waving to the blonde next door before circling around and opening my door. I didn't move. He leaned in, unhooked my seat belt and then stood back up, but I still didn't move. After a few minutes he leaned back in again.

"I'm going to punish you, Carlotta, for being disobedient. The longer you sit here, the worse it'll be. It's up to you."

"What? Are you going to spank me?"

"No, because I think you'd like it too much."

"You're *not* going to spank me, Devon," I hissed, unwilling to make a scene.

"That's twice you've mentioned spanking." He eased back down, sitting on the edge of the car beside my seat and running a hand through his hair.

"Don't ever spank me. Ever!"

"How do you think I should punish you?"

I laughed even though my more rational side knew he was serious. "I could scrub your floor. Huh? Like a little Cinderella?" Like my mother.

"That's not exactly what I had in mind . . ." He stood back up and offered me his hand.

I took it, letting him lead me through the house to the kitchen. He dropped his keys on the counter and began removing the kitchen chairs from around the table, setting them in the living room. Next he got out a bucket and filled it with hot water and floor cleaner, throwing a sponge on top of the suds. When he was done, he stopped in front of me. "But your wish is my command. Strip."

My laughter echoed through the house, but I did it. Stripped down to my bra and panties, tossing my jeans and blouse onto the living room floor behind me.

"Finish . . ." He nodded, his blue eyes hard and sharp.

I never took my eyes off of him. Just reached behind my back and unhooked my bra, throwing it on the floor behind me also, because I knew it would bother him. My panties followed as I kicked them to the side.

"Now scrub the floor," he said with a nod. He stepped around me and into the living room. I turned, watching him walk over to the stereo. The sound of Coldplay filled the living room. He walked back into the kitchen and got himself a beer from the fridge. "I'll be out back. Come and get me when you're done."

He pushed back the pale gray vertical blinds, flooding the room with light, then slid the door open and stepped outside. A warm breeze drifted across my skin as I watched him, debating whether I should call a cab and get dressed or clean the fucking floor.

I stepped into the kitchen, wincing at the cold slate against my feet, and lifted the bucket from the sink. "I cannot believe I am doing this."

The light lemony odor of Mr. Clean filled the kitchen as I dropped the bucket with a thunk. Warm, soapy water sloshed over the side and landed on my foot. A memory as strong as Pine-Sol, which I still can't stand, filled my head. My mother on the floor, scrubbing cracked linoleum. My father watching her from his spot at the kitchen table, his eyes bleary with sleep but still filled with disdain.

This was so going to suck. And it did, but I scrubbed, never saying a word when Devon came inside and stood at the counter watching me. Making me feel even more naked than I actually was, if that was possible.

I was almost done by then, with only a wide swath near the carpet left to do. *Thank God he wasn't a pig.* My knees hurt, and I had indentations in the palms of my hands, which were pruny from the water. I'd even broken a nail. But I refused to let Devon see how much any of it bothered me.

From behind me came the low but unmistakable sound of laughter. His laughter.

I turned and stretched, glaring at him the whole time and growing madder as he laughed louder, harder. Before I'd given it a second thought, the scrub brush flew out of my hand. He caught it square in the chest, his eyes tearing up.

"You know there's this place online that sells butt plugs."

"Butt plugs?" *How the hell did I get here?*

"You do know what those are?" he asked, leaning over the counter and tossing the brush into the sink.

"I own one."

He scrunched his face up again, took a deep breath, and said, "I bet yours doesn't have a curly pink pig's tail on it."

"You wouldn't dare." But it was too late. I got the giggles at the mental picture of me on the floor with a pig's tail.

Sighing, he circled around the counter and sank down in a dry spot, his long legs stretched out in front of him. He patted the floor between his legs. "Come here, please."

I gave him a hard once-over, then complied since he'd said please. "Satisfied?"

"Are you?"

"You're insane!"

Laughing, he roughly pulled me up against him and squeezed me. "You chose your punishment."

"I didn't know you were going to take me seriously!"

"I was trying to make a point."

"I get it now: don't ever joke with you about scrubbing your floors."

"No, don't challenge my authority."

"If I wanted a despot, I'd still be living at home."

"Have I hurt you?" he asked, gently pushing my hair off my shoulder.

"You're fucking with my head, and I don't like it, Devon!" I snapped, shrugging his hand off. "You think I don't know? You think I'm stupid or something? You don't have to lay a hand on me to break me."

"I've already told you I won't."

"I don't believe you."

"Because you don't *trust* me."

I was sticky with sweat and floor cleaner, and the tile floor was growing increasingly uncomfortable on my backside. "Why should I trust you?" I turned my head and looked up at him.

"Because I can free you." He never took his eyes off of me as he pressed his lips to my bare shoulder.

"I am free," I insisted, watching him through a tangle of curls. Wasn't I free? I had a job, friends, a life I loved where no one told me what to do—except for Devon.

"Are you?" From the living room came the sound of the Black Crowes while Devon and I had another stare-down. Devon sang a few lines, then started laughing again. "This song reminds me of you. A stubborn wild woman, who just won't be tamed. What were you thinking about while you were scrubbing the floor?"

I glanced down at my red, rough hands and answered his question. "My mother."

"What about her?"

"I wondered if she'd ever scrubbed the floors naked," I chuckled.

This time we both laughed, and he squeezed me again. A gesture meant to comfort.

"So that's why you chose the floor."

"I suppose." I hadn't really given it that much thought.

He sighed, a heavy sound punctuated only by an acoustic guitar solo from the other room. "I tell you what. Tonight, you're in charge."

"You'll take me home afterward?" I eyed him, wary and uncertain about being put in charge. Only because I figured he had an ulterior motive. No, I *knew* he did.

"I'll even let you tie me down if you want. But first," he said, "you need a shower."

When Devon said I needed a shower, I didn't know he meant he was going to wash me. Maybe this was a peace offering or his way of saying he was sorry or whatever, but he scrubbed every inch of me with a big soft sponge. Tension eased from my muscles as he washed away all my anger I had over scrubbing the damn floor. "Don't ever make me scrub your floor again."

His soft, husky laugh filled my ears while his hands glided over my hips. "Then behave yourself. Do you want me to wash your hair?"

Smiling, I reached up and pulled out the ponytail holder.

"Turn around."

I did, and he lifted my hair, letting the shower sprayer soak its way through the dense mass. He gently pulled me forward, and I kept my eyes closed, reaching out with my hands until I came into contact with the flat, hard plane of his stomach. I cupped his sides, sighing in satisfaction, as his fingers gently worked at my scalp. "That feels good."

He laughed again and pressed a soft kiss to my lips. My little moan of happiness ended on a laugh as soap trailed down the side of my face.

"Lean your head back."

Devon rinsed my hair, then added conditioner, gently untangling my hair with his fingers and rinsing it. Once he was done, he pulled me out into the steamy bathroom and toweled me off.

"So what do I get to do to you?" I asked while drying his back.

"Whatever you want." He opened a drawer and grabbed two condoms. "What do you think I'd like?"

"I don't know." And it frustrated me.

He turned and took the towel from me, tossing it over the shower rod before dragging me into the bedroom.

"Do *you* like to be spanked?"

"No," he said, leading me out of the bedroom. "But you seem to have an interesting fascination with it." He was completely uncaring of his own nakedness and mine. I wasn't a prude, but I didn't make it a habit to wander around waving my ass either. Speaking of asses, Devon's was looking pretty good. He stopped just inside the door to the spare bedroom.

"Okay, what the hell is that?" I asked, pointing to the large purple bench in the middle of the room.

"The movers asked the same thing." He crossed the room and stood at its head, crossing his arms and leaning over as casually as you please.

"Oh my God!" I laughed, slowly following.

"It's a spanking horse." He patted the top. "Go ahead, lie down."

"I thought I was in charge."

"Just . . . try it." He pushed my hair off my shoulders, his touch so tender, I didn't have the heart to say no.

I didn't take my eyes off him as I hoisted myself up and stretched out, aware of my breasts, stomach, and pubic bone crushed against the cushy material. Of the very vulnerable position I was in. "Now what? What would you do to me if you could?"

His erection grew, swelled, thick veins standing out in stark relief against pale, smooth skin. He liked seeing me this way. It turned him on, and in turn, turned me on. I clamped the sides of the table with my thighs, fighting the urge to wiggle, to rub my pussy against the butter-soft material, as he sat down beside me and rested a hand at the base of my spine.

"I'd get the shackles from the closet and bind your wrists."

I sat up, aware of the provocative position I was in, and slowly turned onto my back. The bench was barely wide enough for me to stretch out, but I managed. "Then what?"

He placed his hand on the flat plane of my stomach, right on top of my belly button, and the warm weight sank into my skin, spreading outward.

I licked my lips. "What would you do to me?"

"I'm yours to command. What would you like me to do?"

"Get a whip." At his surprised look, I added, "You said you wanted to make love to me with one. Show me."

With a nod, he ducked into the closet and returned with a short one. It couldn't have been more than two or three feet long.

"What is that?" I asked, eyeing the dozen or so navy blue tassels. I had dust rags that looked more threatening.

"It's a flogger. Made of velvet." He trailed it across my leg and stopped at my pussy. The soft, fuzzy material tickled, and my legs opened wider of their own accord.

"You can't hurt someone with that, can you?"

"No." He dragged it up to my belly, slowly spun it around and drew it back over my skin.

My thighs tightened. I couldn't hold back a smile. "That's nice."

"You like that." He quirked one eyebrow and swept it higher to my breasts.

My nipples grew to sharp achy points. More than anything, I wanted to reach up and pinch them, but didn't dare. "I like."

"Now close your eyes and imagine if you were tied up and I was doing this."

I did as he instructed, succumbing to the erotic image he'd given me, and for the longest time all I could hear was the sound of my own breathing while Devon caressed every inch of me. Every nerve was on high alert, anticipating more. *Wanting* more. "Can I do this to you?"

"Of course you can."

I sighed and stretched my arms above my head.

"It's not about the pain, Carlotta. It's about pleasure."

And control, I silently added. God, how I wanted to believe him, and right then I did. "How many whips—floggers—do you have?"

"A flogger is just a type of whip . . . and almost two dozen."

"Why so many? You can only use one at a time." I giggled

and squirmed a bit as he circled my belly button with the flogger.

"Different whips for different things. A heavier whip like a bull hide hurts, but it's also more for show."

"For show?"

"If you were doing a scene at a local dungeon."

It was easy enough to figure out what a dungeon was, so I didn't bother asking. "Does Houston have one?"

"Of course. A flogger, or even a quirt, is more intimate. More personal. You know they even have some made out of rabbit skin. It's not as soft as this"—He circled my breasts, making the tips pucker and tingle—"but soft. Do you like that? Talk to me, Carlotta."

His voice filled my head. I was turned on, every pore in my skin begging for more. "I feel . . . alive," I panted. "Every inch of me, I can't explain it. Just *alive*. My skin tingles and I want to feel it everywhere. I want to *feel* it."

"So you like it." He trailed the tassels between my breasts and across my belly. "Are you wet?"

I snorted softly. "Oh yeah." I felt as if I were running some sort of race, like I couldn't quite get enough air, like I was expanding.

"Stand up." The velvet trailed across my leg, softer than a lover's touch, then disappeared.

I peeled my eyes open, then slowly peeled myself off the bench, sitting up and forcing myself to focus on Devon. I sat on the edge, legs spread, fully aware of how wet and swollen and tender my pussy was. And how hard he was. His erection was a smooth column that bobbed with each step, tapping his abdomen. He came and stood between my legs, his touch on my thighs light but sure.

"Take this." He pressed the flogger into my hand and instructed me to stand up.

I slowly slid off the bench, standing in front of him on shaky legs. "Now what?"

"Turn around."

Turning, I faced the bench, and Devon moved up behind me so we were belly to back, his erection pressed against my bottom as he circled my waist with one arm. "Hit the bench."

I glanced over my shoulder at him and, at his nod, did just that, blinking at the impact.

"A flogger this soft won't hurt, no matter how hard you try. Well, I suppose it would if you really put your back into it, but if you're going to go to that much effort, you might as well use something heavier, like deer hide or pig suede."

"If the purpose isn't to hurt," I said, taking another swing at the bench, "then why use something heavier?"

"After a while you'll become desensitized to it and you'll want more." He wrapped his fingers around my wrist and we swung together this time.

"Why are you doing this? Why so much trouble?"

"Because I think you're worth it. Now pay attention. I'm trying to teach you to bottom from the top."

I giggled. "Come again."

"To understand *your* job, you need to understand mine." We swung again. "You don't just *whip* someone. You have to learn how." His free hand skimmed from my waist to my hip. "You can whip someone's bottom or even the tops of their thighs, but most other places are too sensitive, too close to vital organs. You have more padding here," he said, giving the cheek of my ass a squeeze. "It's like sex, just amplified. When you have sex, you want to please your partner, right?"

"Right." I pressed myself against him and squeezed my legs together. The tops of my thighs were sticky with my own juices, and as much as I wanted to call a halt to our training session, there was something erotic about having him touch me but not, well, *touch me*. I suppose this was another lesson.

"You need to pay attention to the signals your partner sends out." He pressed his erection more firmly against the cheeks of my bottom. "And you take your cues from there."

"So," I said, turning, "if your partner likes to be teased a lot, you'd tease them?" Grinning, I draped the flogger over his shoulder and let the tassels drift down against his arm.

"Exactly."

Other than the two of us, it seemed as if the whole world had ceased to exist.

"Lay down." I watched with my heart pounding in my chest as he stretched out on his back.

Starting at his feet, I let the flogger trail across one ankle, up his calf and over a knee. It drifted toward the inside of his thigh as I dragged it higher, and I watched him for a response. Any sort of response. I didn't get one, other than his hard cock leaking precum onto his belly. "Do you want something more substantial?"

For some reason being in control wasn't nearly as much fun now. I was too interested in his cock and the way my mouth watered at the thought of taking him between my lips. I wanted to lean over and lap up the tiny pool of clear fluid. I wanted to straddle his hips, take him inside me, and relieve the ache he'd started.

"No, Carlotta."

"No, what?" With a flick of my wrist, the tails of the flogger settled at his shoulder and I dragged it across his neck, letting it slowly dance down his chest, back to that pool.

"No, I don't want something more substantial."

"You're mine, right? I can do whatever I want?"

"Right."

"I like you like this." The flogger slowly drifted around his erection and across his balls, which visibly tightened and shifted in their sacs, and the tiny pool of fluid grew marginally larger. "Did you like feeling me up last night?"

"Yeah." A smile drifted across his lips. "Did *you* like it?"

My belly tightened at the memory. "Mmm hmmm. Have you ever had sex in public?"

"Yeah."

"You felt me up . . . why?"

"Control."

"Because you can control me." Tired of playing and lessons, I dropped the flogger and lightly scraped my nails up the insides of his thighs. His muscles jumped just the tiniest bit at my touch, and I smiled at the more obvious response.

"No one can control you, Carlotta. Ever." He spread his legs wider, then moaned as my fingertips glanced across his balls. "My job is to know what you want, and more importantly, to give you what you want."

"I want you."

"I know." He stretched ever so slightly, resting his arms above his head.

"How do you know what I want?" I knelt on the bench beside him and leaned over, pressing a soft kiss to his thigh.

"I can read you like a book." He shifted slightly under me, but otherwise didn't move.

I could smell his sex, the sweet, musky tempting odor of his cum, drawing me in as I joined him on the bench and buried my face in his balls. They were smooth and firm, and I ran the tip of my tongue up the very center. With light, tender licks, I worked my way higher, covering every inch of them, sucking them into my mouth one at a time. Beneath me, his thigh muscles tensed and he arched off the bench by degrees, his moan of pleasure echoing softly in my ears.

I shifted so that I was straddling his hips with my toes curled against the bench's leg rest, and took him inside me. "You like it like this?"

"You're in charge."

"I'm impatient," I ruefully confessed.

He smiled up at me, his eyes barely open. "You'll learn." His cock pulsated and swelled as his smile grew.

"Don't come." I shifted my hips, setting a slow pace as I rode him, amazed at his control. His patience. *How could he lie there so relaxed?*

I wanted him to sweat, to moan and beg. I wanted to break him, but I didn't. And suddenly, as I sat there rocking back and forth with him inside me, I understood what *he* wanted from *me*. What he meant when he talked about pushing my limits and trust freeing me.

But could I really trust him, and what would happen if I did?

5

I'd spent Monday cleaning house, thankful to have some time away from Devon. Time to think. I'd cleaned the condo from top to bottom, then had my broken nail repaired and spent the afternoon picking out new flowers at Home Depot. Oversized buckets of verbena and phlox now lined one side of my driveway.

On Tuesday I went back to the shop Devon had taken me to, determined to buy that yellow corset, but it was gone. The clerk, a man this time, was no help when I asked about ordering another. As much as it pained me, I'd have to write it off as a loss. Frustrated at my lack of success, I drove home, changed and stretched out on a lounger out back wearing nothing but my skimpiest black bikini bottoms and a T-shirt.

Most of the condo community I lived in was made up of people my age, which meant many, if not all of them, were at work. I peeled my shirt off, oiled myself up, and stretched out topless on a lounge chair.

The total and complete silence around me gave me time to think, more time than I wanted. I stayed outside until every inch of me was so hot I could barely breathe and staying outside was no longer an option.

Two messages from Devon were waiting for me when I stepped through the glass sliding door. I wanted a long, cool shower and maybe a nap, but first I'd have to call him back. With a sigh, I poured myself a glass of ice water and sank down at the kitchen table, phone in hand.

He answered on the second ring. "How are you?"

"I'm fine."

"Good. I was a little worried when I didn't hear from you."

"I said I'm fine!" I was snapping. I knew I was snapping, but I didn't appreciate the smothered feeling suddenly creeping up on me again.

"I'd like to see you today." His voice was soft, smooth, and persuasive.

"Want me to come by the house this afternoon?" And if I felt so smothered, why was I offering to see him?

"I was thinking more of the office." His chuckle filled my ear and I reminded myself the smothering was all me. Not him. Devon wasn't the kind to push, not like that, anyway.

Thoughts of Chambers filled my head. I wasn't ready to walk back into that office. "How about the house?"

"How about a date?" he countered.

"Deal. Is this another test?" I squinted out the back window.

"I guess that depends on you."

I had my shower and my nap, then slipped into a pair of Lucky jeans and a sleeveless, pale yellow turtleneck. By the time Devon showed up at 6:30, I was ready to go. He was wearing faded Levi's and another well-worn polo shirt. Before I could stop him, he'd stepped inside, cupped my face in his hand, and pressed a kiss to my lips.

Something about having him in the house, in such close proximity to the DVD, gave me the willies.

I leaned back, snagging my purse from the entry hall table and slinging it over my shoulder. "How was work?"

"Long." He gave me a tired smile, then whipped a long, narrow box out from behind his back and handed it to me. "For you."

My first thought was, of course, the yellow corset, but I wasn't even close. And all I could do was giggle. Lips pursed, I looked up at Devon and giggled some more while pointing to the fuzzy white bundle in the box. "For me?"

Grinning, he moved in closer, slid an arm around my waist, and said, "For you. Like it?"

"My own flogger." I lifted it out and shook it a bit to untangle the half-dozen strips of rabbit fur. "I love it," I said, smiling up at him.

"You do understand that it's for me to use on you."

That bit of news took me by surprise, but how could something that came from a cute, furry animal hurt?

He tucked me into his car, and, to my surprise, took me for a burger.

The tiny greasy spoon was filled with truckers and families, hardworking blue-collar people like the men I was so used to working with. Funny—I hadn't thought at all about my new job or the fact that I had just over a week until I started. From the booth behind us a baby squalled loudly enough to nearly bust my eardrum, and behind the counter what sounded like two dozen plates shattered.

"Feel like getting out of here?" he asked once we'd had our fill of greasy, salty hand-cut fries and equally greasy burgers. They were absolutely heavenly.

Wincing, I rubbed my ear and nodded.

"Come on." Devon tugged at my elbow and stood up.

Outside, the humid night air was quiet, relatively so anyway, with only the noise of trucks speeding up and down the nearby highway breaking the silence. After the noisy diner, I slid into Devon's Passat with a sigh of relief.

Ten minutes later the neon light of an all-night bowling alley pulled me from the carb-induced stupor I'd slid into.

"You're shitting me?" My jaw landed somewhere in the vicinity of my toes.

From beside me, Devon chuckled. "I gather you've never bowled."

"Never." I unhooked my seatbelt and let him lead me inside. This wasn't exactly what I'd been thinking of when I'd agreed to a date. He'd tried nothing at the diner and obviously had no intention of trying anything inside a crowded bowling alley. And judging from all the cars in the parking lot, it was crowded.

Inside, Devon paid for our shoes and our lane, then led me halfway down the alleyway, past families and groups of couples drinking beer and soda and . . . bowling.

The incredible normalness of it almost sent me into hysterics.

"I promise, it's fun." Devon sat at the tiny table and slid his Nikes off, and I followed suit, tying the ugly bowling shoes on my feet.

"I'm taking you at your word." I laughed.

Once we had our shoes on he took me over to a long rack of balls situated behind us and helped me pick one out.

"Not too heavy?"

I shook my head, grasping the neon orange ball to my chest. After he chose his own, we headed back to our lane, where an employee stood ready to set up our game.

"Can we get those bumper thingies like they have?" I asked, pointing to the family of five beside us.

Devon chuckled and gave the girl in the blue uniform a nod. Up went the bumpers. At least I wouldn't have to worry about gutter balls. He went first, knocking down all but two pins on his first try, then knocking those down on the second.

"Your turn," he said with a grin. He knew I didn't know how to bowl.

Sighing, I stood and smoothed my sweaty hands down my jeans before retrieving my ball. I rolled it over in my hand, finally getting my fingers settled in the holes, then quirked an eyebrow in Devon's direction. "Do these come with directions or what?"

With a smile, he led me out to the lane. He held my hand at chest level. The length of him pressed against me reminded me too much of our practice session with the whip. I exhaled, forcing myself to focus and listen. "Don't release the ball here. Release the ball at your hip. For now, just get used to the feel of the ball in your hand. Aim with your eyes and then swing. That's all there is to it."

"Yeah." I slowly nodded my head, then backed up a few steps and let her fly. The ball zigzagged down the lane like a drunken sailor, crashing into the pins in what seemed like slow motion. "Oh look, I knocked some down." I spun around and gave him my cheesiest grin.

Four. I knocked down four. Not an auspicious beginning.

"So"—Devon stood next to the ball return—"did you like being in charge the other night?"

"I suppose," I said with a shrug. *Hurry up, ball!*

He wrapped his fingers around my upper arm before I had a chance to slip past him. "Honestly."

"Honestly? Sort of, but not really." My ball came shooting out the ball return, thudding into Devon's. I walked over and picked it up, cradling it to my chest again. "I liked it. I think. I even understand it all better, but I don't want to be in charge, not with you."

He nodded slowly, his eyes warm with understanding.

For my second throw I knocked down six of the remaining eight pins. Turning to rejoin Devon, I gave him a tiny, smug smile that made him laugh. He motioned me over with a crook of his finger and we stood watching the child in the next lane throw a strike.

"Not bad." He patted my hip and retrieved his own ball. "How do you feel about whips now?"

"The rabbit flogger is cute?" I offered up halfheartedly.

He laughed again and promptly threw a strike. I saluted him from my seat before easing to my feet. "I really do like my flogger," I whispered once he was close enough to hear me over the sound of crashing pins and happy chatter around us.

"I'm glad."

This time I only knocked down two pins. "Looks like my winning streak is over," I said, almost to myself.

Devon sipped his beer and asked about high school as I rejoined him.

"I was too busy skipping class to play sports." I accepted the beer he handed me with a toast of thanks and stood watching as he knocked over seven of twelve, then the last five.

"I would have thought you'd be more competitive," he said when he finally rejoined me.

With a shrug, I took my turn, smiling slightly as the ball arced down the lane at a more respectable speed. "What about you?"

"Baseball and swim team."

"Ahhh, the boys of summer," I quipped, grinning. "Brothers or sisters?"

"Middle son of three." Standing, he handed me his plastic cup of beer to hold.

Damn him, he threw another strike! I drained the last of his beer and refilled his glass so he wouldn't notice, but of course he did. He didn't say a word, just smirked at me as I handed him his cup and prepared for my turn. "How do you feel about anal sex?"

I almost dropped my ball, and then nearly fell as I spun around in my bowling shoes. A glance at the family behind me assured me they hadn't heard his question.

He closed the short distance between us and smiled down at me. "You said you had a butt plug."

"Never with a man."

His howl of laughter drew stares, but I tuned them out and took my turn.

"Would you?" he asked when I turned back to face him.

"Maybe." How could I be turned on by such a casual, non-threatening, conversational exploration of my sex life? I had no clue. Maybe it was the beer.

This time he only knocked down ten of twelve. I stood at the table, watching and sipping my beer. The icy cold brew burned a path down my throat and slipped down into my legs. I doubted it would improve my game much.

We met at the ball return.

"Blindfold?" he asked.

"Probably." I shrugged. "What's a spreader bar?"

"A bar that keeps your legs spread."

Snorting in the face of his cheeky grin, I picked up my ball.

He leaned in, pressing his lips to my ear. "It usually hooks at your ankles but they have some that are made to go just above your knees. They even make them with shackles for your wrists. Interested?"

"Maybe." I grinned, then went and threw my first strike. With a tiny curtsy, I rejoined him.

"Mummification?" he asked, refilling my beer.

"Ew. I'm not even going to ask."

"Me either, but I thought I'd ask." He retrieved his ball, then turned, a pensive look on his face. "Paddles," he mouthed.

"Like wood?" I scrunched up my face to show my displeasure.

He nodded and adjusted his fingers.

"Uh-uh!"

"Leather straps?" He held out one hand and shrugged as casually as if he were asking whether I preferred red wine over white.

"No!"

"I didn't think so." He threw another strike, then rejoined me at the table. "So what do you have against spanking?"

"Children get spanked, not adults." I stood, ready to take my turn, conscious of his eyes boring into me. "Okay, fine," I said, leaning closer so only he could hear me, "spanking gets a maybe."

I lost and badly, but I wasn't a sore loser and Devon wasn't the type to gloat. Thank God.

Once we were safely settled back in his car, he started in again. "Your most secret fantasy?"

Sighing, I wiggled my back against the cushion, stretching out muscles I didn't recall ever using. Who knew bowling could actually give you a workout? "Wha—"

"Fantasy. Secret fantasy," he clarified.

"I . . . what's yours?"

"You."

Citing an early appointment with a new client, he left me at my front door with a kiss that ranked just above chaste.

I was stumped, not to mention horny and miserable, since I wasn't allowed to masturbate. And I had no idea what my deepest, darkest fantasy was.

6

Wednesday evening I coerced Lanie into meeting me for dinner. I'd spent the day driving myself nuts trying to figure Devon out. And of course, the fantasy thing.

Since Lanie's brother joined us, I had to wait until we got to her place afterward for an evening of movies and girl talk.

"I needed this." With a flick of my wrist I finished wrapping a rubber band around her braid. I patted her back and swung my leg over her head so I could stretch out on the couch.

"Okay, so spill it. How are thing going with Geek Meister? Or should I call him Kink Meister now?" Lanie swung her head around and rested it on the couch cushion so she could look up at me.

"I now understand the meaning of 'still waters run deep.' He, uh . . . he's an interesting man."

One eyebrow slowly rose as she gave me her most skeptical look. "How's it going, really? Are you okay with all this?"

I laughed softly at the memory of our evening spent bowling. "I like him a lot. More than I thought I would. More than I have anyone in a long time."

"Carlotta's in love," she sang, a shit-eating grin on her face.

"I wouldn't go that far." I gave her a stern look and sipped at my wine. "What's really weird is that he hasn't really *done* anything. We talked, we ate, we had sex, we played some . . . He showed me his whips."

Lanie went wide eyed at the mention of whips.

Grinning, I added, "He gave me one made out of rabbit that you'd just love." At that we both howled with laughter, then she scolded me for not bringing it with me. "He's played some head games. I guess it's normal," I added with a shrug. "Otherwise, the only thing he's really made me do is scrub his kitchen floor!" I regretted telling Lanie the minute the words were out of my mouth.

"What the fuck! You didn't?" She climbed the couch cushion until she was practically in my face.

I nodded slowly, my face warming in embarrassment, then filled her in on our shopping trip and my bad behavior. I couldn't tell shit like this to anyone but Lanie. Or Lexi.

"That sounds . . . demeaning," she said, wrinkling her nose.

"Yeah, it does, doesn't it? But you know, in a way, it wasn't. I was mad, though."

"I'd be mad too if some asshole made me clean his floor." She held out a Hershey's Kiss, then unwrapped one for herself, popping it into her mouth before she continued speaking. "Talk about cheap labor."

"In his defense, it was my idea." While the candy melted in my mouth, I argued with myself over how much I should defend Devon and whether or not I'd end up sounding like one of those weak women who were always rushing to defend their men. "I don't want to sound like I'm making excuses for him, but I sort of get it. That's not to say I agree. I just get it. Even if I don't get *him*. Hell, last night we went bowling. It's like he knew I needed time to adjust to being his sub."

"Bowling." She reached for the wine bottle on the floor beside her and refilled both our glasses. "What the fuck is that? I didn't even know people still bowled—outside of the Flintstones."

A snicker escaped at the Flintstones reference. "Well, it was fun." I sighed, trying to figure out where to start, how to explain it all to her. "He put me in charge Sunday night and I pushed him while we were having sex. I *wanted* to push his limits. I even told him he couldn't come, and he didn't. That's what he wants from me, and I guess I trust him enough to do that."

Despite our usual proclivity for playing together, neither Lanie nor I felt like fooling around. Though she did get a good laugh when she found out I *couldn't* fool around.

"What's your deepest, darkest fantasy?" I stretched, frowning unseeing at the movie. *Underworld* was one of my favorites.

"I dunno. Maybe an orgy." Shrugging as if it was no big deal, she threw me another chocolate and turned the TV's volume up. "What about you?"

"I dunno." For me, it was a big deal. I lay there giving the movie less than half of my attention, still bothered over the fact that I had no clue about my fantasy. What was that one incredibly forbidden thing I wanted (sexually) but had never told anyone?

"So, do you still get to go out on Friday?"

"Of course!" I gave her a firm nudge of irritation with my knee. "He doesn't *own* me."

"Then bring him to the bar. I want to meet him."

7

By Thursday morning my skin was crawling with need. I swallowed my pride and called Devon at his office to find out if we could get together this evening.

"How about lunch here at the office," he countered.

"How about you skip work and come here?" I stretched out, wiggling my toes under the comforter and wishing like hell I could masturbate.

"Where's the challenge in that?"

"Challenge?"

"Yeah. There's no risk getting caught, no challenge. I'm not saying we can't ever have vanilla sex, but not today."

There was no getting out of this one. "Should I wear my tool belt?"

"How about you and a coat and nothing underneath." I could hear the smile in his voice.

"I could do that, too," I purred, squirming at the thought. "What time?"

"Noon? I'll order lunch."

* * *

At noon straight up I stepped into Devon's office wearing a red thong, a red Ralph Lauren knee-length coat, and matching high heels. A little frisson of tension danced up my spine as I glanced over the ceiling. It *looked* normal.

The entire front of the small office space was tinted one-way glass, and a gray room divider separated his workspace from what I guessed would be a reception area someday.

Devon smiled at me in a way that made me squeeze my thighs together and dismiss my reservations. The young delivery guy tucked a red moneybag under his arm and turned to leave, barely giving me more than a red-faced smile.

"Chicken salad and fresh fruit." Devon pulled paper-wrapped sandwiches and Styrofoam cups of fruit from the bag and fixed both our plates.

"Sounds good." I dropped my purse, containing a half dozen condoms, on the desk and shoved my keys into my pocket. "Should I lock the door?"

"I'm not expecting anyone."

I bit my lower lip in an effort to hold back a grin. "What exactly do you do anyway?"

"I build custom computers, mostly for gamers. And I do some CADD work, some Web site design."

"Couldn't you do that from home?" The coat's soft flannel lining tickled my nipples.

"I could. But I'd probably never leave the house if I did. And I need room to spread my stuff out. Eventually I want to hire a receptionist. Let's eat," he said, pushing my plate toward me.

"Here? Now? I thought—" I'd thought we were going to do the horizontal boogie. I glanced around the sparsely furnished office. Or vertical boogie, as the case might end up being.

"We are, but what's the rush?"

"This is another game, isn't it?" Smiling in understanding, I sank into a chair and accepted the plate he offered. Legs crossed, I balanced it on one knee.

"You catch on fast," he said, a calculated expression on his face.

"So we just sit here like two normal people having lunch . . . or do you want me to blow you while you eat?" I eased back in the chair, letting my coat slide open to the tops of my thighs. Even if Devon couldn't see them from his position behind the desk, I could.

"Eat. You can blow me later." Devon leaned forward, grinning, and a lock of his dark hair fell across his forehead, making him look even younger and more charming.

"Tell me about Annie?" I took a bite of the chicken salad, then watched for his reaction. I wasn't trying to be mean or even to push him, I was just curious.

His eyes widened briefly in surprise and he stared at me for a minute before responding. "I'll tell you about Annie, if you tell me something."

"What?"

"Anything . . . Something no one knows."

"Trust, right?" I arched an eyebrow in understanding.

He nodded slowly and took a bite of his sandwich, chewing as he watched me.

I mulled it over while chewing a piece of kiwifruit. "I hate my mother. I never see her, never call her."

"Why?"

"She's weak. I hate her because she's weak."

"And Carlotta values strength," he said softly, knowingly.

Now it was my turn to nod. "She just . . . *exists*. She doesn't *live*. My papa was a hard-ass. Like I said, he liked the belt, but I could take it." I shrugged. "Mama, she lived to serve. She thought that was enough. That's no kind of life."

"Maybe it was enough for her."

"Maybe it shouldn't have been!"

He gave me a calming smile. "I'm not going to argue with you about how you feel." He pursed his lips and glanced down at the desk before meeting my gaze head on. "Annie was a sweet woman. Sweet and strong in her own quiet way. The quintessential steel magnolia."

I stifled a brief pang of jealousy at the quiet emotion in his voice. "You miss her."

"Just because I miss her doesn't mean my life should end too. She wouldn't want that."

"My friends think I'm crazy, you know."

"Aren't we all a little crazy?"

I set my plate down and stood up, tired of verbal games. Circling the desk, I pushed his plate out of the way and sat in front of him, with my legs propped on either side of his chair. "I suppose so."

"You're supposed to be eating your lunch."

"I'm not hungry." For food. Or talk. "Why won't you whip me?" Frowning, I leaned forward, elbows propped on my knees so we were nearly face to face.

"You're not ready."

"How long does it take?"

"When you're ready," he said with a nod.

"How long did it take Annie?"

"Months."

"Were you a Dom before you met her?" I unknotted the coat's belt and let it fall open. From outside came the chatter of two women passing by.

"Yeah. We met at a dungeon in Savannah." His hands were on my ankles and slowly sliding higher as he talked. "She was a sub, and I was new and curious. I'd trained with another Dom for almost a year but hadn't found the right woman yet. Why are we talking about my wife?"

"I'm curious." I leaned forward and gently combed his hair off his forehead, enjoying the way it slid through my fingers.

"Tell me about the first time you had sex." His hands glided over my thighs, his thumbs gently kneading tender skin and sending soft electrical impulses to my pussy.

"Does kissing a girl count?"

"No." He reached higher, and I arched my hips off the desk so he could remove my panties.

"I was fourteen." Every inch of me tingled, thinking of the parking lot full of cars outside and the unlocked door. Anyone could walk by; anyone could walk in. "He was sixteen. A neighborhood boy."

"Did you like it?" he asked, standing up. The rasp of his zipper was loud even over the pounding of my heart in my chest.

"It hurt."

I felt his cock nudging at my entrance, then grunted as he roughly shoved his way inside, filling me.

"The second time?"

"A girl," I replied, locking my legs around his waist. "My mother caught us." I laughed at the memory and at his cock pumping in and out of me until I could barely catch my breath.

"Tell me." He slowed his pace while touching me with only his cock and his hands that grasped the tops of my thighs. Sweat beaded on his upper lip.

"She lectured me—I was going to hell—and dragged me to confession."

"Little Catholic Carlotta." He grinned down at me, that lock of hair back across his forehead.

"Lapsed," I gasped, then moaned as my head rolled back. The sweet, thick scent of ripe strawberries and cantaloupe filled my nostrils.

"Faithless."

"Hellbound."

"Godless."

"Heathen," I howled, laughing at the top of my lungs. "The boy."

"Huh?" Devon's face had started to turn red and his eyes were tight as he struggled for control.

"He knocked my sister up." With another laugh, I pushed my lunch onto the floor and lay back across the desk, eyes closed as Devon used me, punished me, though I wasn't quite sure what for. I didn't care either. Until he pulled out and finished himself off with his hand, spilling his semen onto my stomach.

I lay there gasping and unsatisfied, but also uncaring somehow. "You miss her?" I murmured. It took him so long to answer, I was afraid he hadn't heard me, and I wasn't sure I wanted to repeat the question.

"Every fucking day."

He sounded hoarse, raw, as raw as I suddenly felt. I struggled into a sitting position, aware of the sticky, cloudy fluid trickling down my belly, and pulled him into my arms. I felt things I hadn't expected to feel as I sat there hugging him. I felt things I didn't want to feel as his warm breath tickled my back and his labored breathing filled my ears.

Hurt, pain, and anguish colored with a tinge of anger, and all of it his.

Not mine. Or was it? I closed that door, refusing to look too closely. "I'm sorry."

He pushed himself out of my arms. "Let's get out of here."

I shrugged back into my coat while Devon, who refused to let me wipe his semen off my belly, got dressed. I followed him in my 4Runner, which I parked in his garage at a motion of his hand.

Neither of us spoke until we were inside, in his bedroom.

"I'm going to shackle you to the bed, Carlotta."

A tingle of excitement ran through me, and desire, sharp and hot, knotted my belly. Words weren't necessary. Instead, I untied my coat and slid it off my shoulders, letting it fall to the carpet at my feet. "My panties are still in your office."

He waggled an eyebrow at me and ushered me to the bed, where he already had the cuffs attached to the headboard.

"You planned this," I said, handing him the box with the rabbit flogger.

"Guilty." He set it on the bed beside a sturdier-looking one.

"I'm going out tomorrow night." I stretched out on the bed and kicked off my shoes, wriggling against the chilly cotton sheets.

Devon disappeared into the bathroom and I heard the sound of running water. I closed my eyes and blew out a heavy breath to calm the pounding of my heart. I tugged at the cuffs where they were attached to the bed, reminding myself to be patient, to be a good slave and wait to see what Devon had in store for me.

He returned naked, his hair mussed, and a red washcloth in his hand. He gently wiped the dried semen off my belly, then instructed me to roll over and get on my knees. He knelt on the bed and placed one of my wrists in the cuff but didn't buckle it.

"I'm not going to strap them . . . this time." Circling the bed, he repeated the process with the other wrist. "So you think you're ready to be whipped?" His hands skimmed across the globe of my ass to grasp my thighs and push my knees farther under me.

Then he picked up the rabbit flogger.

He was right. It didn't hurt a bit as he flicked it across the backs of my thighs and across my back, letting me adjust to the feel of it.

Finally I understood what he meant about being desensitized to it. But kneeling on that bed with my ass in the air and pussy lips spread left me hungry for more. More of anything—everything.

He switched to a suede flogger made of pigskin, and knelt on the bed behind me, massaging my ass with deep, firm strokes.

Then he snapped the suede flogger lightly against my ass. Just enough so I felt it but not so it hurt. He was teasing me. Testing me. I moaned softly, resting my head on the pillow he'd given me.

He massaged my ass cheek again then flicked the flogger, harder this time. Hard enough to make me squeak.

"Too much?"

All I could do was nod and moan and rub my nipples back and forth against the sheets, wishing they weren't so nice, so smooth, that they were rough and coarse and would take away the ache that ate at my skin as he continued to slowly whip me until it didn't sting anymore. Time and place had lost all meaning. It was just me and him and the pig suede. A slow, sweet heat spread outward from my bottom, invading my pussy and setting my skin on fire. I wanted Devon to fuck me like he'd done in his office.

"Breathe, Carlotta." His voice filled my head, and I inhaled deeply, sucking in the taste and scent of sex. My sex.

My fingers tightened around the straps until my nails dug into the palms of my hands, and I blew out a long, slow breath, sucking in another one.

"Breathe."

My belly tightened painfully, and I forced myself to focus on my breathing and not think. Not think about the whip, biting lightly into my skin, about Devon's hands roughly massaging any sting away, about my pussy weeping, begging for release. He hadn't told me I couldn't come and the orgasm, the release building inside me, was big. Huge, in fact. So I focused on that and breathing.

Every inch of me tingled in anticipation of the next blow and the next. I thrust my bottom higher, as high as I could, welcoming each light bite of the flogger into my skin.

"Harder?" Devon's own heavy breathing filled my ears, followed by my own loud moan.

"Fuck me," I ground out from between my teeth. "Fuck me, please."

"Answer me." The next bite of the flogger was almost as good as having Devon's cock inside of me, and I screamed as the shock reverberated in my pussy.

"Yes!"

"Come for me, Carlotta."

I wanted nothing more than to obey Devon's harshly given order, but I wasn't quite there. "Please!" I was so slick, so wet, so swollen and hungry I thought I might die. But Devon never let up, just maintained that same steady rhythm on my backside, on my ass and thighs, and it took three more lashes before I finally came, my pussy empty but the rest of me somehow strangely satisfied by the time it died down.

The last aftershock had barely died down before Devon was inside me, hot and thick. Fucking me in a hard, steady rhythm, his dick driving in and out of me, pushing me right back up that staircase I'd just fallen down. Despite the speed, the depth, and his apparent need, Devon never lost control as he covered my body with his. His skin was warm and sweaty against the hypersensitive skin of my back, and the stubble on his chin scraped my shoulder, driving me crazy. Driving me higher.

"Don't stop!"

His tongue was in my ear, and I squealed, and then he was saying something I couldn't quite make out. He cradled me against the mattress, his warm breath filling my ear as I rested my head against the pillow in anticipation of the climax we both wanted. I bucked against him, driving him deeper inside me with each thrust. "More . . . more."

I wanted more. I wanted it all. I could barely breathe from his death grip on me. The arms squeezing me. I couldn't think. All I could do was focus on pushing him higher, on pushing *me* higher, until the first wave of my climax hit and my grip on the arm restraints tightened. I bucked against him, welcoming each rolling wave, the heat and weight of Devon inside me and on me. Even the soft lambswool padding of the cuffs against my skin heightened the effect.

Devon sagged against me, the weight of him making breathing difficult. "I miss her," he panted softly, so softly I almost didn't hear him, "but I love you."

I couldn't even process his words. Instead, I just lay there trying to catch my breath. Trying to figure out how to respond or even if I should.

He slipped from my body and gently removed my hands from the restraints before he curled up against my back.

"I just want to love you, Carlotta. I don't want anything else." His hand against my back, running the length of my skin down to my hip, was heavy with the weight of his words.

Everything inside me screamed at me to get up, to leave, but I couldn't seem to bring myself to move. I was too satiated from good sex to even think of moving. Slowly, I lifted a heavy hand and pushed my hair off my face. "Devon?"

"You don't have to say anything. I shouldn't have even said—"

I rolled over to face him, and quickly took in the serious, turbulent expression in his eyes. "I've never been in love. I don't even know what I'm supposed to be feeling right now. Or what to say. Other than the truth"—I wet my lips with my tongue—"but I'm not so naive to think the truth will set me free."

"You can be as free as you want." He reached up and cupped my face in his hand, his fingers gentle against my skin—in their own way, as gentle as when he'd used the flogger on me.

"Can we . . . just see how things go?"

He nodded and the furrows in his forehead smoothed themselves out. "I won't hurt you, but I will push you."

I laid my head on the pillow and he tucked my curls behind my ear, gently rubbing my earlobe as he did so. My mind was still screaming for me to leave but my body refused. All my defenses were down but I couldn't seem to bring myself to care. For the first time in a long time I felt safe, like it was okay if he saw inside me because no matter what I did, he'd still accept what was inside me.

He wasn't someone I could keep out no matter how hard I might try, and I didn't feel like trying anymore.

8

The following morning I woke up to the feel of Devon's lips pressed against my forehead. He was dressed in sharply creased chinos and a lime green shirt. The smell of Dial soap mixed with his aftershave tickled my nostrils. I stretched and wiggled away, and then stretched again, slower this time, testing for sore spots. My bottom was a bit tender but otherwise, there weren't any. "Morning."

"Morning." He took a seat, the bed sinking under his weight. "I've got a meeting this morning."

"Wanna do lunch again?" I asked with a sleepy giggle.

"Greedy girl." He reached out and tweaked a nipple. "I can't. Though I'll probably need it after spending the morning with Uncle Doug."

"Chambers?" A shot of fear had me suddenly sitting upright in bed.

"Yeah, he's a friend of Uncle Doug's. I'll be back about four and I'll leave you the extra garage door opener in your car in case you need to go out for anything."

"Thanks," I mumbled absently. I was still stuck on his meeting with Chambers and barely noted the fact he'd left until I heard the rumble of the garage door descending.

Panic descended in a rush that had my stomach doing flip-flops. Rolling over, I dug my cell phone out of my purse and speed-dialed Lexi. If I were lucky, she'd be in her office on her first break.

"Hello?" The sound of heavy machinery made hearing her almost impossible. Apparently, I wasn't lucky.

"Can you have lunch?" I asked in a rush. How could I wait until lunch?

"Not today, babe."

Kicking the covers aside, I sat on the edge of the bed. "I'm in trouble."

"What did Devon do?"

"It's not that! He has a meeting with Chambers today?"

"You don't think—" She didn't have to finish the sentence; I already had at least a dozen times in my head.

"He wouldn't dare. But if I call him, he will for sure. What the fuck am I gonna do, Lexi?"

"First thing, relax! I seriously doubt Chambers would say anything to Devon about the DVD . . . would he?" A door closed, shutting out the sound of backhoes and dump trucks at the construction site.

"He wouldn't dare," I said, almost more to myself than her.

"Maybe you should have told him." Him, of course, being Devon.

"It's too late now."

"I'm sure he'll understand."

"I hope like hell you're right."

While I was backing out of Devon's driveway, I was dialing his cell phone to leave a reminder about meeting the girls tonight at Jimmy Z's. It went immediately to voice mail, and after leaving a message, I hung up and sped down the road toward the interstate, resigning myself to a solitary afternoon of fretting. And not just about Chambers, but about that garage door opener. Forcing oxygen into my lungs, I flipped on the radio and let the sound of the Mambo Kings take me home.

How could Devon be so sure he loved me? That he even knew me? Though I couldn't deny that he did know me. The knot brought on by his declaration of love returned with a vengeance. After a garage door opener came a key.

At home my marigolds were beginning to wilt. I went out to turn on the hose. I felt as if I'd been gone for days instead of overnight, as if I didn't even know my own house, and I tried to see it through Devon's eyes. What had he seen the first time he walked through the door? I sniffed the air. Good, but a bit stale. I slid open the glass sliding door. Everything was pristine, perfect, orderly, like my life had been up until the point I'd met Devon and recklessly decided to fuck him.

I thought of the DVD tucked in the bottom of my nightstand. What were the chances of Chambers saying something? I didn't think he'd dare, but then, I also hadn't thought he'd stoop low enough to tape me in the first place. I called my nail technician about getting my nail fixed and decided to treat myself to a pedicure as well. It was better than spending the afternoon pacing my living room until I was sick, and Marilee's spa pedicures were worthy of a nap.

By the time I dropped my keys on the kitchen counter, I'd convinced myself that Chambers would keep his trap shut and all would be right with the world. But whether or not I should even tell Devon was another matter. Was it moot? We only had another week to go. Then again, I had a feeling we'd end up being together longer than a week.

The caller ID on the kitchen phone showed another call from Devon. I checked my messages and dialed his number, wondering why he hadn't just called my cell phone. All I'd wanted to do was confirm our plans for tonight and let him know where to meet me.

"How did your meeting go?" I collapsed on the couch and propped my freshly pedicured feet on the table to admire the ten perfect coral toes.

"Hello to you too." He sounded distracted. "It was . . . interesting."

"Is that good or bad?"

"Good for business."

Sighing in relief, I sank deeper into the cushions. "That's fabulous! About tonight—"

"I can't make it."

"Oh." A sharp stab of disappointment lodged itself somewhere between my lungs—along with something else. I stared at my feet wondering what to say.

There were ten very long seconds of dead silence on the phone, and I realized how quiet it was. "Why didn't you tell me?" he asked.

Even though I'd been expecting it, dreading it, I felt as if all the air had been sucked out of my little house. There was no playing dumb. That wasn't my scenario anyway. "I handled it," I sighed softly.

"You . . . '*handled it*'?" His voice sounded controlled, too controlled.

"Yes! I handled it. I got the DVD back, end of story."

"He asked me if we'd watched it, and it was everything I could do not to punch his lights out!" By now he was yelling in the phone. Honestly, he was so even-tempered that a mad Devon was completely alien, and very scary, to me. "How could you not tell me, Carlotta? Especially this morning when you knew I was going to see him?"

"I didn't think he'd—I handled it!" I insisted, my own voice rising.

"Like you handle everything? Like you handle your life? When's the last time you saw your mother, Carlotta? Or your sister?"

"What the hell does my mother have to do with any of this?"

"Everything! You sit there happy and content in your pristine house, thinking you've got everything under control, because you're in control. Because no one tells Carlotta what to do! You didn't think it was important enough to tell me? No, don't answer that. You handled it because you're in control. You don't trust anyone to help you, to do anything for you. Answer me this. Are you more like your mother or your father?"

I wanted to be sick but of course couldn't, not on my pretty, expensive rug.

"Good-bye, Carlotta."

The phone hummed in my ear, and when it became annoying I let it fall to my lap. Then it started beeping. I shut it off. The leather couch stuck to the backs of my thighs. I refused to whisper the Hail Mary that nudged me or laugh at the situation I'd gotten myself into, at what my mama would say if I called her up and told her my boyfriend had just dumped me because I hadn't told him about the porno of us my former boss had made, and told her I'd almost said a Hail Mary. A bubble of hysterical laughter threatened, welled up, but I refused to let it out.

Aren't you proud of me, Mama?

9

Inside Jimmy Z's the music was loud, the bar was crowded, and I wanted to be anyplace other than where I was. Then again, the last thing I wanted was to spend another minute alone.

I'd excused myself, hoping that a few minutes in the ladies' room would help me pull myself together and maybe even come up with a reason to leave. At the sight of Lexi sitting all alone and looking more miserable than I'd seen her in ages, I decided staying was a necessity.

"What's the matter?" I asked, giving her a hug.

"They're sending Wade to Kansas." She gave the swizzle stick in her Woo Woo a halfhearted tap.

"I'm sorry, honey, but you knew it was coming." And I really was. I knew how much she liked him and vice versa.

"I know."

"Where's Lanie?" I asked after motioning for a refill.

She pointed to the dance floor, then motioned for Brian to bring her a refill, too. It was so jammed with gyrating, swaying bodies I couldn't see Lanie or Cherise.

Lexi leaned over and rested her head on my shoulder. "If I get too fucked up, will you drive me home?"

"If I get too fucked up, I'll pay for a cab for both of us." Smiling up at Brian, I ordered another Apple Judy: Grand Marnier, vodka, and apple juice.

"What time is Devon due?" she asked, sipping her drink.

"He's not." I leveled a steady gaze at her and let my words sink in.

Her head dipped slightly and she winced, mouthing a distinct but unheard, "shit."

After my third Apple Judy, I left Lexi alone to mope and went in search of Lanie and a distraction. Any distraction. I found her on the dance floor with Cherise, who was busy feeling her up.

I was free. I could get laid tonight without having anyone fuck with my head. I could masturbate, I could fool around with Lanie and Cherise all night long if I wanted. A real girls' night.

I slithered up behind Lanie, who was dressed in a short halter dress that barely covered her ass, and followed Cherise's hands up her bare legs. I grew hornier by the minute, watching Cherise put the moves on Lanie. She smiled at me over Lanie's shoulder and flicked a pink tongue out from between her lips before burying her face in Lanie's neck. Then she backed up and grooved to something by Santana. I couldn't place the song but it sounded Spanish with a bit of blues and hip-hop thrown in for good measure.

Smiling in appreciation, I leaned in and pressed my lips to Lanie's ear. "She's got nice tits."

Lanie turned and pressed her lips to mine, her tongue skillfully dueling with mine. *I didn't care. I didn't care. I didn't care.*

I didn't care if I was supposed to. If I wasn't. If anyone saw or what anyone thought.

I was in charge.

Cherise moved in again, pressing herself against Lanie and slipping a hand under her dress. I danced and watched, a feral grin on my face, enjoying the show until Lanie gave me a look. Following the direction of her eyes, I looked back and laughed and then made myself scarce.

Once Lanie, Jeff, and Cherise were an item, my presence was no longer necessary. I lost myself in the crowd, dancing a few minutes with this man or that before I'd slither away and lose myself in the hot, sweaty throng again. Until somehow or other Lexi and I ended up seeing who could down the most shooters, and Brian poured us into a cab.

Thank God it was Saturday.

My head throbbed with waves of pain. Self-inflicted pain. Did Lexi feel as awful as I did right now? God, I hoped not.

I yanked the covers over my head and burrowed deeper in bed to protect myself from the sunlight sneaking through the blinds, but I couldn't avoid my head, my gritty eyes, or my mouth. *Ick!*

With a sigh of resignation, I slogged out to the kitchen, stumbled through making coffee, and forced down four ibuprofen with a very small OJ chaser. Then I hit the shower, where I stayed until the hard spray had beat the edge off my pounding head and the water had begun to cool.

I just might live, and a steaming cup of coffee loaded with sugar and cream confirmed the verdict. Dressed in a faded pair of black yoga pants and a tank top, I carried my cup out back and sank into a chair with a sigh of relief. I'd no sooner gotten settled in my chair than the phone began to ring. Easing to my feet, I stepped inside and retrieved the phone from its cradle beside the coffeepot.

"'Lo," I croaked, and took another sip of my coffee.

"Glad I'm not the only one suffering," Lexi groaned.

"Morning, Sunshine." I chuckled and cleared my throat. "Did you talk to Wade?"

"I'll see him later this morning. Listen, I know this is last minute, but I was wondering if you'd like to do brunch here at my house tomorrow?"

"Deviate from the norm?" It hurt too much to even arch an eyebrow at the thought.

"Yes, deviate from the norm. Just a little going-away thing for Wade." She sighed, reminding me how miserable she was at Wade's upcoming transfer.

"Absolutely, sweetness. What do you want me to bring?"

We chatted a bit about Sunday before the subject turned to how to get our cars from Jimmy Z's. It was decided that she and Wade would pick me up later this morning.

The bar's parking lot looked abandoned, littered with trash and starkly empty compared to the previous night, except of course for Lexi's truck and my poor 4Runner.

"Thanks again, Wade."

Lexi's voice stopped me before I could slide out of his oversized Ford F-250. "Busy tonight?"

I knew what she was trying to do—run post-breakup interference—but it wouldn't work. "I'm fine." I climbed down, hitting the alarm on my keychain as I went.

Lexi followed, slamming the truck's door. "Are you just gonna let him go?"

"What else can I do?" Shrugging, I yanked open the SUV's door and tossed my purse into the passenger seat.

"You could apologize."

"I did. Devon is the sort who views trust as something sacred." *And I violated that.*

"Well, for what it's worth, I think you should do *something.*"

I nodded, then gave her a hug and firm instructions to screw

Wade's brains out as a thank-you from both of us, before climbing in the 4Runner. Wade, being the gentleman he was, waited until I had the 4Runner started and moving, even going so far as to follow me out of the parking lot, though he and Lexi turned the opposite way.

I think you should do something.

Lexi's words rang in my head. The hangover had been all I could deal with all morning. And of course the hangover was due to getting dumped. Now I remembered why I normally skipped the whole boyfriend thing all together. I didn't like dealing with the issues, the arguments, the jealousies over his time and my time and his friends and my friends, and if I was super-unlucky, he felt threatened by the fact I'd slept with my best friend. Never mind that she was one of the few women I'd ever slept with in my life.

I think you should do something.

What? Beg? Plead? It wasn't my M.O.

Sighing, I cranked up the radio and let Joss Stone keep me company all the way home. In my driveway, I hit the remote for the garage door opener and smiled as the door slid open.

A plan took shape at the very edge of my mushy brain. I still had Devon's garage door opener. Obviously returning it would make a hell of a legitimate excuse to visit, but what in the world would I say? I slid out and closed the door, my mind still on how to shape the plan into something workable.

Digging through the hall closet, I located a short black jacket. It was more of a car coat and barely reached my knees. In the bathroom, I carefully applied a light coating of makeup—just enough to hide my paleness—and slicked an ultra-demure shade of pink on my lips. From the shelves in my closet I pulled down some killer black Jimmy Choo pumps and stepped into them. Last, but not least, I retrieved the DVD of Devon and me stashed in my nightstand.

I stopped and stared at myself in the mirror, debating panties and/or a bra. Wisdom dictated that I should put same on, at the very least, just in case I got stopped by the police. I yanked open the drawer, quickly scanning the rows of matching sets, then again more slowly, until I located the one I wanted. It was a pale yellow, ultrasheer thong and bra, embroidered with delicate daisy chains. The ensemble went well with my choice of makeup. The DVD in hand, I headed out, stopping long enough to call Devon. No answer. I tried the office. Again, no answer. I left a message on his cell phone, letting him know I was on my way over to return his garage door opener. And then I was on my way.

Devon's car wasn't in the drive when I arrived. My stomach tightened with nerves as I hit the button on the remote. The garage door eased up, revealing the moving boxes stacked in one corner, waiting to be unpacked, another stack against the wall, broken down and waiting for recycling day, and a workbench, empty of tools—but no car.

Waving to the woman next door watering her flowers, I eased the 4Runner into his garage and closed the door behind me. Then I tried Devon's cell phone again.

This time he answered.

Swallowing the lump in my throat, I forced out a greeting. "How are you?"

"You could have just mailed me the garage door opener, Carlotta," he countered, ignoring my question.

"I wanted to return it in person."

"I'll be there in five, just go ahead and leave it on the counter."

"And"—I choked down the lump in my throat—"leave . . . the garage door open?"

"I told you—"

"Please?" I'd never begged for anything in my life. It was

new and not a pleasant feeling. It left a funny taste in my mouth. Or maybe that was remnants of last night's drinking binge.

"Please what?" he asked, his voice husky with emotion.

I slid out of the car and entered Devon's house. It was as peaceful and quiet and tidy as when I'd left Thursday morning. "I want to see you. Just for a minute."

His sigh filled my ear. "I'll give you five minutes."

I hung up and quickly peeled off my clothes, lying them in a tidy pile in the easy chair. Then I turned my attention to Devon's television. It was big, a forty-two-inch Sony affair with the DVD player tucked away on a shelf underneath. I dug the DVD out of my purse and slid it into the player before climbing onto the couch, nervously wondering how fast I could get myself turned on. Or if it were even possible considering the state I was in.

After I hit PLAY, the picture that filled the screen showed me naked but for my tank top and socks, while poor Devon just looked shocked and excited. Getting turned on wouldn't be much of a problem.

I shivered and let my hands drift over my thighs while I watched the DVD. They slipped between my legs, spreading my pussy lips, and dipped themselves in the slight dampness of my cunt. On screen I was yanking Devon's shirt off and intermittently playing with myself, teasing him with fingers wet with my juices. The memory helped excite me. I spit on my fingers, anxious now to get the ball rolling, anxious at the feel of my clit swelling slightly under my fingers. Anxious at the sight of myself on TV, bent over Devon's desk and laughingly telling him to fuck me, fuck me hard. He had and I'd enjoyed every minute of it. I was enjoying it again, even more so if that were possible. I made myself concentrate on *me* and not the sound of Devon's car in the drive or his footsteps in the hall. When Devon walked in and found me masturbating on his couch, I made my fingers continue to stroke my clit, dipping them in my pussy and spreading the wetness around. Tension and need coiled in my belly.

"What the hell are you doing?"

My head rolled back, and I smiled up at him. He looked hot and rumpled and sweet. "Forgive me, Devon, for I have sinned." My fingers never stopped.

"How long has it been since your last confession?" He never took his eyes off me as he dropped his keys on the sofa table and circled the couch where he could see me better.

"I don't remember." I wet my lips with the tip of my tongue.

"Your sins?" he practically panted.

"I've been vain and narrow-minded and untrusting." God, I wanted to come. "I kept a secret when I shouldn't have, and I hurt someone I care about."

"How do you think you should be punished?" He pushed the coffee table out of the way with his foot, grabbed the remote, and started the DVD over again before unbuttoning his shirt and kicking off his shoes.

"Spank me."

He was hard, his erection perfectly outlined by his pants. "Keep playing with yourself." He frowned down at me and my fingers instantly stilled. "Don't stop," he whispered, licking his lips.

I sat there, my legs spread, every intimate inch of me exposed. To my surprise, he turned and watched the television for a few minutes before facing me again. I sat there, waiting for him to speak, my heart slamming against my ribs, my pussy throbbing with need. Would he kick me out?

"I have never been so angry, Carlotta. Ever!" By now he was down on his knees beside me. My fingers slowed again. "I didn't say you could stop."

For a minute I wished, hoped, he'd lean down and help me. Instead, he rested a hand on my calf, never taking his eyes off of my face. His hand slid lower, briefly sinking into the wetness of my pussy before sliding lower, to gently probe at my ass.

"Can I come?" God, I wanted to. My hips tightened, thrusting outward, begging for more.

"Can you?"

I licked my lips and tried again. "May I come, please?"

He shook his head. "Do you understand now? Do you get it? At some point, honey, you've got to start letting people in; you've got to realize you're not perfect and you're not always in control. Sometimes you need help. And needing help doesn't make you weak. And as much as I love you, I don't think I want to see you again."

I knew exactly how hard it was for him to say those words, to be so honest, because there was no mistaking the sadness in his eyes. Deep inside me, the need to run ate at me and my fingers slowed again. If I left, I proved him right. But if I stayed, what would I say? What should I say? "Please?"

"Come," he whispered with a nod.

It roared through me, pushing my hips even higher off the couch and a scream from the back of my throat. Finally, I collapsed against the cushions, struggling for air. Devon pressed a kiss to the back of my thigh and softly instructed me not to move. I couldn't have even if I'd wanted to. He returned from the bathroom a few minutes later and cleaned me up.

"What do we do now?" he asked.

His question surprised me since he always seemed to have all the answers. "What do you want to do?"

"I think the bigger question is, what do you want to do?" he countered.

"I want to be with you."

"What's your fantasy, Carlotta?"

"You. Just you." My heart hurt and my eyes prickled, burned. I knelt down beside him on the floor and wrapped my arms around his waist. "Please."

* * *

I woke up early to the sound of my cell phone ringing. Leaning over the edge of the bed, I rummaged around in my purse until I had my hand wrapped around it, and flipped it open.

"You're not at home," Lexi sang softly in my ear.

"No, I'm not."

Devon dragged me halfway across the bed and held me tight against him.

"Are you still coming this morning?"

"What time is it?" I sleepily scrubbed at my face.

"Eight-thirty. You're supposed to bring the croissants, champagne, and orange juice."

"Oh shit. There's no way I can get champagne this morning. Damnit, Lexi. I'm sorry! I forgot!" I sat up, struggling out of Devon's embrace and propping myself on the pillow.

"Relax," she said, "I knew something was up when I tried to call last night and no one answered, so we picked some up already. Just get the OJ and the croissants and get you and Devon here by ten-thirty."

Epilogue

We were all clustered around the sink in Lexi's kitchen while the men—Jeff, Wade, and Devon—sat on the back porch shooting the shit as only men can do. A smile pasted on my face, I sipped the mimosa I was almost too tired to drink.

"I'm exhausted." Lexi sank against the counter with a laugh.

"And how is Wade?" I hated her just for a minute. She looked so damn happy and carefree. Then I reminded myself that Wade was leaving.

"Other than leaving me, he's great." She rolled her eyes, as if she were as disgusted about how happy she was as the rest of us. "The transfer comes with a promotion." Lexi gave me a conspiratorial grin and a wink before turning her attention to Lanie. "So, do you rate Cherise or Jeff?"

I felt more relaxed than I'd been in months, and I wondered what Devon had done to me—or for me.

"Before we talk about Jeff, let's talk about Cherise." Lanie slid onto the counter after a quick glance outside.

"I like her," Lexi said.

"Me too," I added. "I think we should add her to the group." I held up a hand before they could say anything. "Think about it. We can vote next weekend."

Lexi nodded. "Now, what happened with Jeff?"

"The threesome was incredible." Lanie smiled and took another sip of her drink. "Jeff took me out Saturday night but refused to sleep with me, and . . . my dad's a cheating skeezer."

"What?" I stared in shock, wondering what I'd missed. She looked awful happy for someone whose dad was a cheater. And for someone who hadn't gotten laid.

Lexi flipped open the waffle iron, peeled the waffle out, and added it to the stack before pouring more batter.

"Uh, Lex, did you not hear her?" I re-covered the waffles with foil to keep them warm.

"I heard her, and frankly, I can't say I'm surprised. Her dad's a prick."

"A-men!" Lanie slid off the counter and pulled her casserole from the oven. "I think I'm gonna make Jackie my business partner."

"Lan—" I frowned in concern.

"If things continue to go as well as they have," she added, waving a pot holder in my direction.

"Are you okay?" Lexi asked softly, with a glance in my direction.

"Devon wants me to go to some party this afternoon." I smiled from behind my champagne glass.

Lanie snorted softly. "Must be the day for it. I'm supposed to go to some party at Jeff's mom's house, but he didn't mention it last night and I'm not sure I want to go." She shrugged and picked up a knife, slicing the warm egg concoction into twelve even pieces.

"How come you're not going?" Lexi asked. "Might be fun."

"Dudette, I'm just not sure about this whole *dating* thing."

"You never know if you don't give it a shot," I said softly.

"And then there's the fact he wouldn't sleep with me last night," she hissed, leaning across the counter.

I snorted and snuck another quick look outside at the men. They were laughing at something, and judging from their half-full glasses, they'd need refills soon. Time was running out. "If we don't get out there soon, they're going to come looking for us. Did he give a reason?"

"He said he wouldn't sleep with me again until he knew me better."

"Which means you have to play by his rules, or not at all." I gave Lexi a shit-eating grin and turned to get the fresh fruit out of the fridge.

Lexi nodded her agreement.

"Y'all are nuts! His rules mean a relationship."

"What's the worst that can happen?" I asked, clutching the cold bowl to my chest. "He says he loves you, he pops the question? He breaks your heart?"

"All of the above." She scowled mutinously at me.

"Devon said he loved me and the world didn't end." I picked up my glass and took another sip, calmly licking my lips as if I hadn't just dropped a bomb on the both of them.

Lexi squealed. Lanie just stared as if she couldn't get past the shock of it, a frown on her normally smooth forehead.

"What are you going to do?" Lanie stood staring at me as if I'd sprouted another head.

"Let him. What else can I do?" I smiled serenely at the both of them. "And maybe love him back."

Grinning, Lexi peeled off another waffle and added it to the plate, quirking an eyebrow at me. "Let's eat."

1

"My darling, I want to touch you everywhere," Lars whispered.

Miranda shivered as his long, elegant fingers slid down the flat plane of her belly, his skin so dark against her own pale flesh. His hardness stirred against her bare leg and she gasped. Soon he would drive that thick column of flesh inside her. Could she possibly bear it?

A soft mewl escaped her lips as his hand drifted to the delta of springy curls between her thighs. She squirmed in embarrassment as his fingers tickled the entrance of her body, finding her shamefully wet, aching for his touch.

"Oh, Miranda," Lars sighed, groaning in approval as he felt her wet welcome. "Have you any idea how long I've wanted to touch you like this, how I've ached to slide inside the sweet petals of your womanhood . . ."

Lauren put the book facedown on her bedside table and closed her eyes. Her hand slid down to the waistband of her pajama bottoms and inside her cotton bikini panties. In her mind, Miranda's silvery blond hair became a mass of cinnamon curls, and her petite, delicate figure became Lauren's own strong, curvy form. Lars morphed too, his burnished gold hair turning thick and black, his burning blue eyes melting into deep, dark chocolate.

She bit back a cry as her fingers found her slick, hot center, circling her clit, teasing herself so this wouldn't all be over in less than a minute. Her hand became his—huge, strong and callused from work, rubbing, circling her clit, sliding inside her just enough to tantalize. Just enough to make her ache to feel the hot, huge length of his cock driving deep inside her.

A muffled cry squeezed past her lips as she came, arching off the bed, pressing her hand firmly between her thighs to draw out her climax as long as possible.

Before the last tremors of her orgasm had subsided, she flipped over onto her side, hugging a huge down pillow against her stomach. Wishing with everything she had that it was him instead of a pillow.

These ridiculous fantasies about Tony Donovan had to stop, or she was going to put her head through a brick wall.

Never mind that Lauren had been telling herself the exact same thing for seven months now, ever since she'd met him. And, she scolded herself silently, her steady habit of romance novels wasn't helping matters. Could she help it if, no matter how the author described him, every damned hero ended up looking like Tony? She closed her eyes and allowed herself one more glorious vision. Six foot three, a body that should be on the cover of *Men's Fitness* magazine. Thick, dark hair with just the tiniest hint of curl and an adorable cowlick waving off his forehead. And his eyes, big, dark, and liquid. Eyes that made a woman think about drowning herself in chocolate so he could lick her clean.

Cursing, she reached for the remote control and flicked on *SportsCenter*. Maybe that would distract her.

Tony. Her best friend. Her coworker. But not her lover. Never that.

She listened with half an ear as the host made his predictions about tomorrow's Oakland Raiders game. But most of her brain was still occupied by Tony. Wondering where he was, what he was doing. Who he was doing it with.

She should go back to masturbating. At least those images of Tony didn't twist her guts until she thought she might throw up.

Stupid jealousy. So unproductive, especially given how he felt about her. She cringed, remembering his invitation to join him and his brother Mike earlier tonight.

"We're going over to Pete's in Tahoe City later on," he'd said over wings and beers at Sullivan's pub. "Want to go?"

Lauren cast a glance at Mike's wife, Karen. "Are you going?"

"No," the other woman said. "I've been on my feet all day and I'm beat."

Mike rubbed her shoulders affectionately. "Maybe you wouldn't be so tired if you wore better shoes." He'd looked pointedly at Karen's stiletto-heeled boots.

"You love my shoes and you know it," Karen had replied, and pulled Mike's face down for a kiss that made the room temperature rise at least ten degrees.

"Ugh, you guys are gross," Tony said, sounding like a twelve-year-old afraid of cooties. "So, Lauren," he'd said. "You want to go?"

Go shoot the shit with Mike while she watched Tony roll up on some hot young thing? No, thanks. She'd done plenty of that since she started working with the brothers at their building and renovation company seven months ago. But all she'd said was, "Nah, sounds like you should have it be a guys' night."

"Aw, Mac," he'd said with a grin and a squeeze of her shoulder. "You're practically one of the guys."

She knew Tony loved to say things like that just to get a rise out of her, but that comment had stung. Even more than his usual jokes about her masculine profession as a carpenter and her customary workman's attire.

Lauren thumbed the volume up on her remote, trying to drown out the evil voices in her head. *Why are you surprised? You know exactly how he sees you.* Just one of the guys. An athletic tomboy of a girl who's great to hang out and drink beer with, but not a girl he'd ever feel *that* way about.

She sighed and flipped over to *Saturday Night Live.* Hugh Jackman was hosting, and he was almost enough to keep thoughts of Tony Donovan at bay.

She'd see him soon enough, her friend, her buddy, her pal.

His friendship meant the world to her, so she would continue as she had, concealing any inkling of interest and enjoy the time she did spend with him. From the moment she met him, she'd wanted to be his lover, but knew it would never happen. So she'd settled for friendship. Like she always did.

Tony settled next to Lauren on the couch and stretched his arm along the back of the cushion behind her. He snuck a quick, jealous glance at his brother Mike and his wife, Karen, snuggled together on the short end of the sectional. Karen didn't even bother to pretend to pay attention to the game, but rested with her head in Mike's lap as she read a paperback. Mike settled into the corner of the couch, absently playing with his wife's hair.

It still surprised him every time he saw them together. Mike, the least physically affectionate person in the family, couldn't keep his hands off his wife. As though he needed to have constant contact to make sure she was still here. Although, Tony supposed, considering their rocky path to love, he supposed he couldn't blame them.

His lips pursed into a frown. This was *his* couch, *his* house.

If anyone should be snuggling down in front of the game it should be him.

But no, he had to content himself with sitting next to Lauren. Almost, but not close enough for his thigh to press against hers. His hand dangled off the back of the couch. Almost, but not quite touching the thick reddish-brown curls that hung down past her shoulders.

"Yes!" Lauren and Mike shot off the couch simultaneously, arms up in wide vees. "GO GO GO," Lauren shouted, and Tony finally focused on his 42-inch-wide TV screen.

"Did you see that pass?" Lauren looked down at him, amber eyes sparkling with excitement.

He'd missed the entire play. "Yeah, it was nice."

"Nice? It was a thing of beauty." She and Mike settled back on their respective ends of the couches, and Tony was hard-pressed not to pull her flush against him. An urge that became even harder to resist when Lauren stripped off her fleece pullover. The mountain weather had turned chilly in the past week, but Tony's house was plenty warm, just the way he liked it.

"It's a sauna in here, Ton," she said, fanning herself a little before she sat back against the overstuffed cushions.

"I like it hot," he replied, and took a long pull at his beer. He tried not to think about how good she smelled, soft and fresh. And she always smelled good, even after a hot day under the sun doing manual labor. The clean scent emanated from her pores until he wanted to bury his head between her breasts and soak her up.

Oh, bad idea, thinking about her breasts. He shifted and tugged at the leg of his jeans. He nonchalantly rested his foot on the coffee table and bent his knee to shield the rapidly growing bulge in his fly.

But really, she did have a fantastic rack, showcased very nicely today in a T-shirt that read "JUICY." She had a fantastic everything, as far as he was concerned. He shot up off the couch to get another beer, hoping the alcohol would do its part to put his dick to sleep.

He didn't have much hope it would work, but it gave him an excuse to retreat to the kitchen and get a handle on himself. He remembered the first day he'd met Lauren. Mike had hired her after their youngest brother, Nick, moved to Palo Alto to live with his fiancée. Tony had been skeptical about hiring a woman, but she came with great recommendations and proved that first day to be a highly skilled, motivated worker.

Of course he'd been attracted to her, with her comic-strip-heroine's body, all juicy curves and nicely defined muscles. And that hair. A riot of reddish brown corkscrew curls tumbling around her shoulders. With hair like that, you just knew she'd be a fuckin' wildcat in the sack. Topped off with her wide smile and whiskey brown eyes full of warmth, and she was almost irresistible. But unlike most women he came across, she showed absolutely no awareness of him as a man. Besides, they worked together, and Tony didn't sleep with women he was likely to run into on a regular basis.

And the real clincher had come later that week. They were finishing up on a remodel job out in the Lakeview Estates. Mike was pushing them to complete the job so they could have the rare privilege of telling a client they'd actually finished *ahead* of schedule. But at about six-thirty Lauren had started looking at her watch. And by seven she'd mustered up the courage to ask her new boss when he thought they might finish.

Mike's brow had furrowed and he'd shot Lauren that intimidating look Tony knew he practiced in the mirror. Tony knew because he'd once caught Mike at it. "Do you have somewhere you need to be?"

But Lauren hadn't flinched. She'd just smiled that wide, laughing smile and said, "Not really. But the Sharks are playing and—"

"Ah, a woman after my own heart," Tony had said, looping his arm over her shoulders. "C'mon, Mike. If we finish up tomorrow we'll still be two days ahead of schedule. You can come over and watch it on my plasma screen."

Lauren's mouth had gone slightly slack and her gaze blurred. It was a look he'd only ever seen on a woman's face when he was buried deep inside her. "A plasma screen?" she'd murmured lustfully. "You have a plasma screen?"

At that moment Tony had a startling revelation. He'd finally met a woman he liked too much to fuck.

For the past seven months he'd shoved any and all sexual thoughts aside and settled into a comfy friendship. They did almost everything together, from work, to working out, to watching sports on the plasma screen she so openly coveted.

Unfortunately the lust he felt every time he saw her was becoming exceedingly difficult to resist.

First he had to work with her through the hot summer, her long, muscular legs showcased in cargo shorts while her D-cups strained against a tank top. The image was still vivid in his mind, of firmly muscled arms tan and glistening with sweat, khaki shorts hugging the firm curve of her ass. He'd spent the entire summer resisting the urge to yank down her shorts and bury his mouth in the moist, gingery curls of her pussy.

He grabbed another Dos Equis and held the nearly empty bag of chips in front of his crotch for good measure. He settled back on the couch, nearly groaning when she reached into the bag of chips he still held on his lap. Her hand brushed repeatedly against his cock as she rooted around for more than crumbs, and he wondered how the hell she could be so fucking sexy in a T-shirt and jeans hiding those world-class legs. And she had no fucking clue, he thought angrily, as her gaze remained guilelessly fixed on the game.

Karen and Mike were nuzzling and whispering on the other end of the couch and Tony bit back a demand for them to get a room. It was a good thing they were here. God knew what stupid moves he'd pull if he was alone with Lauren.

Moves, he grumbled silently, that had worked without failure in the past. But for whatever reason, Lauren was completely unaware of him sexually.

Which was a good thing, he reminded himself, because if she showed the slightest bit of interest, offered the tiniest bit of encouragement, he knew he wouldn't be able to hold himself back. He had no faith in his self-restraint. And then he'd be down one very good friend, which in his experience was much harder to come by than lovers.

He was startled from his musings by a shrill electronic version of the William Tell overture. Lauren squirmed to get her phone out her pocket and he savored the sensation of her firmly curved hip rubbing against his thigh. Would have been nice if she'd been a few more inches to the left, but he had to take what he could get.

Lauren frowned at the caller ID display and flipped open the phone. "Hi, Mom . . . yeah. Yeah. Of course I'm coming. No, I haven't asked for the time off, yet." She smiled tightly at Mike. "No, Mike's really great, I'm sure he'll let me." She grinned and winked at Mike, who grinned back and mouthed, "No way."

"I don't think so, Mom. I know, I know, I just . . ." Her gaze met Tony's for a half second before flicking away, hidden by a sweep of dark amber lashes. She went silent and cinnamon-colored brows knit furiously over her small, straight nose. "Motherrrrr!" She sounded like an exasperated adolescent. "I know there's nothing wrong with that! Jesus, Mom, give me a break!" She rolled her eyes at whatever her mother was saying. "Well, don't. It's fine. Fantastic, in fact. Yeah, I'll see you in a week."

She flicked the phone closed and let out an exasperated sigh and flopped back against the sofa cushions. "I don't believe it!"

All three stared at her expectantly.

"My mother thinks I'm a lesbian."

Mike and Karen laughed, but Tony just raised his eyebrows.

Lauren brandished her phone threateningly. "If you say anything, I'll pound you."

Typical Tony—he couldn't resist the opportunity to needle her. "I don't know where she'd get that idea. You're so girly and feminine in your denim and flannel." He choked on a laugh as Lauren launched herself on top of him and tried to pin him to the couch. She shrieked as he rolled over and knocked her to the floor.

She made a pretty good show of trying to get away while her struggles afforded her the perfect opportunity to rub against Tony like a cat in heat. She even got a full second ass grab in there under the guise of trying to roll him over.

Sad, yes, but a girl had to get her thrills where she could find them.

And despite her masculine profession and affinity for flannel, she was emphatically heterosexual. She pushed Tony off her and climbed back onto the couch. Not that she could blame her mother for her suspicions. Her mother—well, she had her own ideas about sexuality, namely, that if you were young and healthy you should be doing it as often as possible. Carly MacLean couldn't imagine a world in which a willing woman wasn't getting laid, and often. So if there wasn't a man in her youngest child's life, there must be a woman.

"I could give you a mullet and complete the image, if you want." Karen, a hairdresser, giggled and ducked when Lauren pegged her with a pretzel twist.

"Shut up, it's not funny," Lauren said, laughing. "You don't understand. My mom is obsessed with my sex life, or lack thereof," she said with a roll of her eyes. "And now she's telling everyone I'm a lesbian."

"Why do you care, anyway?" Mike asked around a mouthful of pretzels. "It's not like the gossip will reach here."

Lauren sighed. "My parents are having a thirtieth wedding anniversary in two weeks, with a big reception, renewal of vows, the whole thing. My mom keeps pestering me to bring a date, and now that she's got this idea in her head, no doubt she'll invite some prospects." She sat back and covered her face with her hands. "She even asked me if I go for the more butch or the more lipstick types."

"Oh, lipstick, definitely. And I want to watch," Tony said.

Lauren was about to punch him again, but something in his eyes stopped her. A heated glint lurked behind his amusement. Even teasing her, Tony oozed sexual heat. It was in the tone of his voice, the deep richness of his eyes, the way he moved with lazy athletic grace.

She couldn't believe it. The perfect solution sat next to her on the couch. "Tony, I need you to do me a huge favor. Be my boyfriend."

Tony inhaled a tortilla chip and started hacking.

Not so sexy now, she thought. "Not for real, dummy. Just come to my parents' party with me and pretend. You're perfect."

"Perfect, how?" Tony wheezed as Mike thumped him on the back.

She scrambled to find the right words. She couldn't exactly tell him that he was sex personified. His ego really didn't need any more stroking. "Ummm, you just have that look," she said evasively.

"What look?" He looked at Mike and Karen for help.

Karen rolled her eyes. "The look of a guy who's fucked half the women in California and left them all smiling, despite the fact that you never call them again," she said, and promptly went back to her book.

"Yeah, that look," Lauren said.

"Huh." Tony's expression said he wondered if maybe he'd been insulted.

"Look," Lauren said reassuringly, "You know how you are. You're a player—a successful one, and it shows. You're not the kind of guy to be in a sexless relationship with a woman—"

"I'm in a sexless relationship with you," Tony broke in.

Lauren rolled her eyes. She wouldn't even dignify that with a response, seeing no reason to remind him that he didn't exactly see her as a woman. "If you show up with me, my mom will forget her concerns about whether or not I'm getting laid. And I won't have to spend the weekend politely turning down offers from other women." She pulled the best pleading puppy-dog face she could muster and opened her eyes wide. "Please, Tony. Pretend you're attracted to me for just one weekend?"